Secrets Beyond Dreams

Lauren Marie

Lauren Marie

Excerpt from Secrets Beyond Dreams

"Mrs. Pieper, your husband has left. He signed a legal contract and paid in full the amount necessary to give you instruction. If you should back down, the money and promissory notes are not refundable." Mr. Mansfield placed his hands on the desk. "And, there is a clause stating if you do back down the fee is tripled, for wasting our time. I understand from Mr. Pieper, it would bankrupt your estate and things would get rather messy." He came out from behind the desk. "That said, Mrs. Pieper, I can say without any reservation, your husband is an ass. I explained to him, quite clearly, to tell all to you before your arrival. I can only apologize to you for his obvious lack of care. To bring you into our situation without a word is unforgivable."

Lauren Marie

Dedication:

For Kendra Thompson - thank you for listening with no judgment, and the laughs and tears.

Copyright

Prologue

1976

"Hey, Nick, we've found something up here."

Nicholas Whear looked up the stairs to where his sister, Stella, stood on the top step and held what looked to be a ledger book in her hand.

"We found Mom's journals, all of them. You'll never believe where they've been hidden all of these years." She grinned, twirled around, and then moved to the hallway.

James Whear, their father, passed away late in October of 1975. Catherine, their mother, was very lonely without him, and it really didn't surprise the children when she left them early in 1976. She'd grown quiet when they visited. Catherine listened to the tales her grandchildren told and the stories of her adult children's daily lives. She commented how proud their father would be. On many evenings, when one of them came up from the city to visit, they could tell she'd been crying or they'd find her looking out a window or wandering through the gardens. They wanted to help, but found there wasn't any way to reach her.

The first Christmas, after their father's death, everyone felt sad. They played Christmas songs on the piano and sat around the fire after dinner, but Nick found everything reminded him of his father.

He would always be a part of the manor for his family, and would always walk with them in the hall and land surrounding the home.

When Catherine passed away, Nicholas and his siblings, Jason, Michael, Steven, Jonathan, Jacob and his twin sister, Stella, met at the Whear estate to arrange final decisions. Although they'd all been born in the manor, they decided it would be best to sell off the home and acreage surrounding it. With families of their own growing up in the city, they all agreed they couldn't afford the taxes and didn't have an interest in keeping the land and herds of sheep.

Arranging the time for all seven children to meet was difficult, but they wanted to do it together. They wanted to sit by the fireplace in the main living room and remember their parents. They all told of memories that were cherished and through the tears and laughter, they found a closeness that time apart would never break.

Whear Hall was located in the central part of the county and founded by their paternal grandfather, Edward Charles Whear. The estate was surrounded by hills, with green grass and tall oaks and maple trees. There were deep forests and a large lake which bordered the grounds of another estate, Mansfield Hall. The lake, never named when they were children, was eventually named Lake Tulle by the township's councilmen. The Tulle River ran off the lake heading west into town.

Grandfather Whear herded sheep, grew vegetables and was successful at both endeavors. Their father, James, was born in September of 1890, at the height of their grandfather's achievement.

On the first evening, the Nick and his siblings gathered around the fireplace and tried to piece together what they could of their parents' past. They all thought James had always lived at Whear Hall. He may have left for a time to go to school, but returned to the place he called home to carry on their grandfather's legacy.

They also came to clean out their mother's personal items, including several closets of clothing, shoes, and sundry other items. Nick arranged to have an estate sale in a month's time. In the library, they found files of legal papers and books stuffed on shelves. In dresser drawers in the guest bedrooms, they found piles of letters and pictures of people they'd known, and some they couldn't identify. They looked through some of them, but with little time, they ended up boxing a lot of it. Hopefully, they'd find the time, later, to look through all those things.

Stella, Jason and Nick were in their mother's bedroom, cleaning out drawers, cupboards and the closet. Nick went downstairs to get a glass of water, when everything changed. He hurried back up the stairs, and followed his sister to the master suite.

His brother Jay explained that he'd pulled an armful of clothes out of a closet, when he heard something slam down onto the floor. He'd looked out of the closet at his sister and said, "You're never going to believe this," and sent her to find Nick.

"Stella said you found Mom's journals."

Jay peered up at the ceiling of the closet, and held another volume in his hand. Nick heard him say under his breath, "I just don't believe it."

Stella walked over from the dresser and looked over his shoulder.

"We need a step stool and a flashlight. You're never going to believe this." Jay turned and held up the book.

"If you say we won't believe it one more time, Jason Whear, I may have to beat you." Stella said, and took the book out of his hand.

It was one of their mother's journals. She'd written in them as long as Nick could remember. She'd always been a mystery about what she would scribble in them and the journals would disappear when she'd filled the pages. Nick thought they might find a box of them up in the attic or stored out in the barn.

He walked over to Stella and took the book from her hand. Opening the cover, he found a sealed envelope. On the outside of the envelope it read, My Children.

Jay pointed up toward the ceiling of the closet. "There's a shelf up there. I saw something dark and when I

7

reached for it, the book and note fell off the edge. You don't think it's where the rest of her journals are, do you?" His eyes gleamed and he grinned.

Stella moved away and said, "There's a chair in the next room. I'll get it."

"This is a letter, addressed to My Children. We'll need to share this with the others," Nick said.

Stella brought the chair into the room. She pushed it to Jay, who grabbed the back and moved it into the closet. Nick took a flashlight out of his pocket and handed it to him. Jay stood on the chair. His head and shoulders disappeared into the upper part of the wardrobe.

"Oh my God." He bent down at the waist and looked at the other two. "There must be forty or fifty journals up there." He straightened up and then pulled them down two and three at a time. He'd hand them off to Stella and Nick and, when he finished, there were five separate piles with one-hundred and four journals in all.

They separated the stacks into smaller piles, opening pages and skimming through them. Their mother had dated each entry and they spent some time putting them into date order. After boxing them, they carried them down to the living room. Nick sent Stella to find the others. He wanted to read the letter before they started on the journals.

Within ten minutes, all seven adults sat around the fireplace. Nick explained what happened and what they'd found.

"I'm going to start with the letter." He slid the envelope out of the journal. "I think this is the last journal Mother wrote in before her death. How she managed to get it up in the top of the closet, is beyond me, but she always accomplished what she set out to do. I guess I shouldn't be surprised."

Michael put his hand on his brother's shoulder. "Nick, shut up and read the letter. We're all dying to hear what it says."

Nick smiled and tore open the envelope. Inside was a five page letter in their mother's handwriting. He started to read aloud. "My darling children. I'm writing this to you on January second." He looked up at the others. "That's the day before she passed." Nick continued. "I assume you have found my many journals. Before I explain about the scribbled pages, I want you to know some things which are very important for me to say. Your father and I loved all of you very much. You were our pride and joy every day of our lives." He stopped as his voice began to crack and his eyes went out of focus. "Your Father was a very strong man, but on the day each of you were born, I can honestly say, he shed many joyful tears. He never broke down much, but his dream of family made him so happy.

Nicholas, Jason and Michael, you will always be our Three Musketeers. Your father and I had such fun watching you with your wooden swords, defending us from evil villains and azalea bushes. Although, I worried like crazy one of you would lose an eye, and Jason, there were many times when you worried me to no end, with tree climbing and all of the adventures you went on, you three came out unscathed in the end. Now you are adults with worries of your own and I find myself less anxious than I did when you were young." There was a chuckle in the room.

"Mother always wanted to know where Jay was," Michael commented.

Nick frowned at his brother.

"Sorry, I'll be quiet," Michael said.

"All of you represent the heart and soul of the Whear family now. You all have many gifts and intelligence, and I'm proud of the way you handle yourselves daily. Whether in science, education, the law, or writing ghost stories, you have all taken wonderful steps in your lives and your successes made your father and me stand taller and prouder

9

than we ever thought possible. John, I do want to apologize for not using your partner when the will was amended. Your practice is very successful, but there were personal reasons for it. I hope you will understand.

Now, with regards to the journals, they begin at the time just before I met your father. I started to keep them during my first marriage…" Nick's jaw dropped. "Mother was married before Father? Did we ever know that?"

The others only looked at him with surprise on their faces and either shook their heads or mumbled, "No."

He focused back on the page and continued, "I know you may be shocked to read this, but there are more surprises to come. There were many times, over the years, I thought about starting a bonfire in the back field and burning the journals up. I also contemplated tearing some of the pages out, but in the end couldn't bring myself to do either. The books go in date order and if you decide to read them, keep in mind the times your father and I lived in. It was a different world for us when we started out. I hope you won't be too shocked by our story. I believe, in my heart, you should know the truth about how your father and I met, the little bit of turmoil we went through just to be together and the joy we found in each other.

There were many times one of you would ask how we met. I know we were vague with our answers, for which, I want to apologize. Although, what occurred was in the past, it still lingered in our memories. Even though it brought us together, it was a difficult time. Your father and I never wanted to dwell on it.

We shared a great amount of love for each other and once we were together, it was for good, and nothing could make us part. Since your father's death, I have ached for him. I have looked daily for his smile, his touch or kiss. I loved him with every part of my body and soul. His strength kept me lifted up and safe. Without him, I feel weak and frightened. I have a sense in my heart I will join him soon and, in a way, I can't wait.

My darling children, I love you all and hope when you have finished the journals, you will continue to love each other and your families with the same joy your father and I shared. Hugs and kisses, Mother."

He folded the letter and put it back into the envelope. They all sat in silence for a time, and stared at the boxes of journals on the table in front of them.

"It's interesting to find them. I remember, once, when I was eleven or twelve years old, Mother caught me in the library reading one of them," Nick said.

"Did she get upset with you, Nick?" Jay asked.

"No. She put it back on the shelf and we went to do something else. She said it was too lovely a day to be sitting inside. I remember, not long after that, the journals disappeared from the library. I guess we know where they went. I wonder if Father built the shelf in the closet." Nick couldn't remember a time his father worked on such a job.

"He probably did it when we were in school," John said, and leaned on the couch.

Stella cleared her throat and blew her nose. "I know time is short this weekend, but what if we start out reading them aloud? That way, we can share them at the same time and discuss what we're finding out. We won't get much done around the house, but I'd rather find out what the journals say. I really want to know how Mother and Father first met."

Everyone agreed. Jay walked over to the table and pulled out the first book. He opened the cover and put his hand on the first page. "Book one." He read the page and then looked up. "Amazing, the start date, is January 3, 1920. She passed away fifty-six years to the day."

Jay turned to the first page and the story began.

Lauren Marie

Chapter One

January 1920

My name is Catherine Pieper. I am twenty-two years old. I've been married to Marshall Pieper for three years. I'm not sure how to start a journal. I've never done anything like this. I'm not a very good writer, but I suppose no one will ever read these pages, so it doesn't really matter.

I walked to the village earlier today and found myself in the stationery shop. On one of the shelves, I found this wonderful, leather-bound book with writing paper. Many times in the past, I have tried to remember when something in my life happened and found it hard to remember if it was five years ago or just yesterday. While in the shop, it occurred to me this would be a good way to remember. I will make notations of important events that occur, so in the future I'll be able to refer back and think, *Ah, yes, this was the day it happened.* I've never done anything like this, writing down my personal thoughts, so I'm going to work hard to make it of interest. I have to remember to use many adjectives.

My husband, Marshall, and I were married on a warm spring day in 1917. The war in Europe continued and a world-wide influenza outbreak was happening. It ravaged our little corner of the county and took my father's life in March of 1918. It killed millions around the world. I prayed it would never come back. I miss my father very much.

Now I sit here at my vanity, afraid to look at myself in the mirror. I remember those days when Marshall and I first married. I thought I'd made a wise choice. He seemed romantic, bringing me bouquets of flowers for no reason. We spent hours taking strolls around the countryside and talked about things we wished for in our lives. He desired a family, as did I, and said he enjoyed his work on the estate, particularly with the sheep. He paid special attention to me and I felt happy. Six months into the marriage, my father passed away.

The estate, Layne Hall, was left to me, but main control of the finances and care fell into Marshall's hands. The solicitor explained estates almost never pass to daughters. Since my parents did not have an heir, it would pass to the eldest male relation. If there wasn't a relation, then controlling interest would be held by a trust or passed to the eldest child's spouse. Since I'm an only child, and my uncles felt no desire to take over Layne, it fell to Marshall.

It became apparent my husband's only interest was Layne Hall. Soon after my father's funeral, Marshall began to spend as much time away from me as possible. He disappeared in the afternoon and would not return for several days or weeks. When he arrived back from his adventures, he would look haggard and worn. He did, and still continues, to do his husbandly duties. Besides the estate, he wants an heir very much. However, no matter how many times he visits my room at night, we still have no luck. When he is drinking, he blames me for the lack of youngsters. "We should have at least two by now!" he shouts at me. There are occasions when he becomes mean and I have to watch my every move. If I say something he doesn't feel is correct...

This isn't how I wanted this journal to begin. I've debated for a bit about tearing the above pages out and starting over. Now, I feel I will leave them. I will look back on them in the future, when I might forget how I felt. I suppose on the next pages I will continue to complain about my marriage situation. I will try to be more positive and note down all the wonderful things around me.

The village is several miles away from us. In the spring, summer and fall, it is a lovely walk and can take up to an hour to get there. Of course, if we take a carriage, it takes less time. Marshall mentioned those automobiles, which have become so popular and wants to buy one. The only problem is there is no place to buy petrol in our county. He gets very upset sometimes and calls the village backwards.

The city is farther away and can take a day by carriage. However, a year ago, a train depot and rail line were completed at the village. We now have train service twice a week. I haven't gone to the city on the train yet, but hopefully, one day soon, I'll experience this way of travel.

The weather today feels chilly. There is a delightful blue sky and the sun shines bright. The sun did set early, as it does in the winter months. I think I will sit by the fire this evening and start the book I found in town. It is an old edition of a Jane Austen story, one I have never read. It is called Emma and I'm looking forward to it very much.

January 13
It snowed today and is very cold. I went for a walk this morning and found it too cold to stay out long. I am sitting by the fire in the kitchen, and watching our cooks, Susan and Katie, prepare the food for our evening meal. I'm half the way through Emma and love the story.

Our cook, Susan has lived at Layne for many years. My mother hired Susan when she was still learning how to cook. Katie came to us last year. She is very young, only fifteen years old, and has quite a lot to learn. I care for them both very much. Stella Taylor started as my nanny and pretty much raised me.

Mother passed away after I turned six years old, and my father felt I needed a nanny. Stella was his first choice, and she's been with me ever since. After I married, she took over management of the household staff. She is a dear, and I know it pains her quite a bit, the way Marshall behaves when he is here. She bites her tongue often.

15

Arthur came to the family before my birth. He is the manager of the estate and helped my father with the daily chores and other staff. He is also our carriage driver. When father passed, I think Arthur felt upset for weeks as he and father were great friends. He disappeared for a time and worked out his sadness. When he returned, he agreed to help my husband run things. There are times when I can tell by the look on Arthur's face, he is unhappy with the way things have turned out, but he always does his best.

Marshall is off on one of his adventures and I'm certain with the snow coming down, he won't be back for a couple of days. I guess I should note, a year ago, news came to my attention, in an off-hand way, that Marshall goes to a gambling hall in the city. Arthur told one of the cooks. She then told Stella, who told me.

She felt I should be told what she'd heard. I could tell it made her uncomfortable, as she is not one to gossip, but told me all the same.

However, today she came to me with different news about my husband. Marshall is not only gambling the income from the estate, but is whoring quite often. This news causes me a great amount of hurt. I suppose I should be grateful he hasn't brought home the syphilis disease or some other vile infection. What if he does, though? If something like this comes into my home, I will never have children. I really need to discuss this with him, but am fearful of his anger. I'm going to have to think this over and broach the subject with him carefully.

January 16
Marshall returned home yesterday afternoon and closed himself off in his study for the rest of the day. I spent a terrible night of lost sleep and tried to figure out how I could approach him about his trips into the city. I'm not sure what to do.

January 17

This evening, Marshall came down to have dinner with me. When he isn't here, I usually eat my meals in the kitchen. He became angry I didn't set the table in the main dining room, but with Stella's help, we got it done in no time and he seemed to settle down. After his third or fourth glass of wine with dinner, I told him we needed to have a discussion.

"We do?" he asked.

"Yes, we do," I answered and tried to look as serious as I could. "It has come to my attention, Marshall, that the time you spend in the city isn't all in the gambling hall."

"I see. Do tell me what you've heard, Catherine." He sounded rather sarcastic and I felt my anger grow.

"Marshall, the whoring must stop. If you get syphilis or some other disease, it could affect our chances of having children. You must see that."

He pushed himself away from the table and stood up. I could see he clenched his fists and thought I may have gone too far.

"Catherine, I come to your room and service you on a regular basis." His voice got louder. "You lie on your back and do nothing to even make me feel welcome. It is your fault we remain childless. What do you expect? I've found women in the city who treat me like a man."

"I've tried to give you pleasure, Marshall. You won't let me touch you. You, you…push my hands away. You never kiss me. You lie on top of me, do your business and then pass out from too much to drink." I stood up and let my own voice be heard.

He came toward me fast and grabbed my hair. "How dare you think I haven't tried?" He pushed me away and I fell to the floor. "You are a boring woman, Catherine. You and your books, and that stupid woman, Stella. What do we need her for, anyway? We have no children for a nanny. She should be let go."

"No!" I shouted at him. I got back onto my feet and stared at him. "So help me Marshall, if you do anything to hurt Stella, I'll go to Father Barrent and tell him I'm filing for an annulment. I have more than enough proof."

"Ah, I see. Father Barrent? Do you think the church will side with you? All it will see is a wife who cuts herself off from society and is unhappy. You have no proof of anything." He laughed.

"Marshall, please, I married you. At the time I thought I loved you, but you have made it very difficult to stay in love with you. If you bring home a disease—"

Marshall swung his arm and struck me across the face. I fell back onto the floor, and my cheek burned with pain. "Do you think I would be so stupid? Good Lord, have you never heard of condoms?"

He picked up the decanter of wine and his glass and left the room. I sat on the floor and then picked myself up. Stella rushed in when she knew Marshall had left, and helped me stand.

"Catherine, are you all right?" she asked.

I looked at her and started to cry. "Stella, I don't know what to do. He doesn't want to listen."

She took my hand. "Come with me dear. We need to get something cool on your cheek or you'll have a terrible bruise."

Later that night, drunk as usual, Marshall came to my room. He turned very brutal and hurt me quite bad. At one point, he turned me on my stomach and put his member in my bottom. It hurt so much. I know I screamed, but I think this only excited him more. Instead of passing out, he again did his business and left.

When I woke up this morning, it was hard to walk. The bruise on my cheek isn't the worst of the many dark spots on my body. I won't be able to show my face in the village for a few days and won't be able to go church this week. I'm at a loss.

January 19

Marshall left the Hall this afternoon. Arthur took him into the village to catch the train to the city. It will be nice to have some peace. He's been very angry with me this week. Fortunately, all it means is he isn't speaking to me. I am going to arrange to speak with Father Barrent. I don't want to live like this any longer.

January 21

My friend, Sylvia Carpenter, stopped in this afternoon. She saw the bruise on my face and became very concerned. I spent some time with her and tried to keep her calm. I spoke candidly about Marshall's treatment. She is getting ready to leave for Europe. She'll take the ship in a week and be gone for six months and she invited me to join her, but I know I can't leave at this point. I admitted to her the idea of such an extensive trip made me feel a little overwhelmed. I've never even been into the city, how on earth would I deal with Europe? I'll miss her very much. She's been a dear friend for many years.

Sylvia is also very vocal about women's rights. She mentioned that sometime this year women may get the right to vote and I laughed. I'm not sure who or what I would vote for. She says women's voices need to be heard and counted if the country is going to progress. I envy her when she so clearly states her beliefs. I wish I could find this type of voice.

January 25

The bruise on my cheek is better and now only an alluring shade of yellow. Marshall has been in the city for a week.

Stella and I have put together plans for the work on the garden this spring. In another month, we'll put the seeds in and hopefully by mid-summer, they'll be in bloom and beautiful. She watches over me and treats me like her daughter. I haven't told her all the details about the argument with Marshall, but I think she knows what happened. I've worn long sleeves all week to cover the bruises on my arms. Since it's cold, I don't think she caught on that I'm covering up.

I've decided when I go to church next week, I'll see if Father Barrent will make an appointment with me. I can't continue to live with Marshall. Since divorce is against church policy, I'll need to get all the information I can about an annulment. It will be a bit of an embarrassment to go through the church, but I won't give up my faith. I'm sure I have enough proof about Marshall's affairs in the city to qualify for the marriage being annulled. Arthur will speak in my favor, if needed.

January 28

There are so many things I know I am not educated about. My friend, Sylvia, used to tell me such wild stories of the relations between men and women. Since she went to a women's college in the city, and traveled all over the world, I trusted her information. I wonder though, with my own lack of knowledge, should I consider my relationship with Marshall to be normal?

Sylvia asked me once if he gave me any pleasure or satisfaction in the bedroom. I felt so embarrassed by the question I couldn't answer. It wasn't because the question shocked me or was wicked. It's because I have no idea what she speaks of.

I sometimes hope when Marshall comes to me, he's too drunk to perform. He bruises me less on those occasions and I'm less likely to make him angry. When he is more sober, he seems to relish making me hurt or cry. It excites him to see me in anguish.

I wish he'd speak to me as he did in the first months of our marriage. In those days, such a short time ago, he was courteous and kind. It was after my father died, that the ill treatment started. In those first days, our relations were better and I never developed any bruises.

Chapter Two

February, 1920

Again, I want to tear out all these pages I've written. I read back through them and can't believe I ever meant to write such sad and bitter words. I suppose it's good to keep track of things like this. If my dealings with Marshall change and become better, I can look back and be more thankful.

I went to church yesterday and enjoyed a lovely service. However, that old crow, Mrs. Stewart, was as rude and gossipy as ever. She greeted me with kindness as I walked out of the hall, and said they'd missed me the last two Sundays. I only answered that I'd been busy with the garden.

Her arched eyebrow told me that she found my answer unsatisfactory. She then said, "My dear, I think you should be aware what people in the village are saying. There's been a rumor about Mr. Pieper floating around—quite scandalous—about his behavior in the city—"

"Thank you, Mrs. Stewart," I cut her off. "I'm sure my husband has no idea what it is all about, but I'll be certain to mention it to him." I turned and walked away from her. I knew I would hear about cutting her speech off, but I didn't care.

When I got back to Layne Hall, Stella could tell by the look on my face, I was upset. She asked what happened. I waved her off, and retreated to the garden. The weeds have never experienced such anger. I knew it was cold, but I didn't feel it. After a time, Stella came out with my sweater and as she put it around my shoulders I started to sob. I knelt in the dirt with weeds in my hands. She crouched down, put her arms around me and tried to be a comfort, but I felt lost.

What was I to do?

After I'd calmed down, I told her what happened at church and how embarrassed I felt with those in the village aware of what Marshall's antics were in the city. Stella recommended again I should speak with Father Barrent and find out what I would need for an annulment. She feels the priest would keep anything I told him in confidence. He might have an idea of how best to deal with Marshall. As for Mrs. Stewart and her crowd of gossips, Stella laughed and said to ignore it. Mrs. Stewart stirs things up to keep her blood pumping.

I hate the thought of the loss of my marriage and becoming a divorcee, but I can't live like this any longer.

February 11

I spoke last Sunday with Father Barrent. I explained to him in general about the events which occurred in January. He is very supportive, but thought I was rushing into annulment. He felt I should continue to try communication with Marshall before I make any decisions. He agrees my husband's behavior has not shown any good Christian values, but with prayer and strong faith, I should be able to make things work out for the best. I am to meet with him again next week and let him know how things have worked out with Marshall. I'm still at a loss as to what I could say or do which would make Marshall listen to me.

February 16

After the church services yesterday, I met with Father Barrent again. I spoke honestly about the things I'd been told about Marshall's trips into the city. I told him everything. Again, Father Barrent was supportive, but still thinks with prayer and faith things will turn out for the best. He lectured me a little on the fact that marriage can be hard work and he knew I would put everything I could into saving it. He offered to speak with Marshall, but I'm not sure what effect that would have. Marshall hates the church so deeply I doubt it would make any difference. He would become so angry with me for exposing his little secrets, I don't want to think about what might be the outcome of his anger.

February 29

Stella and I have gotten things ready for the planting season and as soon as the days are a bit warmer we'll begin to work. In the village, I bought some new seeds and bulbs. If all goes well, the flowers this year will be beautiful. I got a new variety of purple Iris which I'm anxious to plant. Of course, they won't bloom until next year, but I'm sure they will be spectacular. I also think the vegetable garden will be abundant. We should have enough to can for all of next winter.

Leap years always seem strange to me. Twenty-nine days instead of twenty-eight, just seems plain odd. I'm sure there's a very good explanation for it, but I've yet to figure it out.

Marshall arrived home a few days ago, but we haven't spoken much. In six weeks or so, it will be sheep shearing time and he's made arrangements for it. The wool will be sold in the city and I'm sure this is the main reason he's so attentive to Layne Hall right now. He just wants the money in his pocket to gamble away. I wonder what I shall do if he drives the estate into bankruptcy?

Secrets Beyond Dreams

Lauren Marie

Chapter Three

March/April 1920

I made a mistake today. Marshall came in early from the field with the sheep. He seemed sober and I decided to try to kiss him. He bit my lip, it bled and I have a bruise. When I held my mouth and looked at him horrified, he laughed and went into the house.

Stella found me crying in my room. When she saw my face she held me in sympathy. I can't continue to endure this. I've got to leave him. I know Father Barrent will not understand any of this and I may lose my reputation in the church, but I can't let him continue to treat me in such a manner. I know there is an attorney in the village. I must see if I can arrange to meet with him.

I guess my journals, for now, are full of complaints. I never meant for them to be this way, but I find I can only write about what is in my heart. I never want to be without hope, but I'm afraid I have lost what little I have left.

Note: March 2 thru end of the month, Catherine discusses the gardens. She and Stella would work pretty much from sun up to get the debris from winter storms cleared. She spoke about the early spring that year, she knew it could turn back to frigid temperatures, but they kept at work.

She also wrote about raising the hems on her skirts, as fashion changed even in their country setting. Stella threw a fit about it and lectured Catherine about the morals of letting her ankles show. There is a section she wrote about sewing a sleeveless blouse. Whether or

not she ever got around to this top, she never mentions.

She didn't write anything further about going into the village to see the attorney or of any more discussions with Father Barrent. (note: from Michael Whear - journal editor)

April 3

Marshall returned home from the city two days ago. He's in an extremely foul temper and I've stayed as far away from him as possible. I'm not sure what happened to him in the city, but he came home with a black eye. I can only guess what might have occurred, but can't find the courage to bring it up with him.

He came up to my room last evening, but didn't stay long. He stood in the middle of my bedroom, stared at me for a moment, and then left. I'm not sure what to make of it.

April 11

I sat in my room this morning and was working on a hem, when Marshall came in, his hands clenched into fists. He looked angry.

"Your dear Father Barrent just paid me a visit, Catherine."

I only glanced at him and didn't give any reply.

"He was quite arrogant and lectured me on the ills of drinking." Marshall laughed. "He said if I prayed, I could find my way back to the good Lord. Just what I want to achieve." He started toward me.

I stood up and backed away from him. Holding my sewing scissors, I brought them up to defend myself. Marshall stopped when he saw them in my hand. He stared at me and his eyes tightened their gaze. I knew I only made him angrier, but didn't care. I wasn't going to let him lay a hand on me this day.

"Are you going to stab me, Catherine?" he asked.

I continued to remain silent and held my ground. He eventually turned and left the room. He drank himself into a stupor this afternoon and hasn't come out of the library.

April 16

I missed the last couple of days because I didn't feel well enough to write. Things have been tense around the Hall. Marshall spends most of his time drunk.

I've stayed either in the garden or in my room, but, this evening, decided to go down to the dining room. Marshall came out of the library to eat. I knew I should keep silent, but asked him why he was in such a mood. He drank most of the afternoon and said it would be best if I minded my own business.

"Being concerned for my husband's welfare is my own business, Marshall. You came home with a black eye and in an ill-temper. I'm concerned."

He looked around the room. "Why am I in an-ill temper? I get threatened by my wife and"—he moved his arm around and pointed at the room—"this place is so dull," he said.

"If we replaced the piano, I could play some music for you in the evening."

"Some more of those melancholy dirges you like so well? I think not." He drank some more wine. "Perhaps if I brought a couple of the whores from the city out here, it would stir things up!" he shouted. "Then you could learn how to treat a man."

"Marshall, please keep your voice down. The staff will hear you."

"This is my home, why should I care what they hear?" He pushed himself up from the table and I jumped. "What? Are you afraid there will be gossip about you in your precious village?"

"No, I'm worried about our marriage. I can't

29

continue on this way, Marshall. No matter what I say or do, it always seems to make you angry." I stood up to try and face him.

"What do you mean you can't continue on this way? You've got it so very easy. You do your gardening and sewing!" he shouted. "I'm the one who does the work around here. Who else would go out and deal with those damned sheep? Who would hire the workmen to do the shearing? Who? Me, that's who. Your continual bleating like a sheep is going to make me crazy. If you can't continue, then why don't you leave?"

"This is my home, too, Marshall. Your whoring and gambling has gone on long enough. It's worn me out and I can't stand anymore. If I lose Layne Hall in a divorce, then so be it. If I have to get a divorce and lose my place in the church, then so be it." His fist swung up and hit me so fast, I didn't realize it until I sat on the floor. He hit me with the hand he wears his Mason ring on, the one with the diamond. I put my hand up to my cheek, felt something wet and realized it was blood.

"You and your Father Barrent. I'm sure he loved it when you whined. You have lost your mind to think he'll help you. What do you think the church is going to do for you? They'll shun you, Catherine. They'll throw you out and lock the doors behind you. Barrent is such a pious ass. I can't see him doing you any good."

"Why should you care if they shun me? You never attend church. You could care less about the place," I said, and tried to lift myself off the floor.

Marshall laughed. "You have that right. All they want is to rob people blind. Giving tithes? What a bunch of nonsense." He looked down at me with a leer, bent at the waist and grabbed a handful of my hair.

"Come with me, my darling wife. I'm feeling very hard. Let's see if we can find some of the pleasure you think you give to me."

Marshall dragged me out of the dining room and into his study. He pushed me away and locked the door. When he turned back around, he took off his dinner jacket and threw it toward a chair. I backed away and ran into his desk.

"What say we have some fun, Catherine?" He started toward me.

"Marshall, please, what are you doing?"

"You said you wanted to give me pleasure, remember?" He grabbed my hair again and pulled me against him. "I know of a way you can give me pleasure. It will be new and exciting for you, too." He unzipped his trousers and pulled his member out. "The lovely women in the city do this for me and you'll learn to love it with time."

"Please, Marshall, stop this," I begged. He put his hand on my breast and squeezed it so hard it hurt. "You're hurting me, please stop."

"Get on your knees woman. You're going suck my cock like the sluts in the city do. If you're good, well have a night of it."

I felt shocked by what he'd said I couldn't think of anything to reply. What he asked made me feel appalled. He pulled at my hair and pressed my shoulder down so hard and I tried to fight him, but he is much stronger than I.

He leaned toward me and whispered maliciously in my ear. "If you don't get on your knees I'll kick them out from under you."

With that said, he kicked my right shin. It hurt so bad my knee buckled and I went down. When I refused to open my mouth, Marshall pinched my nose closed with his other hand. It made me open and he pushed his member into my mouth and down my throat. It made me choke and I started to heave. I thought it would serve him right if I threw up on him. He kept a tight grip on my hair and started to move himself and me in a rhythm. It made no difference to

31

him how much I choked.

After a time, he withdrew himself and pulled me up to face him. "Was it satisfying? I think not," he said, and pushed me onto his desk face first. He forced my head down and bent me over it. I hit my bottom lip on the corner of a wooden pen holder and felt blood in my mouth. His free hand pulled my skirt up and my under drawers down. I heard him spit and felt his hand in the crack of my rear. He then pushed his member inside my bottom and began to pump me.

Tears flowed down my cheeks. The edge of the desk cut into my upper thighs with each thrust and it burned severely. He withdrew and pushed himself into my vagina. He leaned over me and said, "If I cum in your ass we'll never have children, will we?" He began to pump again and did what he meant to do. He pulled back and I heard his zipper. I tried to straighten, but my legs hurt so badly I was afraid to let go of the desk.

I heard him laugh. "Look, you've bled all over my ink blotter." He went to a side board, pulled a decanter out of the cabinet and poured himself a drink. He guzzled it down it two swallows and turned to me. "Get out of here, I have no further use of you this evening," he said.

I pushed my skirt down and made my way to the door. The key was still in the lock and it turned easily.

"Marshall," I said, and faced him again, "why are you such a bastard?"

"I'm shocked to hear such language from your lips, Catherine. What am I to do with such a foul-mouthed wife?" He smiled.

I left the office and made my way up to my room. I'm bruised once more from the hand of my husband. When I hit the pen holder, it re-injured the area on my lip where Marshall bit me weeks ago. My upper legs have dark blue, swollen marks. I cried for a long time. I am certain now of what I have to do. I should have done it long ago.

April 21

Marshall left Layne Hall a week ago. I hope he never bothers to return. If I could put a curse on him, I would. After this last go round, I am planning to go to the solicitor in the village and find out what I need to do for a divorce. I'll lose Layne Hall, but at this point I don't care. I'm not worried about losing my membership in the church, either. Marshall enjoys his ill treatment of me and the cruelness is not attractive. I don't feel it's necessary to put up with it any longer.

This last week I've been so depressed. I haven't wanted to work in the garden or read any of the books on my shelves. Stella finds me starring out the window. I haven't said anything to her about this, but I should. Since I know I will go through with the divorce, it will affect her, too. She'll have to look for another position elsewhere. I know she won't wish to stay on at Layne, working for Marshall. He has so little regard for her, I doubt he'd keep her on.

I wish my father were here. He would know the sensible way to handle all of this.

April 22

Marshall returned from his latest trip to the city. I've spent most of the day in the garden just to stay away from him. After our last meeting, I want nothing further to do with him. I will go into the village tomorrow and find the solicitor to discuss divorce.

It is so strange though, once you've made a decision about something, another thing comes along to make you doubt your original decision. It never seems to fail.

This evening, before dinner, I was working in the garden trimming some early daisies to bring inside, when Marshall appeared. I said nothing to him and only glanced up once.

"Good evening, Catherine," he said.

"Marshall." I continued trimming.

"Catherine, I need to speak with you, if you have a moment," he said.

His demeanor sounded different than the week before. I felt taken aback. I stopped trimming and turned to him.

"The last time I was here my behavior was unforgivable. I treated you like a beast. I must apologize to you and hope you can forgive me. I've realized the alcohol changes me and turns me into a horrible person. I've decided to give it up. I know I've made your life miserable and, again, I'm very sorry I've done this. I also realize if I continue behaving as such, I'm going to ruin our marriage forever. I hope we are not beyond the point of repair. I know you'll find this unbelievable, but I do love and care for you. I don't want to lose you, Catherine." He put his hand up to my face and touched the area on my lip where the cut still healed. He grimaced. "I'm so terribly sorry for this."

I thought I could see his eyes tearing up. I pulled away from him. "There's a lot for us to work on, Marshall. I don't really trust you now."

"Yes, I haven't done very well with instilling trust. I would like to work on this with you. I've been such a monster, I'm amazed you're speaking to me at all."

I gathered up the daisies and put them in a basket. Marshall insisted on carrying them into the house. He asked if I was going to have my dinner in the kitchen and could he join me. He'd understand if I preferred not to have his company.

His behavior was a surprise and very confusing. I decided to have dinner with him and let the cooks know to serve it in the dining room. I excused myself to clean up and told him I'd see him shortly.

After I washed my hands, I sat at my vanity combing my hair and getting it put back up. As I looked at my reflection in the mirror, I thought I heard a voice in my head saying be careful, be very careful. I wasn't sure at all what happened with Marshall. When he apologized, I felt surprised. In the three years we'd been married, I don't think he ever went this far. There was much to apologize for, but the simple fact he'd taken a first step, was astounding. Still, I felt on edge. It made me wonder what caused his conversion.

I went back downstairs to the dining room, where I found Marshall. Standing, as I entered the room, he pulled the chair away from the table. I thanked him as I sat down and he nudged the chair forward a little. He then sat down, too.

Katie brought in a couple of trays from the kitchen and served us. I asked her to bring me a glass of wine and looked at Marshall to see if he was tempted. Katie looked at him, too.

Marshall turned his attention to us and smiled. "Nothing for me, thank you."

During our meal, we spoke about things to do with the Hall. He talked about the sheep and how good the wool looked this spring. The price of wool per pound also looked good and he felt we would bring in a decent amount. He spoke about some things he'd like to do around the estate. Some repairs from winter storms will be needed in the barn. He even felt we'd have enough to hire some extra help on a regular basis and perhaps purchase another piano. He apologized for selling mine, he said he had no right to this and would like to replace it. I listened to all of this, but kept feeling watchful and waited for something to go wrong.

I finished my dinner and started to excuse myself, but Marshall asked me to wait a moment.

"A gentleman by the name of Jacob Mansfield has invited us to a reception at his estate. It's in a week's time, on the thirtieth. I haven't accepted for us yet, but wondered if you'd like to attend?"

"How are you acquainted with Mr. Mansfield?"

"We have done some business in the city. He owns sheep and we've compared notes about our mutual herds."

"What business have you been conducting in the city?"

"Well, not really business. Mr. Mansfield owns one of the gambling establishments in the city which I've been a guest at."

"Gambling, I see. What is the reception for? I'd rather not go somewhere to gamble."

"I'm not clear on the reason for it. One of his family members has been away in Italy or Spain and will return this week. He wants to welcome them back. Since this would be at his estate, I doubt very much there will be any gambling. We'd leave around mid-morning, attend the reception, and return the next day. You wouldn't have to pack very much."

"Is it formal?"

"No, not tuxedo formal, but we are expected to not be casually dressed."

"I'll think on it and let you know." I stood and started to leave, but stopped myself. "Marshall, what is going on with you? You haven't acted this civil in two years. I don't understand."

"I've had an awakening and realized the stupidity and immaturity of my behavior. I'm well aware I have a lot of mending to do. First, and foremost, I wish to repair things with you. I think if you are able to spend time with me, I'll be able to regain your trust. To prove myself worthy of your love again is most important to me." He walked up to me and took my hand. "Let's attend the reception. Some dancing and good food will make for a lovely evening. If you want to, perhaps we could be gone longer than over night and go up to the North Country. We never did have a honeymoon, perhaps it would be a good starting point." He kissed the back of my hand. "Catherine, may I come up to your room this evening?"

I pulled my hand away and backed up. "My door is locked to you right now. I'll let you know what I decide about the reception." I thought I saw a shadow on his face, but he nodded and looked sad.

I left the room, walked up the stairs and here I sit, in quiet reflection. It's late, going on midnight. I'm tired, but I can't get my brain to quiet down. I am trying to figure out what Marshall's change in attitude could mean. I'm very unsettled this evening. The voice in my head is still telling me to be careful. Perhaps I'll discuss it with Stella in the morning. I trust her opinion.

April 25

I've finally spoken with Stella and told her all which went on for the last week. She reminded me it is important never to lose hope in people or situations. She did, however, agree with my inner voice and asked me to be careful. I knew I needed to give Marshall some answer. I decided to go for a walk into the back fields of the estate and let nature help me make the decision.

As a child, I had secret places around the land where I could hide and daydream or think things over. The green fields have a way of calming my mind. There is a group of giant oak trees which are my favorite. They must be hundreds or thousands of years old. They have character. I can get lost with them and cry or laugh and the trees make no judgments on me.

I made my way across the field to the hill where they stand. I found my much loved place, put down a blanket and sat. I listened to the birds sing and tried to catch sight of them up in the branches. There was a slight breeze blowing and I closed my eyes as my hair caressed my face. The afternoon was too lovely to think about serious matters, but I knew I needed to give my decision some thought.

Marshall still waited for an answer from me about the reception. I found myself bothered about this Mr. Mansfield. If he owned a gambling establishment, he couldn't be a reputable gentleman. I began to wonder if perhaps this person might have caused Marshall's change in manner. We hadn't spoken about what caused Marshall to give up drink and become civil. I found myself coming up with different scenarios and became more confused than when I'd originally sat down.

Finally, after several hours, my stomach made a growling sound. I wanted lunch. Standing, I folded my blanket and started back to the Hall. As I crossed the field, I saw Marshall working with the two hired rovers. They were bringing in part of the herd. I watched them from a rise in the field. The two men who worked with Marshall were stripped from the waist up. They were very tan and muscular. More so than my husband and I found myself admiring their bodies.

When we were first married, Marshall spent more time working the herds and had a very well built body. This changed after my father's death. When the estate turned over to Marshall, he'd quit going into the fields, lost his muscle and grown thicker around the middle from too much drink and food.

I watched them for a time and then realized Marshall spotted me and waved. I raised my hand to wave back and continued on. Maybe he was trying to change his ways. I started to think I should give him the benefit of the doubt. As Stella said, we must not lose hope.

The afternoon, I spent in the garden. Stella had some pepper seeds she felt determined to get planted. I told her my decision about attending the reception with Marshall. I told her it might be ignorant, but felt I needed to give him a chance. He did try to work things out with me and hadn't been drinking all week. Stella didn't comment on my thoughts. We worked quietly throughout the rest of the day.

When we quit in the early evening, we'd made much headway. We will have a huge crop of peppers in a few months time, if they do well.

At dinner, I found Marshall again waited in the dining room. Again, he held my chair and seated me.

"I've thought about going to this reception at your business acquaintance's estate. I won't know any of the people you associate or do business with, so I'm counting on you to introduce me."

He smiled. "You've decided to go?"

"I believe so, yes."

"Good, good. That's wonderful, Catherine. I think you will have a wonderful time. Mr. Mansfield is quite the gentleman."

Marshall, again, didn't have anything to drink with dinner. We sat at the table and talked for a while. I even found myself laughing a little when Marshall made a joke.

The voice in the back of my mind screamed, but I tried to silence it.

April 26

Marshall has respected my privacy all week. I invited him to my room last evening, but he declined. He said he thought we should wait and treat the trip to Mansfield Hall as our honeymoon. We could make it a time to start over. It seemed silly, but I agreed. After our last get-together, I'm not sure I'm ready to let him touch me. He was so brutal that night. My instincts want to trust him, but the other half is being very cautious. I remember how it was before we married. He acted this way, sober and very kind. He returned to the man I fell in love with. The first time I pointed out his different, he found it amusing. It's all I can do at this time.

April 29

We leave for Mansfield Hall tomorrow. I've packed up a valise and will throw in this journal. I want to keep up to date with it and I might see some interesting country on the ride over. It will take about three hours. I'm certain to see some things I'll want to note down. We won't be able to do the North Country on this trip. Marshall is too busy with the herd. It will be a new start for us, though.

Stella met me out in the garden this afternoon and hugged me. She said she hoped the trip would be very pleasurable, but she asked me to take care and be ever watchful of Marshall. She felt he tried, but she still wasn't sure about his honesty. He does have a long way to go to gain my trust back, but I think he may have even further to go with Stella.

His change in attitude has been miraculous. He's spoken with me about plans for expanding the herd. Just a short time ago, he wouldn't have even mentioned it. I'm still not certain what to make of all this.

Secrets Beyond Dreams

Chapter Four

May 1 - Mansfield Hall

I should have known better. I hate myself for believing this marriage might have a chance. I'm furious for letting Marshall pull the wool over my eyes. I'm an idiot. I shouldn't have agreed to this excursion. I believe now Marshall is quite mad and should be thrown into an asylum. I know I'm ranting, but I've got to get this out before I go any further. I'm certain Marshall planned this all along. He arranged to put me into the strangest situation. I have no idea what will become of me. I know I need to calm down, I can barely read my own handwriting.

We left Layne Hall yesterday around ten in the morning. Arthur, our carriage driver, followed Marshall's instructions. I understood the trip would take about three hours. We'd arrive at Mansfield and have enough time to relax and rest before the reception. The road we took to the estate was beautiful. It wasn't overly warm, but the sun shone and as long as the carriage stayed in the sun, it felt warm. Spring flowers were just starting to come out, as were the leaves on the trees. We passed several estates along the way and I felt some satisfaction that their gardens were no further along than ours at Layne Hall. I'd never been on this particular road before and I found the beauty joyful. I hope someday to find that joy again.

Marshall became quiet during the journey. He looked away from me and barely acknowledged my presence. I tried to start a conversation with him, but got a curt, "Not now, my dear." I even tried to touch his hand, but he pulled away from me.

I became unsettled by his conduct, but said nothing

further. In my mind, I started making excuses for him. Perhaps he acted this way due to the lack of whiskey. If there was alcohol at the reception, what if he drank? Would he turn mean again?

The carriage turned off the main road and headed down a private lane. Ahead of the carriage, I could see a rather large lake surround by woods. Ducks and geese swam along and dived under the water. We passed by one of the edges of it and then turned another direction heading into the trees. Passing through a wrought iron gate, we came upon a rather ornate manse. It was built with red brick. A fenced walkway around the roof looked framed in more wrought iron. The lawn and shrubs were well tended. It struck me as a lovely dwelling, but I thought it contained a mystery and hoped to find out why I'd think this.

The carriage stopped in front by the main door. It struck me that there were no other carriages or automobiles in the drive. Marshall opened the door and stepped out of the carriage. Another clue something was amiss hit me. He turned to our driver, Arthur, and told him to wait here. He started to walk up the steps to the main door without offering to help me step down from the coach. His gentlemanly manners from the last week disappeared. I didn't move from my spot and watched as he turned back. He looked perplexed. He'd been so attentive to me before and, now, a sense of foreboding hit my chest.

He came back to the carriage, offered his hand and hissed, "Catherine, please don't make me angry." He stared at me and I saw his madness.

Finally, I gave him my hand and stepped onto the gravel drive. He let go and grabbed at my upper arm. When I tried to pull away, he tightened his grip.

"You're hurting me, Marshall."

He sneered at me and led me up the stairs to the front door of the mansion. He used the knocker to make those inside aware of our arrival. I felt a headache start, but said nothing. I wondered why Marshall behaved in such a manner. We'd barely spoken on the ride to Mansfield and I felt sure I'd not said anything which might annoy him. I'd had about five minutes of hope he really tried to change his ways, but my suspicions grew stronger as we waited for the door to open.

A butler opened the right side of the entrance. He was an older man with graying hair. He stood with his left arm behind his back, and looked at Marshall.

"My name is Pieper. I am expected by Mr. Mansfield," he said.

"Yes sir, please, come in." The butler opened the door farther and motioned us in.

We walked into a large entryway which looked nicely decorated. There was a large, round table in the center of the room with a lovely bouquet of flowers. I wondered for a moment where the flowers came from. It seemed too early in the season for some of the varieties. The lighting in the room seemed dim and I realized the sun must be on the other side of the house at this time of day.

Marshall let go of my arm and I knew there would be another bruise, he'd held on so tight. I walked away from him and looked at the flowers in the vase. It bothered me that there were no other carriages in the drive. I thought we must be the first to arrive, but then wondered. From what Marshall told me, there were supposed to be many other couples attending.

"I'll inform Mr. Mansfield of your arrival, sir," the butler said and left the room.

We waited for some time. Marshall paced back and forth across the tile floor. I decided to sit on one of the chairs in the entry. I looked up at the wall across the room from where I sat and noticed several paintings. The lighting in the room made it difficult to determine what they represented. I squinted at one of them and thought I saw a man looking down at a child. The child handed something to the man, looking up. The longer I looked at the painting, I could see differences about it. I thought I'd stand and get a closer look, when it occurred to me what the scene showed. There wasn't a child in the painting, but a woman and she wasn't handing something to the man. The something I looked at was the man's member standing erect from the crotch of his trousers. My breath caught in my chest and the room grew warm. The setting in the picture made me feel shocked.

Just as I thought to say something to Marshall, the double door opposite the front of the house opened. A very tall, dark-haired man stepped into the anteroom. He smiled and sounded soft spoken.

"Good afternoon, Mr. Pieper." He turned to me and came to where I sat. "Mrs. Pieper, it's a pleasure to meet you. My name is James Whear. Please come this way. Mr. Mansfield is ready for you now."

Marshall put his hands behind his back, walked through the doors and left me behind. Mr. Whear offered me his forearm. "Mrs. Pieper, please allow me to show you the way."

"Thank you, sir." I put my hand on his arm, stood and he led me through the doors into a large library. It occurred to me later in the day what Mr. Whear said about showing me the way had a double meaning. I never would have guessed.

Behind a desk, sat a man who was Mr. Mansfield. He looked to be older, in his fifties or sixties. His hair was gray and his eyes a very clear blue, covered by glasses. He spoke to Marshall in a voice I would have thought for children. I heard him say, "And where is your wife, sir?" All Marshall could do was point at me. Mr. Mansfield stood behind his desk.

"Mrs. Pieper, please, let me introduce you. This is

Mr. Jacob Mansfield. He owns the estate and the school," Mr. Whear said.

Mr. Mansfield stepped from behind the desk. He put out his hands and took one of mine. He kissed the back of it and then cupped it in both of his.

"Mrs. Pieper, I am pleased to make your acquaintance. Have a seat and make yourself comfortable." He motioned to a chair and after I sat down, he walked back behind his desk. He sat and folded his hands on the top. Mr. Whear moved behind Mr. Mansfield and stood, his hands clasped in front of him. He continued to look at me with a pleasant smile on his face.

"Mrs. Pieper." Mr. Mansfield smiled across the desk at me. "I'd like to welcome you. As I'm sure you understand from what your husband has explained to you...I'm sorry, have I said something funny?"

I laughed. "I'm sorry, sir. When you said what my husband explained to me, it struck me as funny. It occurs to me since we are the only ones here...I mean, I understood we were coming here for a reception this evening at the home of one of my husband's business acquaintances." I looked at Marshall who stared straight ahead. "As I started to say, it occurs to me since there are no other guests here at this time I have been misinformed or misunderstood our reasons for coming here."

Mr. Mansfield sat back in his chair and stared at me. He turned his gaze toward Marshall. His brow folded between his eyes and he turned back to me. "Mrs. Pieper, you have no understanding why you're here, have you?"

"No sir, I'm afraid I am at a loss."

Mr. Mansfield seemed to be working out the situation in his head. He pursed his lips together.

"Mr. Pieper, when you signed the contract, I explicitly told you to be very clear to your wife what her stay here would entail." Marshall made no reply.

"My stay here? Sir, it was my understanding we would be here overnight only and return home tomorrow. What is this contract you speak of?"

Mr. Mansfield's eyes narrowed. He motioned to Mr. Whear without shifting his gaze. "James, why don't you take Mrs. Pieper out to the sun room and give her some refreshment? I need to speak with Mr. Pieper."

"Yes sir." He walked back to me and, again, put his arm out for me to take.

I put my hand up and said, "Wait a moment, sir. Mr. Mansfield, if my husband has lied to me about the reasons we came to your estate, then I wish to know." I turned my eyes toward Marshall. He still refused to look at me. "I'm sensing very strongly he brought me here for some purpose, but has lacked the strength to tell me what the purpose is." I turned back to Mr. Mansfield. "Sir, what is this place? I realize what I saw in one of the paintings in the entryway. Is this some sort of brothel?"

"No, no, Mrs. Pieper, I assure you, this isn't a brothel—" Mr. Mansfield started to say.

"It's a place to teach you how to be a better wife to me," Marshall finally found his voice and interrupted Mr. Mansfield. I could tell he tried to keep his anger under control.

Mr. Mansfield stood. "Mr. Pieper, if you please. Had you explained this properly to your wife, we wouldn't have this present situation to deal with." He tried to quiet his tone. "James, please. Mrs. Pieper, go with James out to the sunroom. I must get a few things straight with your husband. All will be explained, I promise."

I hadn't stopped staring at Marshall. I thought perhaps I'd misheard what he said and felt confused. Mr. Whear leaned over and took my hand. I stood and let him lead me into another room. He put his hand inside his jacket and pulled out a handkerchief. Handing it to me, he then turned toward a sideboard with decanters on it and said something, but it didn't register in my head. I looked at the clean, white piece of fabric he'd given me. I didn't realize I cried and couldn't understand why. Marshall's behavior shouldn't be a surprise, but what he'd said about being a better wife, stabbed me in the heart. Why should I feel this way? I hated him more than at any other moment in our three years together. What was I crying about? I couldn't comprehend any of what happened and tried to ebb the flow from my eyes. With my back to Mr. Whear, I walked to the window and looked out at the garden in the back of the house. My mind raced all over the place and I realized I didn't see anything but darkness.

Mr. Whear moved over to me and put a glass with brown liquid in front of me. "You didn't answer, so I poured you a brandy."

I took a sip and the warm fluid went down too fast and caused me to cough. Mr. Whear patted my back and looked concerned. I tried to smile. "Sorry, I don't drink much but wine at Layne Hall."

"Why don't we have a seat, Mrs. Pieper? Perhaps I can answer some of your questions."

Mr. Whear seemed a nice gentleman. For the first time, I believe I really looked at him. His eyes are a beautiful caramel brown, warm and attractive. His countenance seemed peaceful.

We sat on a couch and I tried another sip of the brandy. This time it went down easier. "Mr. Whear, I'm not sure what to ask. I have a notion of what kind of place this is. I'm wondering at what my husband said about making me a better wife. Do you teach how to make the dining table arrangements more presentable or do more complex needlepoint? Or is it a school to help show me how to arrange dinner parties or some such nonsense?"

He smiled. "No, ma'am. We show ladies ways to

please their husbands in the more personal ways."

"Oh, I see. I'm not certain I should be discussing this with you, no offense meant."

"No offense taken. Can I reassure you if you're thinking this is a brothel or house of prostitution, it is not. There are things which occur here between two consenting adults. What happens during this time stays here and isn't discussed again, unless you discuss it. There is a structure involved, but it's only to help increase a couple's pleasure and open their eyes to the possibilities. Have you ever been to Rome or Paris?"

"No."

"Things happen in those places out in the open. The morals are different in those cities. There are museums with the most beautiful nudes of men and women. I'm afraid our country is still a bit in the dark ages. We're brought up to believe any kind of sexual pleasure is a sin. There are those who would frown greatly upon our instruction. They'd say we are treading into a couple's private life too much. This is one of the reasons for confidentiality."

"Private lives? This is all sounding like the Marques De Sade," I commented.

"Have you read the Marques?" he asked.

"No, no. When I was younger, a friend of mine heard about his stories. She eventually did visit the Left Bank in Paris and got to read some of his writings. She told me many wild stories herself."

Mr. Whear nodded. "I see. The Marques was quite mad, but some of his ideas about eroticism weren't all bad."

"You've read his writings, sir?"

"Some of them, not all. Some of his publications are still banned in this country."

"What exactly is your job here?"

"I instruct on technique, positions and other things. I am also a guide. I'll be with you the whole time to assist you and answer questions you might have."

"You instruct? You mean you are a teacher?"

"Yes, in a sense."

"Mr. Whear, this has got to be the most preposterous conversation I've ever experienced. I'm a lady, sir. If my husband thinks I'm going to do this, he's become madder than the Marques."

"We'll have to see what Mr. Mansfield decides. He holds his contracts very dear and your husband did sign one to have you trained."

"Does this mean I have no say in the matter?" I asked.

Before Mr. Whear could answer, a butler came into the room and whispered something in his ear. "Thank you, Thomas." He stood. "Mr. Mansfield has asked us to return to the library, ma'am." He put his hand out to help me up.

I smoothed my skirt down as I stood. I wasn't used to drinking hard liquor and it made me feel a bit light-headed.

We went back into the library where we found Mr. Mansfield sitting at his desk. His hands were clasped together with his chin resting on them. I sat in the chair across from him and Mr. Whear stayed behind me.

"Mrs. Pieper, your husband has left. He signed a legal contract and paid in full the amount necessary to give you instruction. If you should back down, the money and promissory notes are not refundable." He placed his hands on the desk and pushed himself up. "And, there is a clause in the papers stating if you do back down, the fee is tripled, for wasting our time. I understand from Mr. Pieper, it would bankrupt your estate and things would get rather messy." He came out from behind the desk and leaned against the front of it. "That said, Mrs. Pieper, I can say without any reservation, your husband is an ass. I explained to him, quite clearly, to tell all to you before your arrival. I can only apologize to you for his obvious lack of care. To bring you into our situation without a word is unforgivable."

"Thank you for your thoughtfulness, Mr. Mansfield."

"You may not want to thank me when I tell you, if you refuse the course, I will hold your husband in default. I am a businessman and can't let people get away with this kind of behavior. It tarnishes my reputation."

"Let me be certain I'm clear on what you are saying, sir. You are threatening to take the estate to pay off this contract my husband has signed? All, if I don't participate in the program here at Mansfield Hall?" He did not answer. I stood, went to one of the bookshelves and tried to keep my mind calm. I turned back to face Mr. Mansfield. "This is unbelievable."

I thought of Stella. What would she say about all this? She would have a fit and worry herself sick when I didn't return home at the scheduled time. If Marshall showed up without me, she would think the worst.

"Mr. Mansfield, it would seem I am at an impasse. To lose Layne Hall over something my husband did willfully is ridiculous. He must feel it's necessary for me to learn these things and I suppose, as his wife, it's my duty to at least try. Appalling as it may be. Sir, I'll need to send a message to Layne. I have a housekeeper who is very dear to me. She'll be concerned when I don't arrive home tomorrow as expected."

"Of course, Mrs. Pieper. James, go tell young Daniel to saddle a horse and then come to the library." James left the room. Mr. Mansfield opened a drawer in his desk and pulled out a sheet of paper. "Ma'am, please, use my desk to write your note. We'll send it out as soon as the ink is dry."

I sat down at his desk. Dating the paper, I put down *Dearest Stella*, and then got stuck. How was I going to explain this to her? I wrote, I'm writing this so you will not

51

worry when I do not return home tomorrow. I looked up at Mr. Mansfield. "How long am I expected here, sir?"

"A month to six weeks, ma'am," he replied.

I looked back at the paper. *No matter what Marshall says about my absence, do not believe it. The man is a liar. I will be home in about six weeks and will explain all to you then. Rest assured, though, I am fine. Love, Catherine.* I folded the letter. Mr. Mansfield offered me an envelope. I put Stella Taylor on the cover and sealed it with wax he offered.

At this time, a young boy, who looked about fourteen years old, entered the room in front of Mr. Whear. He took off his cap and looked attentive. I handed the note to Mr. Mansfield, who passed it to the boy. He put his hands on the boys' shoulders and looked him in the eye. "Did Mr. Whear explain where you need to take this note, Daniel?"

"Yes, sir."

"Good, good. Ride like the wind. I want it delivered today, you hear?"

"Yes sir," the boy Daniel said. He tipped his hat and ran out of the room.

Mr. Mansfield watched him go and I heard him say, "Good lad."

I realized he and Mr. Whear watched me and I set the pen down and stood. "I'm feeling a bit like Alice down the rabbit hole, sir. If a smoking caterpillar shows up, I won't be much surprised."

"Mrs. Pieper." Mr. Mansfield walked over to me and took my hands in his. "I promise you, nothing here will hurt you. James is a very gentle instructor and he'll watch over you and make sure you are safe." He turned and looked at Mr. Whear. "James, why don't you escort Mrs. Pieper up to her suite and get things started? Ah, ma'am, I do need to ask you one very delicate question. When was your last cycle?" I must not have answered him quickly enough. He then added,

"We want to ensure no unwanted pregnancies."

"Ah, I see. It was about two and a half weeks ago," I answered and felt my face flush.

"Thank you. Now off you go, I'll see you around the grounds before long." He turned back to his desk and I heard him sigh.

I followed Mr. Whear out of the library to the main stairwell in the outer room. On the second floor we turned several corners and came to another set of double doors. He opened the right-hand side and stood back, waiting for me to enter the room. My brain raced and no matter how hard I tried to calm myself, nothing worked. I felt on the edge of panic. I looked up at Mr. Whear who continued to wait. Putting my head down, I walked across the threshold into the room.

I looked around the room and discovered it was decorated very tastefully and attractive. It sat on the corner of the mansion and there were many windows which made it well lit. On the right-hand side, was a large, four poster bed, larger than mine at Layne Hall. There were several chairs, over stuffed and straight back with a table near the windows. To the left was another room. I could see a cast iron, claw foot bathtub and tiles on the floor, and I assumed I'd seen the restroom.

I realized Mr. Whear watched me and I stopped in the middle of the room and felt unsure which way to go. "It's a lovely room, sir," was all I could think to say.

"Yes, I think so, too. May I call you Catherine or Kate? Do you prefer Cathy?" he asked.

When he spoke, I looked up at him. I wasn't certain what I'd heard. My ears buzzed. "I'm sorry, what did you ask?"

"May I call you Catherine?" he asked and smiled. The informality perplexed me, but I agreed. "Good," he said. "I'm going to give you a little time to look around and get

53

used to the room. I will make arrangements for some lunch to be brought up. I imagine you must be hungry?"

"I haven't even thought about food, but, yes, I could eat. Thank you."

"Good, I'll be back in a few minutes." He turned to leave the room.

"Mr. Whear?" I stopped him.

"Forgive me, please. Call me James."

"Sir," I stumbled with his first name. "When my husband left, did he by any chance leave my valise?"

Mr. Whear thought for a moment and said, "I'm not sure. I can check. I don't believe you'll need it, though. We provide everything you could want."

"No, in the bag is my journal and pens. I'd like to have it, if I may. If he left them here, I'd be very grateful."

"Of course, yes. There should be no problem. If he didn't leave it, we can provide another journal for you."

"Thank you, James."

He smiled and left the room. I heard the lock click in the metal plate below the door knob. I walked to the door and tested it. Locked. I turned my back to the door, leaned against the wood and knew how trapped animals felt. Looking at the room again, I walked over to the windows and looked out. The view was appealing with a beautiful garden. Some of the flowers were in bloom and the colors seem so vibrant and alive. I also noticed toward the back of the yard a glass building which must be a green house. It explained the flowers in the vase in the main entrance. It did seem too early for some of the blooms down there. I saw several bird feeders with sparrows and finches feeding. Men worked around the outer edges of the patch. They pulled weeds and tilled the soil, which I wanted to do.

Anger began to build at what Marshall arranged for me and I didn't think I should let myself get worked up. I couldn't fathom why he felt it necessary. Was he trying to offend me so deeply that I would divorce him? He would get his hands on my father's estate and would find this outcome satisfactory. However, it made no sense. He hated the estate. All he really wanted from it was the income. It occurred to me that if we did divorce, the estate would become his and he'd be able to sell it for quite a profit. That and the wool from this year's sheep shearing, would be a very tidy yield. He'd be able to gamble to his heart's content.

After a time, I turned my attention to the restroom. The floor was tiled with small beige squares running half way up the walls. Above the beige, the walls were painted a pale green with a darker green border. I thought there might be some meaning behind the design, but my brain wasn't going to worry about deeper meanings at this time. I felt too tired to figure out anything. The white, cast iron tub looked huge and there were pipes for running water. The sink also had water. It was quite modern.

I heard a noise come from the other room and a different butler wheeled a cart with covered trays toward the table by the windows. He looked younger than the other man, with darker skin and very dark eyes. He had a Spanish look about him. Mr. Whear followed him into the room.

"Catherine, let me introduce Marco. He'll be assisting us in the up-coming weeks. If I'm not here, Marco will be able to help you out."

I nodded. Marco smiled and I did the same. I noticed Mr. Whear held my valise in his hand. He handed it to me and I thanked him. It somehow felt comforting to have the bag in my hands, as though I could protect myself with it. I didn't want to appear weak though, so I set it down on the foot of the bed.

"You're welcome." He unbuttoned his jacket and took it off. "Why don't you have a seat? Cook has made some heavenly smelling beef stew. The aroma in the kitchen is almost overwhelming." He walked over to the closet and hung his jacket. I noticed a row of something white on hangers in there, but he closed the door too fast to see what they were.

I pulled a chair out. Mr. Whear moved to my side, took hold of the chair and held it for me to sit. I did and he sat across from me, asking Marco to begin serving. The stew steamed and my stomach made a loud rumble.

"You are hungry," he said with a smile. "You said you drink wine at your home. I went ahead and chose a Cabernet, which I think will go well with the stew. Would you like a glass?"

"Yes, thank you."

Mr. Whear handed over a basket of biscuits and Marco set out two glasses, pouring the wine. We silently ate and I thanked Marco for the wine. It did go well with the stew.

"Agreed, thank you, Marco, this will do for now." Mr. Whear excused him. Marco bowed and left the room.

While we were eating, we said nothing. Mr. Whear continued to watch me and, as my bowl emptied, I realized looking down wasn't going to work much longer. There was nothing more to see in the bowl. I drank two glasses of wine, but still felt fidgety. His staring made me uneasy.

"Mr. Whear—" I started.

"Please, call me James." He smiled.

I looked across the table at him and tried to convey the seriousness I felt. "You are staring at me, sir. I'm quite uncomfortable to begin with. The staring isn't helping."

"Catherine, I'm sorry. I don't mean to cause you unease, but you must understand. You are an attractive woman." He put his elbow on the table with his chin in his hand.

"Thank you for the compliment, sir."

"You're welcome. Let's have a chat and get to know each other a little better."

"Chat? Is this the way things would normally go?"

"Well, no." He straightened in his chair. "I spoke with Jacob and he believes we should go at a slower pace today. Since your husband didn't explain to you about the arrangement, you'll need some time to adjust. We want you to be comfortable and trust we aren't going to do anything to hurt you."

Although I was confused, I started to feel angry. "What would be the normal arrangement?" I asked. I saw Mr. Whear frown. "Sir, I don't want to be treated any differently because my husband didn't have enough courage to tell me the truth."

"I understand, but we don't need to rush things. Do you ever wear your hair down?" he asked.

I was taken aback by this question and felt certain he'd have more which would seem as odd. "At night, I keep it down when I retire."

Mr. Whear stood and walked behind my chair. He started to pull the clips out of my hair and let it fall to my shoulders. I could feel him finger the ringlets. He kept his hand in my hair and knelt down beside my chair. His touch in my hair was very gentle.

"You have beautiful hair, Catherine. When it's up in the bun, it makes your face too severe, but with it down, you look much softer and sensual." His words and voice were quiet and calming. He put his fingers up to my lip and touched it, then took my hand and started to kiss it. He slid his tongue between my fingers and licked the palm. I pulled my hand away from him. He looked up at me with his brown eyes and I felt warmth in my body.

"I'm sorry, Catherine. I don't mean to be pushy. You are so beautiful"

"Sir, you must forgive me. I know you said things didn't need to be rushed. I'm still in the dark as to where all of this is going. I'm thinking there are going to be many

57

Lauren Marie

things I'll be experiencing in the upcoming days which I've never known before. It's making me very nervous. There is very much I need explained, but first, would you mind very much going back to the other side of the table?"

Mr. Whear touched my cheek, got up and did as I asked. After he sat, he leaned forward and examined his glass of wine. "Catherine, I'm going to ask you some questions. Please, answer them as honestly as you can, all right?" he asked. I nodded. "Good, tell me about the sexual relations between you and your husband."

"Sir, I...what has this to do with instruction?"

"It has everything to do with the instruction, Catherine. Oh, I understand now. The instruction you're thinking of is from books."

"Yes, of course."

"We'll also be putting the book teaching to work physically."

"Physically?" I asked and he nodded. "You'll be touching me?"

"That and more." He smiled. "Now please tell me of your relations with your husband."

I took in a breath and stared at him, completely shocked.

"Catherine, I know this is not comfortable for you, but it will help me in how I go about with your instruction. Please, tell me in the best way you can."

I looked down at my hands. "Marshall is the only man I've ever been with. He comes up to my room. After he is finished with his business, he falls asleep and leaves sometime during the night."

"Finishes his business? That's a terribly mechanical way of saying making love or sexual intercourse. Do you never just sleep together? Do you ever feel any pleasure when he's fucking you?"

I'd heard this word before from Marshall's mouth,

but never in conversation. It sounded terribly wicked. "I'm not sure what you mean by pleasure?"

He put his wine glass on the table. "Have you ever had an orgasm?"

"I'm not sure." I began to feel very small. He looked at me and I could see a touch of sympathy in his eyes. "I'm rather pathetic, aren't I?" I asked.

"No, no. Not pathetic at all, just held back from wonderful feelings and experiences." He sat back. "An orgasm takes your breath away and gives you a charge in your body. It's a sensation like no other. I've even heard for some women it makes their toes curl. Does your husband ever take your breath away?"

I looked away from Mr. Whear. As I thought about it, the only time Marshall took my breath away was on our wedding night and those occasions when he hit me in the stomach. "No," I answered with a weak voice.

Mr. Whear lowered his voice, "Catherine, does he ever kiss and suck on your breasts? Does he caress your most secret areas? Do you ever give him head or suck his penis?"

A vision of the last time I'd been with Marshall flashed in my head and my throat started to tighten. "Mr. Whear, I assure you, I have only ever had my husband lying on top of me. The last time he threw me over his desk and got his pleasure from my rear. He forced me quite recently to…to put his member in my mouth and I cannot remember getting any pleasure from it. I only had bruises to show for it." I couldn't believe what I'd just said and started to sob. This is never going to work for me. Sitting and discussing all of these private things with a total stranger felt too much to handle.

Mr. Whear was again on his knee by my chair and held me in his arms. I wept for several minutes and he stroked my hair. I created a large, wet spot on the sleeve of his shirt.

He spoke softly. "I want to show you what you've been missing. I know it's difficult for you now, but, trust me, let me give you this gift." He moved my head up and pushed my hair back. He then put his lips on mine. I felt his mouth open and his tongue touch my lips. I kept my mouth closed. There was no force. It was the gentlest kiss I'd ever experienced from a man. His tongue moved and he pecked at my lips with his, finally pulling back and opening his eyes.

"Why do you have such a difficult time calling me by my first name?"

I picked up a napkin and wiped my eyes. I laughed and looked back at him. "I only met you a couple of hours ago. I don't think I know you well enough." I laughed a little more and thought my words seemed stupid. "I thought we weren't going to rush this?" I asked.

"Hmmm...I think we'll just take things as they come. You didn't want to be treated differently, remember?" He pushed my hair behind my ear. "May I brush your hair?"

"I'm sorry. What did you just say?" I felt sure I hadn't heard him right.

"I'd like to brush your hair, Catherine. And then, perhaps wash it, in there." He pointed toward the washroom. "Without clothes, in the tub. Nothing here at Mansfield will hurt you. There will be no bruises. Once you've experienced some of the things I'll teach, you'll never want to turn back. Hopefully, you'll be open minded enough to grab on and never let go."

"Mr..." I started and then stopped. "I'm sorry, James, I'm very frightened."

He put his hand on my cheek. "I'll be with you every step of the way. I promise nothing will be painful. I think I understand now you've been brought up a certain way. There were topics never discussed and particular words never used. They are only words. They mean nothing and in some cases they mean something entirely different than our current usage. People should use their dictionaries more often."

He stood and went to the chest of drawers. Opening one of the drawers, he pulled out a brush and then returned to the back of my chair. He began to brush gently and I could feel his hand touch my neck and head as he brought his hand up to feel the curls. "Your hair is so soft, Catherine. It feels so smooth," he whispered.

He finished and put the brush on the table. Kneeling down beside my chair, he put his hand down on the legs and pulled me around so I faced him.

"Show me the bruises," he said.

"What?"

"You said the last time with your husband, he forced himself on you over the desk."

I nodded and began to pull my skirt up to expose my legs. I couldn't believe I did this. When the hem hit the high part of my thigh, I started to move one of my stockings down. The bruises weren't as dark as they'd been. The spot turned a greenish yellow color, but still showed. I rolled the other stocking down.

James put his hands on my knees and looked at the marks. "Do they still hurt?"

"Not so much, no." I watched him.

He ran his hands over the bruises and then leaned forward and kissed each bruise. He looked up at me and asked, "Now?"

"No."

He kissed them again, and I felt his tongue tasting my skin. I thought, for some reason, I could trust this man. For a moment my brain let me believe he wouldn't give me any false perceptions about Mansfield Hall. He would be clear and honest at all times. After the morning with Marshall and his lies, James honesty was appreciated.

Lauren Marie

He stood up and held my hand. "Come with me," he said, and pulled me up. He directed me toward the restroom. "Let me show you something," he said, and guided me to the mirror above the sink. He made me face it and look at myself. He stood behind me, with his hands on my waist. "Look at how beautiful you are, Catherine." Pulling me tight against his body and I could feel his member pressing against my buttocks. His right hand came around to the front of my skirt and his left came over my shoulder and unbuttoned the top of my blouse. His hand slid down inside my shirt, into my camisole and found my breast. Massaging it, he pinched the nipple and I caught my breath and began to perspire. I couldn't take my eyes off of his and felt I'd been hypnotized. I closed my eyes and leaned back into him. I'd never felt anything like this before. James was correct about getting my breath taken away. I would have known if something like this happened before.

He leaned his head down and kissed the side of my neck. Then, he whispered in my ear, "Before I wash your hair, may I make love to you?"

I looked at him in the mirror. The voice in my head screamed at me. It was sin and wicked and I'd be cheating on my marriage. It would be adultery and I would have to explain myself before God. I think I nodded yes, but all I could see or hear were his eyes in the mirror and my breaths.

My heart pounded in my chest. James turned me around to face him. He leaned down and put his lips on mine kissing me gently at first, then with a little more force. I let my lips part and accepted his tongue in my mouth. His right hand moved down the side of my skirt and began to pull it up, but I put my hand over his and pulled away from his lips

"I'm not ready for this. Please, can we wait?" I shook like leaves in a breeze and saw his eyes close.

He smiled, and opened them. Touching my hair, he asked, "Are you okay?"

I wasn't able to come up with any words, so I just nodded.

"You're shaking and it would be best to wait. Time for a bath then, I still want to wash your hair and it will help you relax." Holding my hand, he led me into the other room. "I'll go in and get the water started in the tub." He pointed to the closet. "In there you'll find some robes. Most of your time here will be spent wearing only a robe. They are quite soft and comfortable, I'm told. Please, undress and join me by the bath tub." He went into the restroom and I heard water start to run.

I spent a bit of time undressing and felt in shock. My hands shook as I unbuttoned my blouse. This man, who I'd only just met, just asked to be the only other man I'd been with besides my husband. He'd offered me a gift. My body felt numb, as did my brain, which couldn't put words together. My ears were buzzing again, but this time it wasn't from the fear. I only felt this moment. The water running sounded loud and there were no other sounds. I kept repeating over to myself - I can trust him, I can trust him. I felt as though I'd stepped off a cliff into an unknown world. I caught sight of my reflection in a mirror on the closet door and stared at myself. I wondered if the teaching I would experience made me some kind of a whore. I was a married lady and James kissed me. Although, Marshall cheated on me in the city and paid Jacob Mansfield for the training, I wondered if any of it mattered. I almost didn't care.

I slipped on a robe and tied it at the waist. Walking to the bath, I felt as if I stepped out of my body. I must be in a type of shock, I thought. As I put my foot down on the tile floor, the cool surface on my toes woke me up. I looked up and caught my breath again. James had stripped off his clothes and stood by the tub. His body is muscular and his shoulders quite broad. The upper part looked tan and hard. I couldn't bring myself to look down.

He heard me take in my breath and turned to me. His chest was well built and tan. The room got hot when I moved my eyes to his waist and below, and saw his body was beautiful. He turned off the water and came over to me. He untied the belt holding on the robe and let it slip off my shoulders. I felt very shy and put my hands and arms up to cover my chest.

"Catherine," he said and moved one of my arms down. "Don't think, just relax and feel."

I looked up at his eyes and tried to not let my brain over take me. "I'd like to see your body," he said and moved the sleeve off my arm. I closed my eyes and stood very still. I felt the robe land in a pile around my feet and knew he looked at me. His hand caressed one of my breasts and as he moved around me, it softly felt its way down, around my waist and cupped my bottom. His lips brushed my shoulder and sent a shiver through my system. I took in a deep breath and tried to swallow.

When he stood back by my side, he took my hand and I opened my eyes. He led me to the tub, where I stepped in and sat down about half way down the length of it. I pulled my knees up to my chest. He stepped in behind me, moving his legs on either side of mine. I felt his warm hand massaging my back and shoulders.

Pulling me back to his chest, I straightened my legs a little. He wrapped his arms around me and put his lips on my neck.

"You are so beautiful," he whispered and moved his arm to a shelf by the tub and took hold of a small pitcher. Putting it into the water, he brought it up and poured the warm fluid on my head getting my hair wet. While he washed my hair, I began to cry again. He treated me so gentle and tender and whispered words of comfort. Once the soap was rinsed, he only held me.

I felt afraid to say anything and illiterate and

uneducated in what was happening. I finally found words.

"Why did you do that?" I asked, between sniffs.

His hand moved down my arm. "Why did I wash your hair? Has your husband never done this for you? Did it hurt you?"

"No," I whispered. "You didn't hurt me. Marshal never did anything like it."

"It was only the first. Give yourself some time, you'll be all right."

When we got out of the bath, he brought out a large white towel and dried me off. He wouldn't let me do anything or wrap up. He then brought out a brush and combed my hair. Finally, he let me put the robe back on and I felt grateful to be covered again.

We went back into the other room and it surprised me to find it dark. I heard him click a switch on one of the lamps in the room. I sat down in one of the overstuffed chairs pulling my knees up under my chin. I tried not to look at him. James did not re-dress and his nudity made me uncomfortable.

A knock sounded on the door and Marco came in with dinner on a cart. He asked if I'd like a glass of wine or would I prefer something else. I asked for wine, but it came out a hoarse whisper. James moved his chair closer to mine and when he sat down he became less distracting. With his lower body below the table, I found I could look at him again.

James struck a match and lit the candles on the table. It cast a warming glow in the room and I got out of the overstuffed chair to set the table.

We ate the dinner silently, but I found I wasn't very hungry and after a few bites, put my utensils down.

"Catherine, is the food not to your liking?"

"No, the food is fine," I said. "I'm not very hungry. We just had stew a little while ago."

We began a conversation about unrelated things. He asked me about my interests, wanting to know if I enjoyed needle craft, sewing or cooking. I told him about the garden at Layne Hall and what a pleasure it was to work in the outdoors. He agreed and said he liked working the soil and watching plants grow. I went over my history some and told him about Stella, and the others who worked at the Hall for many years. I mentioned my love of reading and he asked who my favorite authors were.

"I like Austen and the Bronte sisters."

"Ah, the romantics. They are quite good."

"You've read their works?" I asked.

"Yes, some of them. Austen, I like particularly. She has a way of poking fun at the upper class snobs which I find amusing."

"This last winter I also read Alexander Dumas and J.F. Cooper. Those are wonderful authors, too."

He tilted his head and said, "That does surprise me. Which Dumas did you read?"

"The Three Musketeers. Why?"

"I would think books such as The Three Musketeers and Last of the Mohicans would be more enjoyed by menfolk."

"Don't be silly. They have rugged heroes who'll do anything to save their ladies. I would consider them to be as romantic as Austen."

"I just thought they'd be a little too rough and tumble for your tastes. I see I have many secrets yet to learn," he said, with a bit of tease in his voice. "I'll have to remember to call you milady."

"She was quite evil, remember, and lost her head for her sins," I replied. I tried not to laugh and act perfectly serious.

We spoke for several hours. He told me about what to expect in the coming weeks without going into too much detail. He said I'd have the mornings to myself and I could use this time to write in my journal. He also said Mr. Mansfield owned quite an extensive library and if I'd like to look for a book to occupy some time, it wouldn't be any problem. The afternoons would be spent learning new things and the evenings would be for putting those subjects to practice.

After a time, James got up and went to the nightstand where he'd put his pocket watch. He clicked it open and looked at it.

"What time is it?" I asked.

"Just after eleven o'clock." He put it back down, came to my chair and put his hand on my shoulder. "You've had a very trying day, Catherine. I think some rest would be good." He held his hand out, but I didn't stand right away. "I should let you know there are others here who will be working with me in your teachings. When the men are having vaginal intercourse with you, they'll be wearing condoms and they'll never kiss you on the mouth. I'm the only one who'll have that pleasure. They'll never cum in your birth canal either. As Jacob said, we wish no unwanted children to come out of the learning you'll have. Ah, you've gone silent again."

I looked up at him. "May I ask a question?"

"Of course." He pulled his chair next to mine and sat.

"How long have you been doing this? Teaching woman about intercourse and such?"

"About eleven years, but I've lived here at Mansfield for eighteen years. My father died when I was twelve and Jacob took me in. Remember Daniel, the boy who delivered your message?" I nodded. "His is a similar situation. Jacob is a bit of a softy when it comes to us orphans."

"Is he attracted to boys?"

"No, nothing of the sort. I think he would have lots of children if he'd found the right wife. Jacob's never been married, but he does love women. He goes into the city often, to a particular brothel, where I think he has a favorite. Anyway, Jacob educated me. I had tutors for everything. When I turned eighteen, I trained a little myself, but didn't need too much. I'd picked up a lot of technique from the other men who were around. I didn't begin teaching until I was nineteen, when Jacob felt I could give a woman the best training. This place used to be busier, but in the last year it's slowed down. I think Jacob is slowing down, too. He mentions retiring to Greece every now and then."

"Are there any other women here now?"

"No, you're the only client."

"What would you do if he stopped this business?"

"Milady, you've gotten more than a question and you are looking extremely worn out." He stood and held out his hands.

I took them and as I rose from the chair the room shifted a little. "I think the couple of glasses of wine have gone to my head. I am tired."

"May I take your robe?"

I felt my forehead crease. "What am I to sleep in, sir?"

"Your skin only, you'll get used to it and according to other ladies, 'it's nice not having a dressing gown wrapped around my waist and stomach in the morning.'"

"I see." I opened the robe and slipped it off. Turning, I moved under the sheet and put my head on the pillow. I watched James as he blew out the candles, turned off the lights and made his way to the other side of the bed. I lifted up onto my elbows. "Are you sleeping here, too?"

"Yes, I also need my rest," he said and slid under the covers. He switched off the bedside lamp on the nightstand and moved over to me in the darkened room. I rolled over to my right side with my face away from him. I felt his hand come up under my arm and he pulled me to his chest. He kissed my ear and whispered "good night". I didn't think it would be possible to sleep, but sleep I did. Before drifting off, I thought how different it felt to have a protective arm holding me. If Marshall passed out, he never stayed for long. We'd always lived in separate rooms.

I've written so much this morning my hand is cramping. Yesterday was such a long day and so much happened. I'm going to continue to fill these pages with the upcoming days. The good Lord only knows what they will bring.

Lauren Marie

Chapter Five

1976

Nick and his brothers and sister all sat and stared at each other. Then Nick, set the book on the coffee table and stood. He walked over to the front window and looked out at the cars parked along the drive.

Stella sat back on the couch, hugging a pillow. "It's the School for Scandal. Samuel Barber would be very proud," she said, half mumbling.

"Dear sister, the School for Scandal was originally a play, not a symphonic piece," Michael commented, and glanced at her.

"I know that, dear brother. It was the first thing that popped into my head." She put her head back on the couch.

"I need a drink. I'm taking orders." Michael stood and stretched.

"Bring the bottle," Nick said. He turned from the window and walked back to his seat. "I guess we know how mother and father first met now. It seems so surreal. Were there really sex schools for adults in their time?"

"I have heard of such things," John said, and stretched his legs out in front of him. "I never did believe they actually existed, but I guess they did."

"What do you mean you've heard of them?" Nick asked, and sat back down by Jay.

"When I was in college, there were some erotic books floating around that hinted at such places."

"You didn't read that crap," Stella said and sat up looking angry.

"You need to remember, I was nineteen or twenty years old. The guys I studied with brought them in and we thought we were being extremely rebellious. It wasn't the best literature in the world, but we were hormone crazy back then. It was early in the 1950s, you know?"

"Lord have mercy, John. Next you'll be telling me you subscribe to Playboy magazine," Stella said.

John started to answer, but Michael interrupted when he came in carrying a tray of shot glasses and a bottle of whiskey. "If he doesn't, I have some I can show you. That is if you're interested, Stella," he said, and put the tray on the coffee table.

"That's very funny, Michael, ha, ha," she huffed.

"Now, come on, you guys. There's really no way to prove if the schools existed. Our mother wrote about one such place, and we know for a fact Mother never lied or stretched the truth," Nick said.

As Michael poured the whiskey, Nick and the others watched him and accepted the glasses as he passed them around.

"I, too, have heard of such schools. They are considered by some to be extremely disreputable and, for that reason, they keep things very hush-hush. I was in a bar in New York with some editors years ago and after a few rounds, heard the most fascinating stories." Michael looked at his siblings and smiled. "You should be aware that people only go to them if they choose to go. No one is ever forced."

"You're joking," Steven said. "Those places really existed?"

Michael nodded and drank his whiskey in one swallow. "And, still do exist. That's how I understood it, anyway."

"Her first husband was such a jerk," Stella said,

taking a sip. "It's no wonder mother never talked about him."

"She could have been protecting Uncle Jacob, too. Imagine if it had gotten out at that time. It would have created such a scandal in the community. They all would have been outcasts. It is as mother said in the note. They lived in a different time." Michael put his glass on the table and sat back on the couch.

Nick looked at his youngest brother. "Jacob, you've been awfully quiet. Do you have any thoughts about this?"

Jacob looked around at the group and frowned. "No, I'm not ready to judge anything. We still only know a little of what went on with Mother and Father. It is a bit embarrassing to hear their relations so graphically read to us. I find, though, I want to hear more. I'm going to make arrangements with the college to be out for another week. Tomorrow's Sunday and I'm certain we won't be able to finish all of these journals by then. I want to know the whole story."

"I have to agree. Mother's journals have opened a can of worms," Michael said. "I'm fortunate that I don't have anywhere important to be right now. I can stay."

Nick and the others agreed. They would call spouses and work and make arrangements to stay at the estate longer.

Lauren Marie

Secrets Beyond Dreams

Chapter Six

May 2, 1920

Yesterday was certainly a strange day. I'm still unsure of what to make of the entire goings-on here at Mansfield.

When I woke up in the morning, I still lay on my right side with James' arm thrown over me. I listened to him breathe for a while and, I could tell he still slept. Somehow, I managed to get out from under his arm without waking him. Grabbing the robe off of the chair, I put it on and made my way to the restroom.

I washed my face and scrubbed my teeth with my finger as best I could. Drying off with a towel, I stared at myself in the mirror, unsure of the person I looked at. I saw a familiar face, but my mind felt confused and frightened. I found the brush James used the day before and brushed out my hair. My clips were on the table out in the other room and I didn't want to go retrieve them, but knew I couldn't stay in here all day.

I opened the door and started into the other room. James sat up in the bed and smiled.

"Good morning, Catherine," he greeted me. I froze in the middle of the floor and looked at him. "Would you like for me to brush your hair?"

I didn't realize I still held onto the brush and looked at it. "You asked me a question yesterday which I didn't respond to. The answer is no." I moved my eyes to him.

He sat up a little straighter on the mattress and looked confused. "Which question would that have been?"

I walked to the window and gazed out the glass panes. I couldn't look at him "My husband never puts his mouth on my breasts. He squeezes them with his hands and I often end up with bruises…" My voice faded and my mind cried out. I leaned my head against the cool glass, it felt comforting somehow. I closed my eyes and tried to concentrate, but my mind told me too many things.

I hadn't heard James get out of the bed, but his hands were on my shoulders and he stood behind me. He reached around and took the brush out of my hand, setting it on the table.

Continuing to stare through the glass, I started to say something, but so many words ran through my brain, I got lost in them and closed my mouth. "I think this must be what it feels like to be in shock, sir," was all I could come up with.

His left arm wrapped around my chest and pulled me to him. "Catherine, it will be all right. I promise you. Although, I'm feeling your husband should be the one here, learning how to treat his wife better."

"Thank you," I said.

We stood this way for some time. He massaged my neck with his free hand and at some point, I realized I'd brought my hands up to hold his arm.

"I need my clips. I should put my hair up," I said.

"Why? I think it looks better down. Please, don't put it back in that bun."

I looked up at him and he smiled, again.

There was a light knock on the door and James pulled away from me. I didn't turn, but could smell coffee and bacon. Apparently, the butler or Marco or someone, brought a cart up with breakfast. At the feel of my stomach rumbling, I woke up and turned around.

After breakfast, James got up to leave the room and

said I'd be on my own until lunch time. Then we'd get down to work. He disappeared into the hallway and I noted this time he didn't lock the door. As I wrote in my journal, I heard people out working in the garden. Watching them out the window, I saw James out there in the midst of it all. His shirt was off and, I must admit, I found some enjoyment in watching his muscles move and remembering what he looked like by the tub.

I went through the closet and found other clothing. The skirt and blouse I'd worn yesterday were nowhere to be found. There was a pull over dress in the wardrobe, I took off the hanger and looked at. It was a pale blue linen garment and I took off the robe and put it on. There were slits up the sides to just above my knees. I could not find my shoes though and I didn't much like the idea of walking around without them. I sat back at the table and continued to write in my journal.

Sometime later, James came back in. He carried a pair of slip-on shoes and asked if I'd like to come out and see the garden. He said he liked the dress I'd chosen to wear and it looked very nice, but didn't show off my figure enough. He knelt down and picked up my foot to slip on one of the shoes. He said they looked like they fit and wanted to know how they felt. They were comfortable enough.

"Where are my shoes, sir?" I asked.

"I put them in your bag. It's on the floor of the closet, Milady." He smiled up at me.

"Oh, thank you." I must have overlooked the bag.

He showed me around Mansfield and took me first out to the garden. We walked a lovely path looking out on the green fields surrounding the estate. I asked him about the lake I'd seen on the way in yesterday. He acknowledged it, but said it had no name. He liked to fish there and Jacob allowed the tenants around the estate to use it freely.

We came to a fork in the road and James lead me to

the right side, saying this path would take us back to Mansfield. I asked where the other path led. He got a sad look on his face, but then smiled and said it went to another estate. I wondered about the look, but as we continued on, the path took us into some trees and I forgot about it entirely until now. I'm going to have to ask him about the other estate and why it made him sad.

When we got back to Mansfield, he showed me the library. The collection was quite impressive. I found books in languages I'd never heard of before. Apparently, Mr. Mansfield is well versed in many languages and has a knack for picking them up. James wasn't sure how many he could speak.

I chose a volume by Edgar Allan Poe which I hadn't read, called the Pit and the Pendulum. James wondered if Mr. Poe might be too frightening. I said things in the real world were scarier than fiction stories in books. He told me I was too rational. I found myself comfortable at being honest with him.

After lunch, James brought in a large volume of what I thought was an art book. It was beautifully bound with a leather cover. We sat at the table in my room and he opened the book. It was an art book, but the paintings and drawings were not standard art. They depicted people in various sexual positions, some of which seemed to go against any way the body could ever bend. There were pictures of one man with one woman, two men with one woman, one man with two women and so on. Part of me felt appalled by the pictures, but another part was curious and found them rather interesting. When I told James I didn't think my body could bend like this, he laughed and said I'd be surprised what the body could do. When I asked what he meant, he decided to show me.

Leading me to the bed, he sat me down and lay me back with my knees over the side. He lifted one of my legs bringing my foot up to his mouth. He kissed my ankle and put it on his shoulder. He then moved toward me so my knee sat on his shoulder and his weight was being held by my leg. My other leg frogged out and he pulled the lower half up on the back of his thighs. He looked down at me and raised his eyebrows. He said the thing he liked most about this position was being able to see my face, to watch the expressions as excitement built. When Marco was with us, he said, I would be amazed at the positions he could acquire.

Today would only be James and myself, though. He said it would be better to have me get used to him, before complicating the training.

We got back up and returned to the table. I told James my leg felt like it had been dislocated. He said this was another good reason for taking it slowly. He didn't want to injure muscles I wasn't used to working.

We looked at some more of the pictures and came across one of a woman with a man's member in her mouth. It was only a painting, but I could see by the look on the woman's face she felt happy about the act. You could see one of her hands holding the man, her other hand was down between her own legs. I grabbed at the book cover and closed the volume with a thud.

James asked what I found disturbing about the painting. It made me feel as though I would gag as the memory of Marshall forcing his member into my mouth, and holding my nose closed, flooded my brain. I wondered about the happy look on the woman's face and couldn't believe it would be enjoyable. I asked James about the woman's hand between her legs, trying to veer away from the other part of the picture.

"Have you never heard of masturbation?" he asked.

"Yes, of course. I've heard men do it, but…"

"Women can do it too, Catherine. Have you never touched yourself and felt a little pleased?"

"No, not in this way."

"Sometimes it's the only way a woman can enjoy orgasms. Men can be lacking the education to pleasure a woman. You must not feel as though you're lacking in any knowledge. It's a basic misunderstanding which goes on around the world." He re-opened the book to the wicked page. "Was that the only thing you found disturbing?"

I glanced back at the picture. "James, she looks happy."

"When you experienced this with your husband, tell me what happened."

I looked at him and said, "No."

"Why not? I'm not going to judge you or find fault, Catherine." He pushed my hair away from my cheek and touched my lip. "Is it how you got these bruises?"

I put my hand up to may face, covered it and pulled away from him. I felt nothing at this moment. "I didn't think you could still see it."

"I can only see it a little. It's an unusual shade of yellow, different from the rest of your skin color."

"My lip was from an error in judgment. Marshall hadn't been drinking and I thought I'd give him a kiss. He bit me. I re-injured it when I hit a pen holder on his desk. My cheek came from being hit at the dinner table." I looked back up at him and saw sadness in his eyes. "He then dragged me by my hair into his study. When I wouldn't get on my knees, he kicked me on my leg which made my knee buckle. When I wouldn't open my mouth, he pinched my nose," my voice started to fade to where I only whispered. "It didn't seem to matter to him if I couldn't breathe or choked. It seemed to make him more excited." I swallowed and took in a breath. "I'm sorry. I didn't mean to go into this."

"No, Catherine, don't apologize. Your husband should be castrated for treating you in such a manner. It's appalling. Thank you for sharing. I want you to know I don't approve of such behavior. It's a man's way of feeling powerful and it is sick." He closed the book.

I looked up at him. "Thank you."

"Why are you thanking me? I've done nothing?"

"No, thank you. Just thank you." He took my hands and kissed both of my palms. "James?"

"Yes."

I wasn't sure what I wanted to ask. There were so many questions, but they seemed to be in a jumble again. "Nothing, never mind," I said and pulled away my hand that he held. "You listen well. It's greatly appreciated."

He looked at me creasing his brow a bit, but said nothing. He turned his attention back to my hands and began kissing them again. He kissed my wrist and then ran his tongue up to my elbow.

"Catherine, I'd like to touch your body and kiss it. May I?" he asked.

I found this a courteous question, but almost laughed. He has an odd way about him. "I suppose you may, since it's supposed to be part of the training," I replied.

He pushed his chair back and pulled me onto his lap with my back against his chest. My legs were spread on either side of his and he pulled my linen dress up over my head. He did it so fast I didn't have time to think that I sat naked on his knees. Dropping the dress on the floor next to the chair, he put his hands on my thighs.

"Put your hand on your pussy," he whispered and licked my ear.

"I…but…wait," I stuttered.

"No. Put your hand out like this."

He held his hand up flat and I did the same. His moved his on top of mine and put it down on my most secret place. I felt his middle finger push mine down and the warm and wetness swallowed my finger. He moved our fingers in circles over what felt like a nub and the room began to grow warm. Feelings flooded my body and it became difficult to draw in breath. Continuing that movement, he brought his hand up to my breast and played with the nipple which cause my mind to go crazy. I couldn't think or say any words, the feeling flamed throughout my body and I arched my back looking up at the ceiling.

I think I moaned, but am not sure. The feeling that hit me was like nothing I'd ever experienced before and never with Marshall. It caused me to soar.

"Catherine, I want you to turn around and face me," he said.

With his help, we got me turned and his brown eyes searched mine. He kissed my mouth and brought his hands up to my breasts. I felt myself lean back and his lips left mine to move down to the center of my chest. He kissed and licked the cleavage made by his hands. Putting his mouth on the nipple of one breast, I sucked in my breath and tilted my head back. I closed my eyes and focused on only the moment. I blocked every other thought out of my head. I could feel his teeth nibbling on the skin of my breast and then his mouth moved to the other side. He ran his hands down and up my legs and took my hand in his and put my middle finger in his mouth.

"I want to taste you," he said around my finger then closed his lips. I could feel his tongue licking my finger and giggled.

He put his hand on the back of my head and brought it forward to put his mouth on mine. Again, I wasn't thinking and I put my tongue into his mouth and felt his tongue on mine. I sensed a growing pressure in my pelvic area and found myself wanting him very much.

He pulled back and I opened my eyes to look into his again.

"Catherine, please, unbutton my trousers."

I looked down at his crotch and could tell he was

getting excited. I did as he said and opened the top button. I felt surprised to find he wore no under clothes. I could see a patch of hair and part of his member. I looked back up at him. He smiled and whispered, "You may touch my penis. Be gentle though."

I put my hand down into his trousers and wrapped my fingers around his already solid member. I moved it up and out. It felt hard, yet soft and warm to my touch. James leaned a little forward and pulled his shirt off. I couldn't take my eyes off of him. Marshall never allowed me to do this. He'd push my hand away. I moved my thumb a little and touched the top.

"There are braces on either side of the chair. Can you put your feet on them?"

I moved my feet around and felt the cross bar on the chair legs. "Yes."

"Good, plant your feet on them and lift yourself up a bit." Again, I did as he said and put my hands on his shoulders for balance. He looked up at me and said, "You know where my penis goes. Put it there."

I knew what he asked. The words came back into my head. Wicked, whore, cheater. I shut them off and adjusted my position and moved his member to the opening of my vagina. As I slowly let myself down, I felt it slid into me and I sighed. Without James telling me to do so, I began to push up again and began a rhythmic movement. I never would have believed my legs were strong enough to do this, but I did for as long as I could. James put his lips back on my breast and sucked it hard. He put his hand up to the other and pinched the nipple between his fingers. My heart pounded and I realized I'd stopped feeling nervous.

When my legs grew tired, James lifted me up and lay my back on the table. He pushed the book out of the way. His member started to slide out, but he pushed it back in. I wrapped my legs around his waist and put my hands into his hair. He rested on his elbows on either side of me and pumped again. I thought for a moment it would have been nice to try the position we'd seen in the book, but he stopped pushing in and straightened up. He put up a finger and said to wait one moment and not to move. He went to the dresser, opened a drawer, and removed a little package. Opening it, he pulled out what looked like a small sock. As he moved back toward me, he put it over his member and I realized it was a condom. In no time he'd reentered me and stood, moving his body in and out. The pumping quickened and he leaned back over me and moaned in my ear. He pushed a couple more times and then stopped.

I'd been so engrossed watching him that I realized I'd lost my breath. As did he. James moved to straighten up, again. His member pulled out of me, smaller, and the condom dropped to the floor. He pulled me up and kissed my mouth. With both of his hands in my hair, he massaged my neck and ran them down my back. He whispered in my ear, "You've just passed on your first position."

I kissed his cheek and then his lips. "Oh."

"Milady, it will get better and better. I promise."

"Milord, please pardon my ignorance. I didn't realize there was a count." I tried to smile, but found myself mesmerized with his lips. I kissed them again and again.

We spent the rest of the evening exploring one another. I learned so much last night. Things which can be done with touch, with tongue, and with the body came to me as natural as anything. I pushed all other thoughts out of my mind and just lived for one moment. When James lips and tongue found my secret places, I placed my own hands on my breasts and can say I know what an orgasm is now. It so amazed me, James ability to keep himself excited. He did his job well and made me feel so much.

When we curled up on the bed sheets together, I didn't even remember we'd never eaten dinner. Waking up this morning, I found I was starving. The food tasted heavenly and I looked at James with a different eye. Whatever nerves I'd suffered through two days ago, were gone. I decided he is one of the nicest men I have ever met. I wish he could train Marshall on how to treat a woman. It would make being at Layne Hall worth living for.

Chapter Seven

May 13, 1920

I haven't written anything in the last several days. My mind went spinning and I've spent a lot of my spare time trying to sort out my feelings over the events of the last days. Embarrassingly, I must admit a part of me is enjoying the physical contact I've experienced with James. He is gentle and kind. There is warmth in his eyes, I find comforting in a way. I know it's only been a week or so, but I trust him and know in my heart he would never do anything to hurt me.

There is also a voice in my head saying I've sinned and cheated on Marshall. That same voice also angrily says Marshall's cheated on me and he did it first. I'm feeling a bit childish. I want to stomp my feet and pout and scream that I shouldn't feel guilty.

The one thing I have realized is it would be very easy to become spoiled by the attention I've been receiving. It is like nothing I've ever experienced and I have to remember it won't always be this way. It makes me a little sad, but I know I have obligations at home. I must remember that.

Yesterday, I started my cycle a week early and things slowed down. James said he didn't want to cause me any embarrassment, knowing this time of the month can be uncomfortable for woman. Despite it, we've still studied the pictures of positions in the books. He still kisses and caresses me at night. I've also found things I can do with my mouth and James let me approach his penis on my own. I did put it in my mouth, but not too far. It caused him to suck in his breath and moan. His response did amaze me. At first, I thought I'd hurt him, but he told me no. It felt wonderful. From my past experience, I couldn't fathom any pleasure from it.

He took me down to Jacobs's library to let me look, once again, at the multitude of books. Jacobs's selection is impressive. I picked up one of the art type books with graphic pictures in them. A couple of times, I felt my face blush and the room got very warm. I brought the Edgar Allan Poe book back and picked out a copy of Mary Shelley's Frankenstein to read. I found my brain spun too much over the last week to concentrate on reading. Frankenstein, I'd started a long time ago, but never finished. I couldn't remember why I stopped. It may that I was too young and it scared me. Perhaps this would be a good time to try again and see if I could get it read through.

Jacob also has a beautiful grand piano. I hadn't noticed it when I first went down to the library. James said he wouldn't mind my playing, so I sat down and began playing a piece from memory. The musical instrument sounded wonderful and I could have gone on playing all afternoon. At one point, I looked up and saw Jacob across the room leaning on one of the bookshelves. His eyes were closed and his mouth turned up in a smile. It surprised me so to see him that I pulled my hands off the keys and stopped playing. He opened his eyes and sighed, "You play very well, my dear. Please don't stop."

"Thank you, sir. I'm afraid though, if I continue, I won't want to stop."

"If you continue playing as you were, then you may play anytime you wish. That was lovely." Jacob smiled and nodded. He then turned and left the room.

James smiled. "It was lovely, Catherine."

I touched the keys lightly. "Marshall says I always play dirges. I've never thought of "Daisy Bell" as a dirge. It's a love song." I looked back up at him.

"It isn't a dirge and, unfortunately, we don't have a bicycle built for two."

His reference to the lyrics of "Daisy Bell" pleased me. I smiled and looked down at my hands. For a moment, I felt a little shy and then realized how silly I was being. James had seen me without my clothes. I looked back up at him and became entranced by his lovely eyes.

I've also spent a couple of mornings working out in the Mansfield gardens with James. It's been nice to concentrate on something other than my body. He provided a pair of trousers to wear outside. It's the first time in my life I've worn slacks, and I must admit it makes working in the dirt somewhat easier, even if they are a few sizes too large. I needed to cinch them up with a belt. James put a couple of extra holes in the leather for me and I've even gone so far as to throw off my shoes while working out there. By the end of the day, my feet were filthy. James enjoys washing them in the evening and gives wonderful foot massages.

Those couple of evenings were relaxing. James taught me about giving back massages and showed how to follow the line of the muscles. He taught me how to use my thumbs and the palm of my hand. He laid flat on the bed while I straddled his thighs and rubbed his back using oil. He said I learned how to do this well and seemed to enjoy is.

"James how tall are you?" I asked, one evening.

"Hmm, about six-foot-four-inches. Why do you ask?"

"I was just wondering that's all." I continued rubbing his back.

"How tall are you?"

"I don't really know. I haven't ever been measured as I remember."

"I'd say you are probably five-foot-six or seven. I could always track down a measuring stick," he chuckled. "Who did you get your beautiful ash brown hair and blue eyes from?"

"More than likely my mother. My father had darker

89

hair."

"Didn't you know your mother?" he asked.

"She passed away when I was little. Stella is really the only mother figure I've ever had."

"Hmm…"

At this point, I brought my hands down across his rear and barely touched his skin. One of his hands shot behind him and grabbed my wrist which startled me. He propped himself up on his other elbow and looked over his shoulder. "Milady, sorry to scare you, but my bottom is the one ticklish part of my body." He looked at me with a frown, but winked.

"I'm very sorry, milord, that's quite unusual." He let go of my wrist and lay back down. "How very unusual," I said and felt my eyebrow shoot up.

I looked at my hands and had an evil thought. I pressed my knees together a little tighter on his thighs. Using the tips of my fingers, I started to tickle him again on his buttocks. He began to laugh and tried to roll over. I held him down only a few seconds before he'd rolled me over and looked down at me. He held my hands over my head.

"I told you milady was evil." I looked up at him innocently.

"Should I punish you for tickling me?"

"Milord? Please, don't say you didn't enjoy it. I'll be heartbroken," I said, with all the drama I could muster.

"Ah, a pox on my black heart for treating you ill. May I ask if milady is ticklish?"

"Not at all, sir." I looked away, trying not to laugh.

"Not even in your stomach or ribs?" He tried to poke me in the ribs, but when I didn't react, he stopped. He sat up, stared me in the eyes, and cocked an eyebrow. "What about your feet? Let me think. I have cleaned the mud of your feet after working in the garden, but you never reacted."

"If you know what's good for you, sir, you'll leave

them be."

He stared at me with his mouth opened. "Like hell I'll leave them alone." He flipped me around onto my stomach.

"No! Stop it now." Before I knew it, James held my foot and tickled my toes. I laughed so hard my eyes watered.

Finally, he stopped and kissed the bottom of my foot. He turned and smiled at me. "That should teach you." He smacked my bottom.

I stopped laughing. "I'm sorry, but I've never heard of anyone having a ticklish bottom before. It was much too tempting." I turned over on my back, laid my head on the pillow and sighed. "James, it would be so nice to stay like this forever. Just sunny, warm days working in the garden and lying in bed with nothing to distract."

"Yes, it would," he said. He moved next to me and put his arm cross my stomach.

"The reality of it though, is depressing me. The thought of going back to Layne Hall and Marshall." I sat up and pulled my knees up to my chin. He moved his arm and sat up next to me. "I'm not certain I like reality very much." I looked at him and he put his hand on my arm and wrapped his other arm around my shoulders.

"There's something I've been meaning to tell you. I have to confess, I broke your confidence."

"What do you mean?"

"When you first arrived, I told you everything which happens here, in this room, stays here. Last week when you told me about your husband's behavior, I spoke with Jacob. He'd already figured some of it out, so he wasn't much surprised. I broke your trust and I want to apologize."

I stretched my legs out and leaned on him. "There's no reason to apologize. I was near hysterics. You had to be concerned."

"I was."

"What did Mr. Mansfield say in response?"

"He too is concerned and said at some time in the next week or so, he'll speak to you about it. He did say, perhaps, if you should choose not to go back, you could stay on here at the Hall. He thinks he could find something for you to do."

"Stay? Oh, I couldn't possibly. I'll have to return and see where things stand with Marshall. If I don't return, it will leave too much hanging and I'd end up feeling guilty. I just hope we are accomplishing what he wants." I lay back down on the bed. "James, may I ask a question?"

"Of course." He lay on his side next to me.

"The other women who've been here, after they leave, have you ever heard or been told how things are working out for them? Are they happier? Are their marriages much more successful?"

"Jacob has received news, things work out better for some. Others have a more difficult time. Some husbands realize, too late, what their wives have done here and they become jealous. They can't deal with another man being in their place, even if I am just a surrogate. What goes on here can cause irreparable damage." His brow furrowed and he looked away from me. I felt something coming from him and sadness pierced my heart.

"James, what is the matter?"

He looked at me and tried to smile. "Sorry, I'm just worried about sending you back to the situation. I fear your husband's behavior to you."

I put my hand up to his face. "Thank you for your concern. We'll cross that bridge when we come to it, right?" James took my hand and kissed my knuckles. He lay down, wrapping his arms around me.

"Catherine, I…" He stopped. "No, never mind. It's not important."

He held me a long time this particular night and we

stayed silent. I wonder still what he would have said, but didn't feel it was my place to push him with more questions. I've also been thinking on the word "surrogate." I know its meaning, but in the first week, never would have put it to use. James has come to mean a lot to me, if it's possible in only one week's time. We've continued to talk and laugh this week, but I sense something is gnawing at him. Again, I'm not sure it's my place to ask what is bothering him. There are times when he seems far away.

Lauren Marie

Secrets Beyond Dreams

Chapter Eight

May 15, 1920

After working in the garden today, James and I went for a short stroll around the Mansfield grounds. Today was a beautiful, cool day, but the sun shone and some of the early spring wild flowers were blooming. It felt wonderful. We made our way down to the lake with no name and sat by its banks watching the ducks in the water and the clouds in the sky. We talked about things other than the training.

James told me a little of his childhood. His father raised sheep and vegetable crops and was quite successful. When I asked about his father, James became quiet and stood up by the water. He began skipping stones. Leaning over to grab a handful of rocks, he said, "My father was not a very strong man." He looked back at me and fingered the rocks in his palm. "I don't mean physically. He was very strong. I mean mentally. He gambled too much and got into some trouble for it." He turned and threw the rocks forcefully into the water. "We should head back. Those clouds over the ridge don't look too promising."

He helped me stand and we started to go back. Before we got back to the Hall, the skies opened up and began to pour down. We ran along the path and he cut down a different direction and we came to a barn. Running through the doors, we were both drenched and I realized my linen shirt clung tightly to my body. For once, though, it didn't make me feel shy and I didn't cover myself.

The inside of the barn looked odd in a way. There

were benches in the middle of the floor with metal rings on the seats. A post with chains and leather cuffs hanging off stood in the middle of the dirt floor. James stood by the door and watched the rain outside.

"James, why are the benches placed oddly and what is this post?" I pointed at the chains with cuffs. He turned to me and smiled. Leaning against the wall next to the door, he crossed his arms and looked at me. "What?" I asked.

"Your blouse is quite alluring in this light," he replied.

I could feel my shoulders pull back as I looked down at my body. "Do you think?"

His eyebrow arched up and he continued to smile. "Yes, I do," he said. He moved away from the wall toward me and came up close to my face. I could feel his warm breath on my cheek. Placing his hand on my breast and feeling it through the wet linen caused me to catch my breath. "I don't think, until now, I have truly realized how beautiful your body is." He unbuttoned the top buttons, slid his hand in and leaned his head down to mine, brushing my lips with his. I could feel his other hand on my lower back, raised my hand to his arm and could feel his strong muscles tighten as he applied pressure to my nipple.

"Come to the post," he whispered in my ear. He pulled his hand out of my shirt and led me to the post in the middle of the floor. He turned me so my back pressed against it and took one of my hands in his. He brought it up to his mouth and kissed the knuckles and then continued moving my hand up until it was raised above my head. I couldn't concentrate and I didn't realize what he did. I felt the leather strap wrap around my wrist and looked up.

"Oh," was all I could say. I closed my eyes and tried to breath.

He took my other hand and kissed the knuckles again. This time, he licked my palm and put my index finger into his mouth. Withdrawing my finger, he started to move my hand up and did the same with it as he did the first time. I felt him pull my blouse out of the slacks I wore and undo the rest of the buttons. His warm hands felt inside the wet material and both his palms found my breasts and squeezed. He leaned toward me and said, "I know you are still bleeding right now. Would you be too embarrassed if I made love to you?"

My breath caught in my throat. I opened my eyes and found him staring at me. My voice didn't work and all I could do was shake my head no. He undid my trousers and slid them off with my under garments. He then took off his slacks and leaned against me. Lifting me a little, he said, "Grab the chains." I looked up and did as he told me to do. He parted my legs and brought them up around his waist. I'll never understand how he managed it, but his penis found its' way inside me. It felt exquisite. I couldn't defend myself as I hung there and I now know what it feels like to be helpless.

Because of his strong arms there wasn't much pressure on my arms and he moved to hold me with one arm, while his other hand came up to my breast and he played with my nipple, once again taking my breath away. He began to pump and despite the rough feeling of the post on my back, I felt almost weightless. His fingers moved down my side and he wedged his hand between our stomachs. His finger found my spot and began to circle it. He'd apply a little pressure then lighten his touch. My pelvis blazed from his teasing.

As he moved his hips, something came into my mind and I leaned my head down to whisper in his ear, "You can cum in me, you know?"

He pulled back, looked at my eyes and smiled. "I know." He put his mouth on mine and kissed me hard. I readily opened my mouth and accepted his tongue, touching it with mine. He continued moving for some time and I heard him moan as he pumped harder. We both were out of breath and as I tightened my legs around his waist, I felt his final push into me. My heart just about exploded inside my chest, when I felt his hot seed release into my canal and felt the orgasm envelop me.

James leaned against me and I could feel his warm breath on my neck. He sighed and his penis fell out and my legs dropped to the ground. As he undid the leather straps, my arms felt very heavy. I hadn't realized my fingers were going to sleep and they started to tingle. I shook them and flexed them in and out.

He bent over to put his trousers on and when he turned back to me, he smiled. "Thank you, Catherine."

I slipped my clothes back on and re-buttoned my shirt. "Thank you for what?" I asked.

James came over to me and took my hand in his. He kissed the palm and then held it to his face. "Some ladies don't feel comfortable having physical contact during their cycles. So, thank you," he said.

"I see," I replied. "I guess it just shows how uneducated I am in the finer points of love making. I've never done it during my menses. Marshall refuses to touch me. I didn't realize it was supposed to be uncomfortable, because it wasn't."

He walked over to the door and looked out. "It's stopped raining." He turned back to me, as I made my way to his side. "Are you ready for some dinner?"

I hadn't even thought about food, but found myself starving. "Yes, I am, as a matter of fact." He took my hand and led me out of the barn to the path back to the Hall. "James, I'm curious about the barn. Is it used at all for animals?"

He laughed. "The barn is sometimes used for animals. The area just inside the door, though, is kept as clean as possible for other uses."

"Is it used for training?"

"It is."

"I see." We continued along the path. "Was our moment in the barn part of the training?"

"Yes and no."

I stopped and looked at him. I could tell he teased. "Will I or won't I be given credit for my performance?"

"No, you'll get credit for it," he said.

I crossed my arms over me chest. "No points off for bleeding, right?"

James chuckled and shook his head. "No points off." He held out his hand. "Come on. I'm starving."

We found our way back to Mansfield Hall. After getting cleaned up from our outing, we sat down and ate a lovely meal. We talked for several hours and I felt James seemed more relaxed than usual. I wasn't sure what to make of it. We didn't talk about the training at all and just learned about each other. He asked Marco to bring a Gramophone up to my room and several phonograph records which he played.

At one point we even danced a waltz. He held my waist and spun me around the room. As we finished waltzing, I asked, "You said yes and no. What did you mean?"

He looked at me confused. "When?"

"This afternoon on the path to Mansfield. I wanted to know if our encounter in the barn was part of the training and you said yes and no. What did you mean?"

He smiled and nodded. "I remember now. You asked questions about the barn."

I raised my eyebrows and tilted my head.

James swirled me around and bent me over backwards in a dip. "You weren't supposed to experience the barn quite so soon." He stood me back up and we stopped dancing.

I squinted my eyes at him. "And?"

He let me go and walked over to the table. Picking up his glass of wine, he took a sip. I could tell he stalled.

"And there will be a barn experience?" I asked.

He turned back to face me. "Let me ask you this, did you enjoy your experience in the barn?"

I thought about the question for a moment. "Let's, for the moment, say I did enjoy it. Will there be more moments like it to enjoy?"

"Would you like there to be another moment in the barn?" he asked.

"You're not going to answer my question are you?"

He set the glass down and came to me. Putting his arm around my waist and holding my hand down at his side, he started two stepping and whispered in my ear. "No."

"Why?"

"It's not the right time."

I leaned back and felt his arm tighten around my waist. "You're being a brat, you know?"

James continued to smile, but said nothing.

"All right, may I ask another question?"

"Yes."

"Have you ever been married?"

"No."

"Why?"

"Well, Mansfield isn't really the proper place for a wife. It wouldn't be comfortable for a lady to have to share her husband with other women."

"Yes, I see. Do you ever wish to get married?"

"One day, yes, when I'm finished here, I hope very much to marry. I'd also like to have a herd of children, too."

"A herd of children?" I almost started to laugh. "What do you mean when you're finished?"

"I don't intend to do this forever, Catherine."

"What do you really want to do?"

James got a thoughtful look on his face and smiled. "I one day would like to have a herd of sheep and farm, the way my father did. Only I don't gamble, so if I work hard, I'm sure it will succeed."

"I see. Will you tell your prospective wife about the entire goings on here at Mansfield?"

"That is a hard one to answer. I suppose it would depend on the lady and if she were opened minded enough to accept these kinds of activities."

I looked up at him and realized we'd stopped moving and stood still. "Is there a prospective lady you have your eye on?"

"Yes, there is."

"I see. I didn't know you were courting anyone." I didn't mean for this to sound as surprised as it did. A strange feeling welled up inside of me and I could swear jealousy attacked my insides. I had no experience of this feeling to compare it.

James pulled me up into his arms and gave me a tight hug. He whispered in my ear, "It's funny. You keep saying I see, but I don't think you do see."

I pulled back from him and looked in his eyes. "I do now, I think…" I thought I knew what he spoke of, but didn't feel we should begin to go in this direction. I had commitments at home to honor and couldn't begin to think of anything other than those. "I think we should dance some more this evening."

I didn't ask any more questions for the rest of the evening. We did continue to dance. I buried the feelings I became aware of for James and tried to not let them carry me away. As much as the thought of going home made me frightened and being in James arms made me feel safe, I couldn't let this sway me. I needed to be strong.

Secrets Beyond Dreams

Lauren Marie

Chapter Nine

May 17, 1920

I haven't written much in the last couple of days. James keeps me so busy during the morning I haven't found the time to sit down and scribble any thoughts. It has been an amazing week though. Where to start?

After my cycle finished, we started the training sessions again. Interesting and educating is all I can think to say. James brought in Marco and introduced a blindfold. I never in my wildest imaginings thought of being touched by two men at once. Such it was, though, and I have to admit I felt frightened and excited all at once. Having two males to deal with at once was almost more than I could fathom. I know I should write more of it down, but I think I want to keep it to myself and off these pages. Now I really feel as though I've been cheating outrageously on Marshall.

May 18, 1920

I had a moment of pure evil last evening. I knew James planned out the evening and intended to work in the suite. I'd stared out the window as the sun went down and latched on to what I thought a brilliant idea.

James came up to the room after finishing some business with Mr. Mansfield. He'd gone into the bath and I could hear water running in the sink. He must have shaved or washed up. After a few minutes, he came out. His shirt hung out of his slacks and I watched his reflection in the window. He turned on a light by the bed and then looked up at me.

I turned from the window and leaned against the cool glass. "James, I'd like to do things differently tonight if it isn't too much trouble."

"Oh?" He smiled. "What does milady have in mind?"

"I wondered if we could go back to the barn."

He straightened up and got a curious look on his face. "Why do you want to go there?"

I thought for a moment and moistened my lips. "I'd like to show you something."

"What are you thinking about?"

I decided to act nonchalant. "It's nothing important. I thought it would be fun to do something different. If you think it's not a good idea, that's fine."

He walked over to stand next to me. "The barn. Do you want to be taken against the post again?"

I smiled, but kept silent.

"Milady is full of mystery this evening." James put his arm out for me to take and led us out of the room.

We picked up a lantern on our way out of the Hall. He walked confidently toward the path. We stayed quiet on our walk in the night air. It felt cool, but I thought with the right motivation we could warm things up.

When we arrived at the barn, he slid the door open and walked in. I followed him and stood across the room from him. He set the lantern down on a wooden shelf and turned, standing by the post. I must admit, with his shirt hanging out, he looked handsome and I could feel myself growing warm.

"Milady." He smiled and bowed.

"James, you've given me so much since I arrived, I don't feel I've repaid you very well. I want to give back to you this evening."

He squinted his eyes. "Catherine, you know it isn't

necessary?"

"I know. I just want you to relax and let me do the work this time." I walked up to him and put my hand up on his shirt. Grabbing a handful, I pushed him back to the post. I almost panicked as I realized I wasn't tall enough to reach the cuffs on top. I glanced around the room and saw a wooden bucket. Turning it over, I placed it in front of him and stepped up. I faced James eye to eye.

He started to bring his hands up to my hips. "Don't touch me," I said, quietly.

His brows furrowed, but he put his hands down to his sides. I leaned toward him, kissed his neck and licked up to his jaw. I heard him let out a breath. Bringing my hands up to his shoulders, I continued kissing him and brushed his lips with my tongue. I unbuttoned his shirt and slipped it off his shoulders. After unbuttoning the cuffs, I let it fall to the ground.

I ran one of my hands down his arm and brought his fingers up to my lips. I took one of his fingers in my mouth and sucked on it. He watched my movements as I kissed his palm and then brought his arm up to the cuff at the top of the post. A huge smile appeared on his face and he started to say something. I shushed him and put the cuff around his wrist. I did the same with his other arm and stepped off the bucket moving it aside.

Standing in front of him, I untied the dress I wore and moved it off my shoulders and let it fall to my feet. I could tell from the movement in his slacks I'd gotten his attention. I walked back up to him and put both my hands on the tight muscles in his chest. I kissed and licked his skin and heard him moan. Running my tongue up his stomach to his nipples I looked up at him and brought my hands down to the top of his slacks. I undid the button and moved the zipper down. I put my hands on his waist and moved them around to his rear.

Lauren Marie

His bottom felt tight and hard like the rest of his body. I massaged the cheeks and continued kissing his ribs and licking his nipples. I glanced up and saw his eyes were closed. He breathed through his mouth. When I brought my hand around to the front of his trousers, he sucked in a deep breath and held it. I found his penis very hard and warm. Holding it in one hand, I slid his slacks down with the other.

I moved down into a crouch and ran my hand down his leg. I glanced up and he looked at me. After the way I'd been introduced to this act, I never thought I would want to do it again. For some reason, earlier in the evening I wanted to try again and started to move my mouth toward his penis.

"Catherine, you don't have to do this," James said.

"I know," I whispered. "I want to. Now hush." With that, I put him in my mouth. I know I probably thought too much, but I didn't want to gag as I did before with Marshall. Taking a deep breath, I let him slid all the way to the back of my throat and came back holding his head with my lips. I sucked on it and he moaned as I continued these movements. At one point, I put my hands on his behind and pulled him toward my face. I held him in my mouth and throat and swallowed.

This caused him to moan again. I did this for some time and then let his penis out of my mouth. I kissed and licked it and felt it with my hand. My body was on fire and as much as I would have liked him to cum in my mouth, I wanted it in another part of my body worse. I moved my hands up to his stomach and started to stand up. Bringing the bucket back, I stood on it and licked him all the way up. I then planted my lips on his. His hard penis pressed against my stomach and his breathing sounded rapid. Running my fingers through his hair, I pushed my tongue in his mouth and his touched mine and they danced in swirls.

I ran my hand up his arm and without looking I undid the cuff. His arm fell to the side and then wrapped

108

around me. I did the other arm and he put it on my bottom. We continued to kiss and feel one another.

"Lay down on the bench, milord." He let me go and did as I asked. When he was prostrate, I straddled his pelvis and lowered myself down to him. I adjusted his penis putting it to my opening and pushed down. It slid in easily and felt wonderful. I pushed down as far as I could, and wanted it in as deep as possible. His knees came up behind me and I started to moved. His hand came up to my pelvis and he found my clitoris. I was in heaven. The sensations running through my body were so fantastic. I brought my hands up to my own breasts and played with the nipples.

After several minutes, James growled deep in his throat. I looked down at him and he started to pump his hips up. Although he seemed on the verge of orgasm, his finger twirled on me and continued until I felt release. My head arched back and I know I moaned. I leaned against his legs feeling everything go tight in me. I believe it was the best orgasm I'd ever experienced and my breathing was rapid and I let out a long gasp.

When I opened my eyes and looked down at him. Bringing his hand up to mine, he pulled me down on top of his chest and wrapped his arms around my back. It occurred to me his penis was still hard.

I pushed up and looked in his eyes. "You didn't have an orgasm."

He grinned. "Not yet. Milady, may I take over for just a moment?"

"I didn't want you to work tonight, James."

He started to sit up, which caused me to move to stand. "This is definitely not work, my darling." He bent over and picked up my dress, folded it and laid it on the bench. He moved behind me and pointed at the bench. "Put your knees on your dress, and your hands half way down the bench. Hold on to the sides with your fingers."

As I moved into the position he described, I looked over my shoulder at him. He put his hands on my rear and leaned over kissing my cheeks. He then stood straight and I felt him put his penis to my opening. He pushed in slow, and I almost moved back to get his entire length in quicker. I savored ever inch of him. With his hands on my waist, I felt him start to lean over me and his fingers moved to one breast and the other to my clitoris.

"Oh James, please, take me."

"I have every intention of taking you, milady. I want you to orgasm with me. I'm so close to exploding, but I'm not going to move until you're ready," he whispered.

His finger swirled on my clitoris and as he pressed hard on it, he pinched my nipple. I would have thought him mean, if it didn't feel so wonderful. His finger lightened and then pressed harder and I could feel the rush beginning.

"Oh God, it's starting, now." I moaned.

James began to pump into me harder than ever before and I could hear myself shout as his finger brought me to release. At the same time I yelled, James began to groan and smacked my bottom with his hands as he pumped jets of warm semen into my vagina.

He pulled me up and held me tight to his chest. He kissed my shoulder. I could hear his heavy breathing begin to wane and I opened my eyes.

"Oh my, that was nice, very nice," I said.

He stood me on my feet and leaned his head on my shoulder. "Nice is an understatement. That was earth moving and I'm very impressed with you."

I looked up at him. "What do you mean?"

He put a warm hand on my shoulder. "I didn't think you'd be able to give me oral pleasure after what your husband put you through."

I tried to think of a reasonable explanation. "It needed to be the right situation."

James played with my hair and ran his fingers down my spine. The situation seemed peaceful and safe and I felt wonderful.

"Milady, we didn't use a condom this evening," James said.

I opened my eyes, but didn't move. "I didn't even think of it." I turned around and put my hand on his chest. I hadn't thought of anything like using a condom. I looked at him and smiled. "My cycle just finished. We should be all right. I don't believe I'm able to have children anyway. My husband and I have tried, but…well, I don't think we need to worry." I saw his brow crease. "What?"

"Did you ever consider it might not be your fault you remain childless?" he asked.

I moved from his arms and put my hand on my forehead. I never thought of that possibility and I'd always felt the guilt was my own. "I suppose that could be a valid, but still don't think there is anything to worry about. Thank you for your consideration."

James ran his hand through my hair and touched my face. "Catherine, you amaze me. That was incredible."

I bowed my head to him. "Your servant, milord."

He laughed and pulled me back into his arms. "Servant, my ass. You were in complete control." He leaned over me and put his arms around my shoulders and kissed my lips. "I've never had anyone do that before. Thank you."

"It was my pleasure." I realized we'd built up a sweat, but with the lack of movement I started to get chilled. "I should have brought a blanket," I thought out loud.

"Are you ready to go back?"

"Yes, I'm getting cold."

James put on his trousers, while I slipped my dress over my head and tied it around my waist. He picked up his shirt and brought it to me, placing it around my shoulders. He got the lantern off the shelf and we headed back to the house. As we were walking the path, he put his hand around my waist. "How does a nice warm bath sound, milady?"

"Heavenly." I smiled up at him. "Don't we have lessons tonight?"

"I believe you deserve the night off and I think I should wash your hair, too. You've somehow managed to get hay in it." I felt his fingers up in my hair, pulling strands of hay out.

"I guess this would be one of the tough parts of servicing, milord. I didn't go near the hay and still get debris in my hair," I said.

"Easily corrected, milady." He grinned.

When we arrived back in the suite, James ran the bath water and I brushed the dry, brown hay out of my hair. I still couldn't figure out how I managed this and heard him get into the tube. I thought for a moment how much I'd changed in the last three weeks. During my first days at Mansfield, I never would have felt comfortable walking into the restroom and joining him, particularly without my clothes. Now it felt so natural and easy. I put the brush down and went in to join him.

James parted his legs and I stepped into the warm water. I lowered myself and ran my hands down his legs. He'd sat up and put his arms around my shoulders pulling me to his chest. His body felt warmed up from the chill, evening air.

When he finished washing my hair, we sat in the tub for a bit and he played with my breasts. "You know, Catherine, you have very beautiful breasts."

I laughed and thanked him. My face felt flushed.

He sat up a little looked down at me. "You're not getting shy are you?" he asked. He relaxed back down and continued playing with my nipples. "You certainly weren't timid earlier this evening."

"I believe I might have been possessed by an evil

spirit." I felt a smile pull at my lips.

"An evil spirit? I want to meet this spirit and thank it for your actions."

"I'm sure something could be arranged." I put my hand on his and brought it up to my lips. I kissed his palm and sucked on his fingers and thumb. After a time, I could fell his penis awakening and hardening into my back. I turned my head and looked at him. "Milord, I believe the spirit may have returned."

James laughed and hugged me. "Good thing it decided to come back. I want you again."

I reached my hand to his neck and pulled myself up a little, so I could meet his lips. I kissed his face and chin, and came back to his lips. He parted them and gave me a very passionate kiss. I felt myself grow warm again.

We made love several more times that night and every time James waited for me to come before he allowed himself release. Where he gets the strength from to hold orgasms back is beyond me. Late into the night we lay in bed and touched one another and talked.

"I can't believe it's possible to have such feelings. I don't know how I'm going to leave this. I'm Alice back down the rabbit hole, James." I put my head back on his chest.

"Will you, won't you, will you, won't you, will you join the dance?" he quoted quietly.

When I heard the phrase from Alice's Adventures in Wonderland, my head popped back up. I looked at him. "The Lobster quadrille, you've read Alice? Well, when one's lost, I suppose it's good advice to stay where you are until someone finds you…" I quoted back.

"But who'd ever think to look for me here?" he finished the quote and smiled. "I read it many years ago. It seems funny to remember those quotes just now." He rubbed my shoulders.

Tears rolled down my cheeks. "This evening hasn't turned out quite the way I had planned."

James pulled me tight in his arms. We were quiet for the rest of the evening.

When I woke up this morning, I thought about all which occurred. I feel I could easily get used to being treated with the kindness and gentleness James shows me. I know, though, I will have to return to Layne and Marshall. I can only hope this is what my husband wished when he sent me to Mansfield. I must to try to reach him and show him the pleasures we can experience, but realized I am going to miss James. His arms around me, his touch and care, have become very important in such a short time. I will remember him forever.

After we got up and ate breakfast, James said there wouldn't be any training until this evening. He thinks I should take it easy today, but won't go into any details of what to expect. After working for a time in the garden, I'm sitting here wondering what the nighttime will bring.

Secrets Beyond Dreams

Chapter Ten

May 21, 1920

The last two days have turned out to be a most unusual. A couple of days ago, I wrote James said I should take it easy during the day, as the evening activities were going to be very exhausting. I tried to read Frankenstein in the afternoon, but found it difficult to concentrate. I asked James what would happen in the evening, but he wouldn't say and I decided to go down to the gardens and wander. The sun was out, but it wasn't too hot. There were big, fluffy clouds moving above my head.

I walked the lawn to the rose garden and found a bench to sit on. The roses were beginning to bud and would probably come out after I left Mansfield. It would be beautiful and I would miss not seeing them.

The warmth seeped through my dress and listening to the birds sing, I closed my eyes and heard footsteps, crunching the gravel behind me. I opened my eyes and turned to see who approached.

"Ah, Mrs. Pieper, are you enjoying the sun?" I heard a familiar voice.

"Good afternoon, sir." I smiled. Mr. Mansfield stood by a rose bush. "Yes, the sun is lovely today."

"Yes, yes it is. I don't wish to disturb, but may I join you?" He gestured toward the bench.

"Of course." The bench was long enough I didn't have to move for him to sit. I thought it nice of him to ask. "It is your bench, sir."

"Yes, it is, but you looked so serene. I really don't

wish to disturb you."

"You're not bothering me at all. The company will be nice." I gazed around at the roses. "You do have a beautiful garden, sir."

"Thank you, yes, it is relaxing out here. The staff does a rather remarkable job keeping up with it all. James works very hard out here, too."

"Yes, he does. I'm also very grateful I've been allowed to do some of the work myself. I love gardening very much."

"Yes, yes," he said and looked up at the Hall. "May I be so bold as to ask you a question?"

"Of course."

"I am aware, if my establishment were known about outside of this little community, most would find it shocking and disgraceful. I think when you first came here you were a bit shocked?" he asked.

"Yes, but more surprised though. I have a friend who has spent some time on the East Bank in Paris. I've heard stories from her which made my ears burn."

Mr. Mansfield laughed and leaned toward me. "Thank the Lord we're more civilized than the French, don't you think?"

I too laughed and never thought learning sexual positions could be considered civil. "Yes, I do agree."

"And the staff has treated you well?" he continued.

"Oh yes, all things considered, the staff has been very helpful and accommodating."

"Good, good." He looked at his walking stick and pursed his lips. "All is going well with James, also?" He looked at me out of the corner of his eye.

"Yes, he's been very kind."

"And his training hasn't been too forceful and he hasn't pushed himself on you?"

"No, he's let me acclimate to the situations at my

own pace. Both he and his assistant, Marco, have been quite gentle. May I ask what this is about, sir?"

"Well, considering the circumstances which brought you here, I just wanted to make sure we haven't over stepped boundaries or been rude to you."

"Mr. Mansfield, I think pretty much all that goes on here over steps boundaries. If we'd had this discussion two or three weeks ago I'm sure I would have a different opinion. My thinking has changed and it's good I'm able to see some things are worth thinking differently about."

He smiled and agreed.

"It is strange. I believe I could become quite spoiled and very obsessed with the feelings I've experienced in the last week alone. Parts of it were a bit overwhelming. At this point, sir, I have no complaints. I only hope this is what my husband really wanted." I took Mr. Mansfield's arm and gave it a squeeze. "I am truly astounded by my own change of opinion."

He patted my arm. "Good," he said. "Mrs. Pieper, James did tell me some of the ways your husband has treated you in the past and it does concern me."

"Thank you, sir."

"I feel if you should wish to stay here at the Hall and not return right away to Layne, we would be able to accommodate you without question."

I wondered about his concern. "Sir, my husband is a brut with me. I do thank you very much for your offer, but I do need to return. I have to find out if I can make my marriage work or not."

He looked back at his walking stick. "I understand and hope all will work out for the best."

We sat for a time and discussed other issues. I found even though he enjoyed a wonderful garden it wasn't really his cup of tea. He knows the bushes are roses, but the particular types he didn't know. It was nice to speak with him and before I realized it two hours passed. I saw James walk down the path toward us.

"There you are. I've been looking all over the estate for you," he said.

"I've been sitting right here."

"Smarty," he said, looking at Mr. Mansfield. "I don't mean to interrupt, but we should head in to get ready for dinner, Jacob."

"Of course, we were just having a lazy conversation. Nothing to important," Mr. Mansfield replied.

I stood and looked down at Mr. Mansfield. "It was a lovely afternoon and the conversation very relaxing, sir. Thank you for keeping me company."

"You're very welcome, my dear." He continued to sit on the bench.

I took James arm and he led me up the path, toward the back of the Hall.

"Did you have a good conversation?" James asked.

"Yes, as I've already said, it was lovely. It's nice having a less active afternoon for a change."

"What did you discuss?"

"That, sir, is none of your business."

We were walking across the lawn and James stopped and turned to me. "Catherine, have I done something to annoy you?"

"No, not at all. I didn't mean to sound snippy. Mr. Mansfield and I just passed the time." I let go of his arm and continued to walk toward the house. "I just wish you'd tell me what will be happening this evening."

"All in good time, milady, all in good time." He caught up with me.

"Now who's being a smarty? Why is dinner so early, sir?"

"You'll want your stomach settled before this evening. And, I think a couple glasses of wine will make it easier, too." We walked onto the patio to the back door.

"Now the mystery deepens. Should I be getting nervous?" I asked.

"Nothing that transpires tonight will hurt you. I promise, there is no reason to be nervous."

We went back up to the room and changed our clothes. I put on a light weight white linen dress with a split up either leg. When James saw me, he said I looked like an angle. I laughed and said I didn't think angles would be caught at Mansfield Hall.

I ate a small dinner and drank several glasses of wine. On the third glass, I began to feel tipsy. I found things around me quite funny and, although I can't remember why, went into a laughing attack. I wish I could remember what struck my funny bone so hard. I finished the third glass and James poured me another.

"Milord, I think you're trying to get me drunk." I laughed.

He smiled, put the bottle down and made no reply. He sat back in his chair.

"Four glasses of wine, I don't think I've ever had this much in a single evening," I said and looked at the glass.

He leaned forward, and his eyes were quite serious. "Catherine, I..." he started to say something, but stopped.

"Oh Lord, you've done it again."

He looked startled. "Done what?"

"Milord, there have been several occasions in the last week where you've started sentences and not finished them. What is it you're having such a difficult time discussing?"

He turned his head away and mumbled. "Nothing, it's nothing."

"Nothing? I think you're telling me a lie. Why do you get such a wrinkle between your eyes?" I tried not to slur my words.

He looked at his pocket watch and clicked it shut. Standing, he took me by the hand. "Let's take a walk."

I held my wine glass and frowned. "I hate it when you don't answer a question." He pulled on my hand and I watched him. I saw something in his eyes, although I wasn't certain what I saw. "What time is it?" I asked and rose from my chair. I took another sip of wine and set the glass on the table.

"Almost eight o'clock."

I realized the time must have arrived and all would be revealed. Even though the wine made me feel light on my feet, my brain started to work.

We went out the back door of the Hall to the patio. Marco waited for us and approached. He handed some things made of leather and a black cloth to James, who took my hand and led me down the path to the left of the patio. It was the trail to the barn. I remembered the day when it rained and he made love to me against the post. I also thought about our recent adventure in that building and felt a smile come to my face. I began to feel warm, and hoped we were going to have a repeat of those days.

Once we were in the trees, James slowed his pace some and started to speak. "There will be some other men taking control of the activities tonight. It will be rougher than what you're used to. I've spoken with the leader though, and he agreed, it won't be as rough as it could be."

"James, you will be there, won't you?"

We stopped and he faced me holding my arm. "No, I'm not allowed."

I thought about this for a moment. "You said, from the beginning, you'd be with me every step of the way?"

He looked down at the path. "I know, I shouldn't have said that. This is a one-time only night. It never will happen again unless you want it to." He put his arm around my waist and we started toward the barn again. "The men involved tonight are ruffians. We only hire their services when they are in the area and they are good with the land and sheep. I know there are people who think they are just thieves and criminals, but they aren't. If we give them respect and honesty, they work very hard. They have been given boundaries tonight. They have at times used masochistic means to bring a woman to orgasm, but they are not allowed to strike you this evening."

I stopped again and pulled away from James. "I have a husband who hits me already. I don't want any of that."

"I know. The men are good to their word once they've given it. They've sworn to no violence tonight and I trust them completely."

"You do believe them?"

"Yes, I do," he said. "Catherine, I need you to understand something very important. I care very much for you and I've gone off the usual track Jacob runs at Mansfield because of this care. I'm not supposed to be involved in this in any way. Jacob wouldn't be happy if he found out what I've done, but done it I have. It won't be a tea party, but the men will take care with you."

"James, why is this part of the training?"

"It's usually used for women who are having a difficult time enjoying themselves. There will be several different men who will desire you. Imagine the power a woman should feel over those men." He looked down at me. "You, on the other hand, gave up resistance after the first couple of days. I didn't think it was necessary, but Jacob disagreed. It will only be one night and I think you will enjoy yourself. I wish I could be there with you." He touched my cheek. He moved his hand down to mine and started walking again. "I won't be far away."

"What if I say no?"

"That is your choice, Catherine."

Even with four glasses of wine my brain became

alert. "James, do you know if Marshall had any idea about this? Did Mr. Mansfield tell him about it?"

"I wouldn't think so, but you'd have to ask Jacob. I'm not sure how much detail he goes into."

We turned a corner and I saw the barn ahead of us. I could see lights shining in the doorway. We stopped at the tree line. I could hear laughter coming from inside the structure.

"Would you prefer to decline this evening's activities?" James asked and became remote.

"I…" I looked at the barn and then up at him. "I am unsure."

"Catherine, I need your dress, please," James said.

"What? My dress, why?" I felt very shaky.

"You won't need it tonight."

Taking in a breath, I thought this is a one night only event. I'd never experience anything like this again unless I chose to do it again. I slipped it off my dress and handed it to him.

"Put your wrists up."

I did as he asked and he put the leather bracelets around each wrist. There was a metal ring attaching them in the middle. I didn't know what these were used for, but felt certain I'd find out.

He put a blindfold over my eyes and tied it tightly behind my head. "You'll want to keep this on at all times tonight." He moved around behind me and put his hand on my naked back. "There's nothing for you to trip over. I won't let you fall." He moved me forward and I did reach out my hands. I knew he wouldn't let me fall, it just felt better having them up.

I could hear the men's voices start to quiet down. Someone whistled. Even though I wore the blindfold a bright light shone ahead of me. I stopped when my hands touched on a hairy chest. I felt James hand leave my back and knew I was on my own. The man in front of me took hold of the metal ring on the bracelet and pulled me forward. After a few steps, I could feel hay on my feet and knew I'd entered the barn. The man who held on to the ring stopped and attached something to it. I heard a gear turning and my arms started to be pulled up.

***

It did turn out to be an intense evening. Having the blindfold on made each touch all the more mysterious. I didn't have any control over the situation and, after feeling scared at first, it did become exhilarating. The men involved were rough and the only time they spoke to me would be to tell what they were going to do to my body. Their hands were calloused and I don't think any of them shaved in a week or more. I felt certain I'd have red patches on parts of my body from just their faces rubbing against my skin. They used several different techniques and positions. After a time, with my arms pulled up toward the rafters, they brought me down, laid my body across the shorter bench and attached the metal ring. My bottom rested just on the edge. I didn't realize that the height of the bench could be adjusted, but soon discovered it could be changed to different, and more accommodating levels. I came several times, which I think made the men enjoy themselves even more. I went from being nervous to not thinking, in no time. The men did their job well.

As I lay on my back, on a bench, with my wrists attached by the bracelet, I realized the blindfold slipped up and I opened my eye. Standing next to the bench, I saw one of the men who'd worked in the garden on occasion. I believe he was called Heck. His hair is bright red and he wore a beard cut close to his face. He spoke to one of the other men and they laughed. Remembering what James said about keeping the blindfold on at all times, I turned my head to the side and rubbed the blindfold on my arm and brought it back down. I just hoped it stayed on.

I don't know how many hours passed. I don't know how many men were there. At some point, I was unattached from the bench and picked up in one of the men's arms. He carried me a few steps and kneeled down. I felt hay on my back and a rough blanket got thrown over me. The man took my hands up and undid the leather bracelets releasing my wrists. I started to bring my hand up to the blindfold, but he caught it and said, "You won't be wantin' to do that just yet, ma'am." I put my hand down.

I felt exhausted and started to fall asleep, but heard footsteps come toward me. I wondered if there might be more and didn't think I had any strength left. I felt hands behind my head untying the blindfold and when I opened my eyes saw James kneeling over me. His brown eyes looked so warm and comforting.

"Catherine, are you all right?" he asked.

I tried to smile and say yes, but whether or not I accomplished it, I'm not sure. He leaned over, picked me up in his arms and we left the barn. Mumbling that I needed to take a bath, I tucked my head onto his shoulder and must have fallen asleep.

I awoke yesterday morning. I wasn't certain how long I'd slept, but saw my room and bed. James washed me, which must have been difficult for him. I could no longer see the dirt and grime on my skin from the last evening. He'd also put me into a dressing gown. Even though my skin was clean, I could still feel and taste the ruffians. I thought about all which transpired the night before. My brain blocked out some of the details, but parts will remain vivid in my memory. I felt some satisfaction with how the evening progressed, but I also felt somewhat disgusted. Not disgust at the amount of intercourse, but with the fact that I'd gotten pleasure out of it. I had no idea who the men were, and they'd given me more pleasure in one night than my husband did in three years of marriage. I would need to work out this dilemma on my own. I knew I'd never be able to discuss this with the pastor at home.

I turned over and felt James slept next to me. His left arm stretched over me and I listened to him breath and tried not to think anymore about the events. The even rhythm of his breathes sounded comforting in a way. Trying to come to terms with myself would be a difficult task.

I looked at James face and watched him for a time. I realized I'd developed deep feelings for him. He worked very hard at his many jobs around Mansfield Hall. He was so strong, but also kind and gentle.

"Are you okay?" I heard him whisper.

I looked at his face. "You've been asking me that quite a lot," I answered.

He smiled and opened his eyes. "I'm just wanting to take good care of you, ma'am."

"Thank you, sir. Have you been awake long?"

"Just stirred. Have you been awake long?"

"A while."

"Just thinking?"

"Yes, just thinking."

"Do you want to discuss anything?" James asked.

I watched him bring his right hand from under his pillow and prop up his head so he looked down at me.

"Exactly how is it the hot water gets up here from the kitchen?"

He laughed. "You're evading my question, milady. I meant about last night."

"I know, milord. I have a good reason for evasion." James raised an eyebrow and looked serious. "I'm having a difficult time separating the actions of the fifty, or so, men I had intercourse with last night."

"There were only five."

"Only five? It seemed like more," I said. "Really, it

is strange thinking of those men being excited by me. It's not as if I really knew how to service five at one time."

"Jacob and I wouldn't have put you in the situation unless we felt you were ready. Catherine, you are very attractive. I would think any man would be excited by you."

I reached up and touched his lips. "I may never walk properly again."

James smiled and ran his hand through my hair. "I'll carry you everywhere." He leaned over and kissed me on the cheek.

"Oh, my goodness," I said.

"What?"

"I must look a mess." I sat up and my legs shook.

James put his hand on my arm, pulled me back down and wrapped his arms around me. "You look gorgeous."

I put my head on his chest and listened to his heart beat. "You're being too kind, milord." I turned my head and rested my chin on him. Looking up at his eyes, I asked, "What's on the agenda today?"

"No plans today. You have a day off."

"Thank goodness. I'm not sure I have the strength to do much of anything."

"I realize the activity from last night probably left you somewhat raw. I don't recommend any sex today."

"What shall I do?"

He looked down at me quite serious. "You could stay in bed all day if you'd like, with me waiting on you, hand and foot. Or go down to the library and play the piano or find a book. However, it is a beautiful day outside and you could choose to spend the day with me picnicking out in the countryside, away from the Hall."

"Hmm, no plans, right?"

"Right. There are some very beautiful places in these parts. We could saddle up a horse and be there within an hour," James said.

"Horses? Saddle? Are there any places closer we could walk to? There's no way my body is going on a horse."

"Sorry, that was dumb. No horses. There are some places closer."

"Good, that is my choice then."

"I'll tell Marco to prepare a hamper." He rolled over and stood stretching his hands over his head. It still took my breath away to look at his body. The embarrassment I'd felt at first disappeared and I couldn't take my eyes off of him. He slid his slacks on and turned to the closet. He put on a shirt and pulled out a linen dress, this one a sage green with embroidery around the neck. He threw it on the bed and said he'd be back in a few minutes and left the room.

I sat up again and stretched. When I tried to stand, my legs started to shake again and were sore. I slipped the dressing gown off and put on the linen. It fit loose with a tie around the waist. Walking to the closet, I found the slip on shoes and put my feet in them. I looked at my reflection in the standing mirror and became horrified. My hair sat in what looked like a birds nest and my face was pale with red blotches. I went into the restroom to wash my face and brush my hair.

When I came back out, James just returned and pushed a cart. "Breakfast, milady?" he asked.

"Yes, I'm starving."

He took my hand, led me to the table and held my chair out helping me sit. Placing a plate in front of me, he started dishing up steaming eggs and bacon. "Where's Marco this morning?"

James smiled. "Marco is preparing a hamper for our picnic and then he gets the rest of the day off, too."

"My goodness, James, will any work be done at Mansfield today?"

"Of course, always lots to do at the Hall."

I don't believe food ever tasted as good as it did yesterday morning. The coffee smelled wonderful and the bacon in particular made my mouth water. After we finished breakfast, we walked down to the kitchen and picked up a hamper.

"Milady, let us not tarry any longer." James held his arm out for me.

I laughed and did my best to curtsy. "Yes, milord."

We left the kitchen and went out the back door of Mansfield Hall. Cutting through the garden, James led me to the path which would take us down to the no name lake. We entered the forest and strolled.

At first, I wasn't sure my legs would carry me very far, but after the first half hour I realized they were loosening and felt stronger. Coming to the fork in the path, I expected we would go to the right as we'd done before. However, James nudged me down the left. We walked this path for just five minutes and came around a corner. Coming out of the woods to a small valley between two forests, James went ahead of me on the path.

He turned and walked backwards. Stopping, he pointed to the valley. "Does milady find this acceptable for a picnic?"

"Yes, milord, it's beautiful."

He waited for me to catch up with him and then put his free hand around my waist and walked beside me.

"Does milady realize I was born and raised in these hills? I know this area like the back of my hand."

We came to another fork in the path and stopped. James frowned looking left and right. He started to the right, but then pulled left again.

"You thought I didn't know which way to go?"

"I thought no such thing, milord. I never said a word," I answered back.

He smiled and led me around another corner to a

clearing on top of a hillside. Before I'd a chance to look around, James dropped the hamper and grabbed me in his arms. He gave me a very forceful kiss and twirled me around. He finished the kiss and leaned his head back leering at me. If I had not known he was being silly, I might have felt frightened.

"Milady has doubted my sense of direction. I must stripe her naked and make passionate love to her until she's senseless." He pulled me close and whispered in my ear. "Milord will ride you gently, because he knows your discomfort."

I leaned back and pretended to fight him. "A pox upon me, milord, for ever doubting your abilities." I straightened up and looked him in the eye. "You did say earlier though you wouldn't recommend sex today?" Stretching up on my toes, I kissed his chin and licked his throat. I moved my hand down his chest to the front of his slacks. We continued to stare at one another. I unbuckled his belt and pulled the zipper down. My hand slid into the opening and latched onto his penis and wrapped my hand around it. James began to breathe a little faster. He turned his head and looked over his shoulder. Taking my hand out of his pants, he kissed it and then led me to a grassy area off the trail.

Lying down on his back, in the shade of a huge oak tree, he said, "Milady, I'm all yours."

I knelt down next to him and undid the button on his slacks. Putting my hand back in, I found his penis and tightened my grip. "Milord, may I ask a question?"

James sucked in his breath when I gave his penis a tug. In a gasp with his eyes closed he said, "Of course, milady."

"Sir, why is it you wear no under drawers?"

James opened his eyes again. "In situations like this, less is best."

"I see. It makes perfect sense to me." I continued to stroke him with my hand. I remembered my first night at Mansfield, James did this for himself.

He put his hands on my legs and I could hear him moan. I continued sliding the member around in my hand and held tightly to him. After a few minutes, I scooted forward and pulled my dress up. I slipped it over my head and tossed it to the side.

He started to sit up and asked, "Are you sure?"

"I'm sure."

"I haven't any condoms."

I arched my back and stretched, then looked back down at him. "You know, Mr. Whear, I don't really care. In fact," I lifted myself up and lowered down onto his penis. It stung some, but it was right where I wanted it. "I would prefer if you would cum in me now and the rest of my time here."

"Catherine," he started to say, but caught his breath as I lifted up and down a couple of times. He went back down and put his hands on my knees. After a few more pumps, I leaned over him, letting my hair surround his face. I kissed his lips. His hand came up into my hair and he kissed me back with more pressure. I felt his knees bend and he moved his pelvis. I began breathing more rapidly and kissed his neck and chest. His hand went through my hair and down my back. Rolling me over, he lay on top of me and pumped harder. I wrapped my legs around his waist. I could hardly believe I felt able to participate. After the last evening's festivities, I was surprised at my own strength.

He slowed a little and whispered in my ear, "Catherine, you know I'm falling in love with you?"

My voice caught in my throat.

James continued to thrust into me. "This is no longer just a job for me. I know it's only been a short time, but I've loved you since first seeing you in Jacob's office. You asked last night why I kept stopping a thought mid-sentence. I didn't think it was right to burden you with these feelings, but I can't hold them in any longer. I love you," he said.

"James," I whispered. It was all I could get out, though, as a flood of emotions and warmth over took me. He moaned in my ear, rammed his penis home, and held the position. I felt the tension release from him and his weight on top of me was wonderful. He started to move off, but I grabbed him. "No! Please, don't move, not yet."

He propped himself up on an elbow and looked down at me. "I'm not crushing you, am I?"

"No." I held on tight and closed my eyes and pulled my head up to kiss him. I looked at him. "I already knew that you love me. I knew in a way."

"Yes."

I put my hand up to his face and touched his lips. I didn't know what to say. He pulled his weight off of me. While he went back to the path for the hamper, I sat up and found my dress. I slid it back over my head and pulled my knees up to my chin. He set the hamper down and opened it pulling a blanket out. He spread it under the tree and then sat down on it behind me. I felt his hand on my shoulder and I leaned back into his arms. He wrapped them around me and put his face in my hair.

"I want to show you something," he said. He stood back up and leaned over to offer me his hand. I took it and he lifted me up. He led me back to the path and around a corner to an area where we could view the valley through a bank of trees. We stood on the edge of a hill side. The rolling grass was green and waving in the breeze.

He pointed to our right and to my surprise I could see a mansion built among the trees. I never would have seen it if he hadn't pointed it out.

"That is the manse of the family Whear," he said.

The place had not been cared for in some time.

Vines took over in the front and some of the windows where covered over. The lawn around the mansion would be as high as my hips. James let go of my hand and walked closer to the edge of the hill. He leaned against a tree looking down at the house. "Remember when I told you about my father passing away?"

"Yes."

I could see tears well in his eyes. He put his hand up to his face a moment and cleared his throat. "When he passed it left me an orphan. Jacob was kind enough to take me in and see to my education and raised me properly."

I walked up to him and put my arm around his waist.

He turned to face me. "I'd like to be able to say my father was led astray, but he knew what happened. Like your husband, Catherine, he gambled. I was twelve years old then and he left behind so much debt, I almost lost Whear Hall. Most of my father's debt was owed to Jacob, who eventually picked up the title to the house. For the past eighteen years, I've worked off what my father owed. Jacob agreed, once I'm finished, he'll give me the title back and it will be in the Whear family again. I loved my father, and it was hard not being able to fix him."

I understood what James felt. The hopeless feeling of not being able to heal a situation was hard and depressing.

"Catherine, you're my last client. When we finish the training, the debt will be paid. Jacob will give me the title and I'll finally be going home."

"Do you trust him to keep to his word?" I asked.

"Jacob may be a crook in some ways, but he is an honest crook. Like the ruffians, once his word is given, he holds to it." James put his arms around me and hugged me tight.

I smiled up at him and said, "I'm very pleased for you."

"Thank you." He took my hand and kissed it. "You

133

could come and be the mistress of Whear Hall." He raised an eyebrow.

I leaned my head against his chest and sighed. "James, have you ever stopped reading a Chapter in the middle and not finished it until sometime later? For a time, not knowing how the story progresses and what is happening to the people involved?"

"Are you trying to change the subject?" he asked.

I put my head up, pulled away from him and moved to the tree opposite of him. I leaned against it and rested my face against the bark. "No, I'm not changing the subject. I'm just saying, it would be impossible to think of going with you at this time." I turned around and looked at him. My own eyes started to fill and I felt a tear escape down my cheek. "I have a Chapter which needs finishing, one way or the other. I have to go back and see if there's any way to fix my marriage."

"Sometimes things can't be fixed," he said.

I nodded and my throat tightened. He started to come toward me, but I put my hand up to stop him. "James, I'm falling in love with you, too. I know I shouldn't say it. I'm only going to cause you pain and heartache. You've been so kind to me these last weeks. I never thought before I came to Mansfield it was possible to feel such sensations and life."

Tears rolled down my cheeks in a flood. James moved to me and wrapped his arms around my waist. He kissed me softly on my cheeks and neck. He found my lips and brushed them with his and took my breath away.

We made love another time this afternoon. We were back under the tree, lying on our backs looking up at the clouds. We played with the lunch in the hamper, but neither one of us felt very hungry. I think we both even fell asleep for a time. We didn't discuss much, as our minds were in turmoil.

I know, from my own standpoint, I am going to have a difficult time saying good bye to him. I have to be honest with myself. I do love James. I want him with me forever and no one else. As he said about his father, James too is a good man. His heart is huge and caring and when his arms are wrapped around me, I feel safe and protected. Maybe one day we will find each other again. I have to return to Layne Hall and see if my life with Marshall is going to survive.

May 25, 1920

This last week has been trying. It would seem there is to be no more of the training sessions. James is only with me in the evenings now. There is a sadness in both of us which seems to be…

Lauren Marie

Chapter Eleven

1976

"How could father do that to her? How could mother allow such a thing?" Stella stood up from the couch. "Five men at one time...what was she thinking?"

"Stella, please, stop shouting. We're all right here and can hear you just fine," Michael said, and leaned over to the whiskey bottle. He poured himself another drink.

Steven closed the book he read from and set it on the table. "That's the end of that one. Who wants to read next?" He looked around at his brothers.

"I'm not sure I want to hear anymore," Stella said and sat down. "These can't be our parents. I just cannot understand any of this."

Nicholas sat forward, put his elbows on his knees and clasped his hands. He, too, didn't know what to think. "Does anyone remember them sneaking off in the middle of the night?"

Michael and Jay laughed, while the others looked at them as though they'd gone crazy.

"I remember many nights when I'd hear the floor boards creaking in the hallway. I looked out the window and saw them wandering off, hand in hand," Jay said.

"I followed them one night." Nicholas continued.

"Do tell, brother." Michael grinned.

"I followed them to the spot I think we just heard about. The one up on the hillside, under the oak trees. I only watched for a few minutes before I started to feel guilty and came back home. They loved each other so much. I watched

137

father take mother's clothes off. She sighed and whispered to him. I never understood what he was doing, but now I think I do understand better." He looked straight at Stella. "Their love and connection seemed strange, but it held strong. Mother trusted him in every sense of the word. If he'd asked her to walk into fire for him, she would have done it, because she trusted him with every fiber of her being and knew everything would turn out fine."

Jacob took his sister's hand and leaned against her. "Stel, we still shouldn't judge them. We haven't gotten the whole story. How did they come to be together?" He smiled at her. "We need to hear the rest."

She relaxed back and shook her head. "Fine, fine, who's going to read next?"

Jay half stood and picked up the next book in the stack. He opened the cover and started.

Chapter Twelve

May 27, 1920

Last night, I ate dinner alone and crawled onto the bed by myself. I thought for several hours, again finding myself in a dilemma. As much as I wanted to stay with James, I knew I couldn't. To try and have a life with him would be impossible, until my days with Marshall were sorted out. I couldn't guarantee James anything and it wouldn't be fair to him.

Sometime during the night, James entered the room. I felt his arm come over me. I brought my hand up to his wrist and touched him. He turned his hand to hold mine. I could feel his breath on my neck as he kissed it. I wanted to tell him I loved him. I wanted to stay with him forever. All I could do though was cry. We said nothing to one another and he only held me in his arms.

This morning I saw Mr. Mansfield down in the library. He said he'd sent Daniel to Layne Hall and asked to have the carriage sent for me tomorrow. I thanked him and returned to my room. I've spent the afternoon crying. I must get my emotions under control and be strong when I return to Layne Hall.

May 28, 1920

Last night was difficult. For the first time since my arrival at Mansfield, I actually felt nervous. James and I didn't speak much during dinner. We sat at the table for a while. It became an uncomfortable silence.

I couldn't stand it any longer, we needed to talk. "James, I know this is hard. Please believe I'm feeling it, too. If things were different…" I found him looking at me with a tight expression on his face and I couldn't continue.

He took in a breath and relaxed some. "Catherine, I know you feel it's necessary to return and try to salvage your marriage, but I don't want you to go. I love you and want you with me."

"You know it is impossible." I looked down at my hands. My throat felt tight and my eyes began to burn. "I'd rather stay with you. Please know that, but I can't," I whispered.

"If anything ever happens you can always come back. I won't be here at Mansfield, but Jacob will know how to find me at Whear. I'll wait for you, forever, if I have to."

"James, you must not wait long. You deserve as much happiness as you can grab on to. Promise me you'll move on?"

He pressed his lips together and shook his head. "No, no promises." He stood and looked out one of the windows.

"These last few days I've been going over and over in my mind the things which have changed for me in the last month. I don't even know if I'll be able to stand Marshall's hands on me. It won't be your touch."

James turned from the window and knelt beside me before I could blink. He put his head in my lap with his hand on my leg. He said, "I know you'll come back to me. I can hope."

The tears came again. I thought I'd used them all up yesterday, but they rolled down my cheeks again.

"If he hurts you again, you leave him." He pulled back up and looked at me.

"No promises, James."

He stayed with me and we held each other close through most of the night. I didn't think I'd be able to sleep, but at some point I drifted off. When I woke up this morning he'd already gone.

Chapter Thirteen

Layne Hall - May 29, 1920

I'm home now. I arrived yesterday and it seems strange being back and alone again. Marshall is away in the city. No one here is sure when he'll return. He's been gone for some time.

Yesterday, waking up without James's body pressed next to me, was hard. I missed talking to him and just the feeling of his warmth and presence created a large hole in the room. I sat up on the bed and looked at the table and chairs by the window where we'd talked and laughed and made love. I felt terribly sad and scared.

The sadness came from never seeing James again after today. Scared about what waited for me at home. I hoped this training would make me the better wife Marshall looked for. I needed to go home with the determination to pick up the pieces and try to fall in love with my husband again. I also knew I had to forgive him if I could make it work, but it's going to be difficult, particularly if he continues to hit me. Time will tell.

I got dressed in the clothes I'd brought with me and they all seemed uncomfortable. Something James said about getting used to looser fitting clothes, came to mind and I smiled. He'd been right. After I'd put on a dress, I took off my panties and felt better, freer.

After I dressed, Marco brought in a cart with breakfast items. Only one plate and silver setting sat on the table and he told me he would be back in half an hour to have my valise brought down and accompany me to a final meeting with Mr. Mansfield.

I drank a cup of tea and ate some toast and fruit. The half hour sped by and Marco came back. He picked up the bag. "Ma'am, if you're ready, I will show you down to Mr. Mansfield now," Marco said.

"Thank you, Marco," I replied.

I followed him down the hallway to the stairs. We went through the main entryway past what I'd originally thought was obscene art. He showed me to the sunroom off of the office. Mr. Mansfield stood as I entered. He asked Marco to let us know when the carriage arrived and then offered coffee or tea.

"No thank you, sir. I have a long ride ahead of me."

"Yes, of course." He motioned for Marco to be on his way. "Please, have a seat." Mr. Mansfield sat across from me and picked up his own cup. "Mrs. Pieper, I hope your time here hasn't been too trying?"

"Not at all, sir. I can say the first week was difficult, but James made the transition smooth, I think. In fact, I wished to thank him too for his courtesy, but he seems to have disappeared this morning."

Mr. Mansfield frowned a little. "Yes, James left early this morning to go to Whear Hall. I believe he showed it to you and told you the circumstances surrounding it. He was very anxious to get things moving over there."

"I see." I felt a pang of sadness enter my heart, but thought perhaps it was best. I needed to fix my own life. "I'm sorry I missed him. If you see him, please, extend my thanks to him."

"I'll be sure to do that for you."

"Mr. Mansfield, may I ask, now that James is gone, what will happen here? Who will take over for him?"

"One of the young men you have met during your stay. I'm going to have to speak with those with seniority. The position will be filled easily though." He frowned. "Mrs. Pieper, I know we discussed this last week in the garden and I don't wish to be inappropriate, but must. I'm hoping all will be well when you return home to your husband.

However, if you ever need any assistance, please, please call on us here at Mansfield."

"Why do you say that, sir?"

He paused and pushed his lower lip out. "When you first arrived, it was quite obvious Mr. Pieper recently struck you."

"Obvious?"

"Yes, the bruising hadn't faded. When I spoke to your husband that day, he denied any knowledge of the bruises. It was apparent he lied and possessed a forked tongue."

"That is something Marshall does very well, but how could you tell the truth?"

"He wouldn't look me in the eye. I've been a gambler for a long time, my dear. I have learned to read people and know when I'm being lied to and, in your case, I'm concerned. That day, I tried to have a long discussion with him. It was obvious he didn't listen to his own words." He shook his head. "I've also heard some things around the city. Needless to say, Mrs. Pieper, I ask you to be careful with him. If there is any sign of his violence returning, get away from him quickly."

"Thank you, sir. I will heed your warning." I wanted to ask what he heard in the city, but then a knock sounded on the door and Marco entered.

"Sir, Mrs. Pieper's carriage is here. The case has been loaded and they're ready to leave."

"Thank you, Marco." Jacob stood up and looked down at me. He held out his arm. "Mrs. Pieper."

I put my hand on his arm and stood. "Mr. Mansfield, I wonder if I could ask a favor?"

"Certainly, my dear."

"If, in the future, we have the lovely chance of meeting again, would you please call me Catherine?"

He laughed. "Of course, Catherine, of course.

143

Please, call me Jacob."

I smiled back at him. "Thank you, Jacob"

He escorted me out to the carriage where Arthur waited. He helped me up the two steps and, as I sat, Jacob bid me farewell.

As we pulled away from Mansfield Hall, I felt a heaviness in my chest and worked hard to not cry. I wished I'd one more chance to look into James's warm brown eyes and have him hold me. I watched the scenery pass by and found I could keep my mind off all which occurred in the last month. I focused on the days coming up and knew I'd have some explaining to do with Stella. Should I come right out and tell her the truth about Mansfield or should I try to come up with another story?

We just passed through the gates and were riding a darkened part of the road thick with trees. We rounded a bend and up a head of us, I saw a familiar face. Just off the road, James stood under a cedar tree. He watched us approach, but made no move. I stared at him as we went past.

"Arthur, stop the carriage," I said.

"What is it, ma'am?" He halted the horses and turned to me.

I opened the door and prepared to step down. "Wait here, I'll be back in a moment."

I walked along the road and came up even with the tree where James stood. "You left this morning without saying goodbye," I said.

"I hate goodbyes." He made no move.

I looked at the ground and found a way to him, moving toward the tree. Glancing over my shoulder, I saw smaller trees blocking my view of the carriage. Arthur wouldn't see us.

When I was about five feet from him, I stopped. "I agree with you. Goodbyes can be horrible."

144

We stood and stared at one another. I wanted to remember his dark eyes most. They held such comfort in them. "I apologize for staring, but I want to remember every detail of your eyes, hair, face…"

Before I could say anything further, James grabbed me in his arms and pushed my back against the tree. He placed his lips on mine and kissed me hard and strong. I felt his hand move down my skirt and start to pull it up. He moved his lips to my neck. I put my hand over his and made him release my skirt.

"We can't do this, James. It's time for us to part," I said. I tried to be strong and, although I wanted him to make love to me desperately, I knew we needed to move forward.

The few minutes passed too quickly and before I knew it, James pulled away from me. He turned his back to me and looked at the road.

"Catherine, I love you and I know you love me."

"I do love you."

He turned back to face me. "Leave him, come and live with me at Whear Hall. We can make a home, have children. We could be so happy."

I put my hands up to his face and kissed him. "Milord, you know I can't. I have to go back to Layne."

James put his hands on my waist and pulled me close. "I'll wait for you, milady. I'll be at Whear Hall waiting for you. Do you hear me? No matter how long it takes."

"I hear you, love. I'll miss you. I'll miss waking in the morning with you and having breakfast. I'll miss watching the sunrise with you." I put my head on his chest and felt I never wanted to let him go, but I did. I looked up into his eyes. "I'm not going to say goodbye, then."

He smiled. "I like that. No goodbyes."

I started to turn away and he took my hand in his. Leaning toward me, he brushed his lips across mine and then down my neck. We stared into each other's eyes. I took a step away from him, but didn't take my eyes off him. I somehow managed to get back to the road without my eyes leaving his handsome face. When I heard the crunch of gravel under my shoes, I smiled one last time and turned, heading back to the carriage.

It was a long ride home to Layne Hall, but we finally arrived in the early afternoon. Stella had heard the carriage coming up the drive and waited outside the front door with her hands folded in front of her.

The carriage came to a halt and Arthur started to get up to help me out, but I stopped him. I got out on my own and turned to him. "Arthur, thank you for coming all the way to pick me up. Get yourself some lunch before you put the horse away."

"You're very welcome, ma'am. Thank you." He smiled.

"My bag can be brought in later."

"Yes, ma'am."

He snapped the reins on the horse and moved away. I turned to Stella who came toward me with her arms out. "Catherine, where have you been?" She hugged me. "Are you all right? I've been so worried."

We walked to the house. I put my arm through hers. "Did you receive my message?" I set my bag on the hall table and turned into the main living room. Layne Hall seemed very small compared to where I'd been.

"That nice young boy brought it, but it was a month ago." She looked concerned.

"Stella." I started to the kitchen and took her hand to follow me. "Come sit in the kitchen with me. I'm very hungry and would like some tea. I'll explain all I can."

We went into the kitchen and I was greeted by Susan and Katie. Within ten minutes, Susan warmed up a bowl of soup and served it to me with thick slices of fresh bread.

After a couple of spoonfuls, I slowed down and started to tell Stella an edited version of my story. I knew the cooks were listening and tried to keep the story a little vague. I knew I would tell Stella everything, but didn't want to share it with the whole house.

"First of all, is Marshall here?" I asked her.

"No, he left for the city about three weeks ago. He hasn't been back since. Things haven't been done here at Layne either. The sheep are past ready for shearing."

"That's fine. Now to answer your question, I've been on a bit of a retreat. I learned some new things while I was there and hopefully it will help me communicate with Marshall better. I was treated like a queen. I had a massage almost every day and special baths." I stopped and looked over at the stove. Susan stood at the sink and listened. "If you ladies would like to sit and listen in, that would be all right."

Both Susan and Katie glanced at each other, then smiled and came to the table.

"It was a nice time. I guess it was like a vacation. I'd do it again in a heartbeat."

"I'm so glad you're safe, Catherine. Even though the young man brought your message, I was still concerned Marshall might have done something to you."

"As you see, I'm fine. I'm exhausted from the trip home, but otherwise, just fine."

She smiled at me and let me finish my lunch.

We talked for several hours. Sitting in the main living room, Stella filled me in on what went on in the village and at Layne Hall. Besides shearing time, I found out I'd missed the lambs being born, which was always a wonderful time of year. Stella frowned and when I asked her what concerned her, the lines around her mouth appeared to deepen and she told me Marshall sold all of the lambs within days of their births. She felt certain he lied to the man who bought them.

"They were too young, Catherine, much too young." She looked down at her hands. "Since he's been gone, nothing much has been taken care of. No one's been hired for the shearing."

I sat up in my chair. "Do you know who he sold the lambs to?"

"No."

"How many were there?"

"At least twenty-five, I heard from one of the men who helped with the birthing."

"I'm assuming Marshall didn't leave any money behind when he left?" I thought about the paltry sum in my own bag. It wouldn't be enough for two or three days work.

"Not anything, Catherine." She looked at me with sad eyes.

"Oh, Stella." I rubbed my eyes. "What are we to do? If the shearing doesn't get done, what are we going to live on this winter?"

She remained silent.

For the rest of the evening, my mind spun. I needed to think of some way to find Marshall and get him to pay attention to the livestock or come up with someway myself. I didn't have the funds to pay for such an endeavor. I couldn't sleep and my mind kept coming back to the fact Marshall left with Layne's capital for the summer and could think of no way to fix the problem.

For a brief time, I let my brain think of James. Lying in bed, I could feel his arms around me, but not his warmth. I even thought I could smell him, but he wasn't there.

Secrets Beyond Dreams

Chapter Fourteen

May 31, 1920

There are some miracles in the world. I've thanked the Lord above all day for his grace and all he provides.

I spoke today with the foreman of a shearing crew which has been working on the estate next to Layne. I explained honestly the problem which occurred with our sheep and that I wouldn't have the funds to pay them until after the wool sold. To gain his trust, I increased the offer by a nickel over the current going rate. He agreed and said the crew could be at Layne by the beginning of next week. He said they'd lost a job elsewhere to another group and would be happy to help us out. I felt so grateful, I almost started to cry.

What a relief. Once we get the wool in and sold, with the sale of vegetables, we should be able to survive the winter months. I'm going to have to find a place in the house to hide the money. It will be gone in a heartbeat if Marshall finds it.

June 1, 1920

Stella and I made a concerted effort to keep the garden going. It is hard work, but I even got Susan and Katie to come out of the kitchen a couple of times to help weed.

I got so frustrated, two days ago, with my silly skirt. In the afternoon, I came into the house, took off my skirt and pulled it to pieces. Using a pair of Marshall's trousers as a pattern, I've put together a pair of slacks to wear in the garden. Stella looked shocked when I walked out the back door today. I saw Susan smile, though. It is making the work much easier, as I knew it would. Ever since doing this at Mansfield, I can't begin to remember how it was working in a skirt. I must have been daft.

June 3, 1920

The shearing crew arrived this morning and will work through the weekend to bring in the herd and get them shaved. The foreman agreed to come with me into the village, when the wools ready, to get it sold. He wants to be sure we get a fair price.

Still no Marshall. I've thought about what I want to say to him when he does return. I'm almost certain he won't want to hear it. I keep praying I'll have the strength.

June 4, 1920

After working in the garden all morning, Stella and I decided to have a quiet afternoon. I'm feeling rather worn today. We sat in the living room where Stella worked on her stitching and I tried to read my book, but couldn't concentrate. I put it down on the table next to me.

"Stella, I have to make a confession." She stopped her needlepoint and listened. "You're too dear to me and I can't lie to you. Not ever." I didn't know how to tell her, but needed to say something. I couldn't live with myself being dishonest. "When I left here a month or so ago, I believed Marshall was taking me to a business associate's estate for some reception."

"I thought it strange when the young man brought your message and then Marshall came home. It was obvious he knew nothing about the message. He just said you would be away for a time. I felt confused," she said and sighed.

I sat forward and put my arm on my knees. "Stella." I stopped. There was no clear way of asking this. "Have you ever heard of schools where a husband can send his wife to be trained in relations and such?"

She looked at me, and asked, "Do you mean etiquette-type training?"

I decided to come right out with it. "I mean schools which train women to be better wives, sexually?"

Stella put her hand up to her mouth and her breath caught. "I've never heard of such a thing."

"They do exist, believe me, and it is where Marshall took me."

"Why didn't you get back in the carriage and come back immediately?"

"It got complicated. Marshall signed some sort of contract with the proprietor. The gentleman, Mr. Mansfield, tried to explain it to me, but I felt so shocked by the whole thing I couldn't follow what he said. What I did grasp though, was if I didn't participate, Layne Hall would have been lost. This may make no difference in the long run. The way Marshall is gambling, we may lose it anyway. I agreed to participate." I looked over at her horrified face. "The gentleman who guided me through the month, treated me very kindly and tenderly, and, yes, I cheated on Marshall with him many times in the month. He is a wonderful man, Stella." My voice became choked. "He showed me all I have been missing in my relations with Marshall." I looked away from her, pulled out a handkerchief and dried my eyes. "I know I was only with him a short time, but I fell in love with him and he with me. At least, that was what he said when I left to come home. I miss him terribly."

Stella dried her own tears and in a small voice asked, "What are you going to do?"

"What do you mean?"

"Are you going to stay here at Layne or run off with this other man?"

"I've come home to try and work things out with Marshall. We have a lot to discuss, if he will, and it's going

152

to be some time before I will trust him, again. Hopefully, all will be fine."

"Why would he send you to such a place?" she asked.

"I'm sorry, Stella, you would have to ask Marshall. I'll never understand why."

We were silent for a time and Stella mulled this over. She looked over at me. "Catherine, what was his name? The man you were with?"

"James Whear."

"That's a good name."

"I think you would have liked him. The last night I stayed at Mansfield, he asked me to come away with him." I tried to keep from crying. "I knew I couldn't. I have to get things sorted out here."

"You don't give in easily, Catherine. I'm very proud of you for the courage and strength you've shown."

"Thank you. I don't know what will happen, Stella. When Marshall comes home...I don't know what to expect. I came back to make a faithful effort with him, but if he continues hitting me, it will be over. I can only take it a day at a time and because of what's happened, I hope you will consider staying here with me, please."

"Why wouldn't I stay with you, Catherine?" she asked and looked hurt.

"I did have intimate relations with another man. It goes against the Lord's moral code."

Stella rolled her eyes. "You're being silly, Catherine. He knows you had no choice and I'm sure he understands."

I smiled. "Thank you Stella. That is a comfort."

Lauren Marie

Chapter Fifteen

June 11, 1920

It's been very busy the last few days and I haven't the time or willingness to write. All has gone so well, though.

The crew worked fast at getting the herd done. It seemed to take them no time at all. Yesterday, the wool got loaded up and I went with the men into the village. After a bit of haggling with the buyer, the foreman assured me we were getting a good price per pound. I received the cash, paid the foreman and had some left in my pocket. I said goodbye to the crew and walked home.

I've put the remaining cash away in a place I don't believe Marshall will discover. I feel proud of myself this evening and drank a second glass of wine with dinner. For the first time since my return to Layne Hall, I actually think I can relax.

June 15, 1920

When I got up this morning I didn't feel well. I've been nauseated all day and figure, from now on, one glass of wine with dinner is enough. I'm not sure what it is, but it made being out in the sun in the garden hard. I only put in an hour, before I gave up and came back into the house. I'm feeling better this evening.

June 17, 1920

Yesterday and this morning, I got up late. I've tried, with Stella's help, to keep the garden in good shape. We're getting close to some of the first vegetables being ripe and ready for canning. Susan lines up glass jars and prepares the kitchen. The squash plants went mad and are threatening to outgrow the garden area. We trimmed them back some today, which should keep them under control.

My arms and nose are turning brown again and freckles are starting to reappear. I'd bent over a tomato plants and must have straightened too fast as I got dizzy and threw up. Stella helped me to the patio and brought a glass of cool water. I tried to drink from the glass, but it only made me want to throw up, again. I stayed in the shade for a while, feeling nauseated and tired.

A couple of years ago, the influenza virus attacked our county. It was the influenza which killed my father. It killed millions around the world and I wondered if it returned and made me feel so ill.

"Stella, what if I have the influenza virus? Have you heard if it's still around?" I asked, when she joined me on the patio.

She squeezed my hand and smiled. "Dear, I don't think it's the influenza. You don't seem to be burning up with fever and other than getting tan from gardening, your complexion hasn't changed. I think you just need some rest. All of the stress you came home to, may have caught up with you."

I've rested most of the day. I think I'll retire early tonight. I may need to go see the doctor in the village to find out what's ailing me.

June 20, 1920
I'm still throwing up. Stella went into the village today to get Dr. Hansen. He arrived after lunchtime and I felt a bit better by his arrival.

He excused the kitchen staff and cleaned up the table, covering it with a sheet. He then handed me a white

156

cotton gown and left the room. I changed into the gown and in a few minutes he returned. He helped me onto the table, looked at my eyes, felt along my neck and checked my throat. He then pulled a device with tubes from his pocket. He placed the tubes in his ears, held the other piece to my chest and seemed to listen. He walked around the table and held the device to my back and asked me to take in breaths. He helped me to lie down on the table and he felt my stomach. I saw his brows crease and then smooth out. He put the tubes back into his ears and listened to my stomach.

Finally, he stood and put his listening device into his pocket. He smiled. "Go ahead and get dressed, Mrs. Pieper. I'll meet you in the living room." He helped me down from the table and left the kitchen.

I dressed as quickly as possible and went to the living room door. Before I went in, I thought, It's got to be all right, he did smile. I felt frightened for a moment and wondered if it might be the cancer. I pushed the door open. Dr. Hansen sat in a chair making notes on a piece of paper. I sat opposite him and waited.

He looked up, folded the paper and put it in his jacket pocket. "Mrs. Pieper, when did you have your last menstrual cycle?"

I sat back in my chair surprised at his question. "Let me think. It would have been the third week of April, I believe." When I spoke those words, I knew and felt like a complete idiot for not thinking of it.

The doctor raised his eyebrows. "I'm going to need for you to come into the village this week and let me do a blood test to confirm what I think you already know."

"Of course, I'll walk into town tomorrow. This is wonderful news, doctor." My heart raced.

He stood, walked over to my chair and handed me a piece of paper. "This is the name of the midwife in the village. There's no hurry to contact her, you're only about four weeks along. You can contact her in a couple of months. She'll go over the delivery instructions with you and later on, she'll want to make weekly visits to check on you. I'll see you tomorrow, then?"

"Yes, yes." I got up and walked him to the door. "What time would be convenient?" I asked.

"Eleven o'clock in the morning should work fine." He smiled. "Congratulations, Mrs. Pieper."

"Thank you, doctor." I closed the door and leaned against it. Dates and things I'd said to James ran through my head. Things James said to me about unwanted pregnancies, started up. I talked the panic out of my head. I was pregnant and felt incredibly happy.

I walked down to the kitchen to get a cup of tea and found Stella at the table waiting for me. "Well? What did the doctor say?" she asked.

"Susan, could I get a cup of tea?" I sat at the table across from Stella.

"Yes, ma'am."

"It's nothing too serious. I won't have much to worry about for a while."

Susan turned from the stove and looked at me, concerned.

"What is it?" Stella asked with panic in her voice.

"I'm afraid we won't really know what it is for several months." Stella sat back in her chair with a confused look on her face. "In fact, it won't be until January before we find out if it's a boy or girl." I smiled at her.

"Good Lord, child." Stella stood and came to hug me. "You can be so difficult sometimes. I nearly worried myself to death."

"None of that now, I'm going to need your help—everyone's help—all right?"

Susan brought my tea and said congratulations. She smiled on her way back to the stove.

After I spoke with Stella, I spent the afternoon in the garden alone. I knew Marshall would come home and, hopefully, be pleased with the news. I wanted to keep it a secret that the baby wasn't his. What he didn't know wouldn't hurt him. The only problem would be timing. Having checked a calendar, I figured it was two weeks or so before I left Mansfield when I told James to stop using the condoms. I checked my pages here and discovered it was on April first when Marshall last touched me. It would be tight. I'd keep praying all would go well and I couldn't believe it, but I actually wanted him to come home.

Lauren Marie

Secrets Beyond Dreams

Chapter Sixteen

June 24, 1920

I came in from the garden this afternoon and went into the kitchen to wash my hands.

Susan turned as I walked in. "Don't know if you've been told, ma'am?" She scowled. "Mr. Pieper has come back from the city. He's in his library."

"Thank you, Susan." I dried my hands, put the towel down on the counter and stared at it for a moment feeling my stomach with my other hand. I took in a breath and headed for the hallway. As I made my way to the library, I prayed to the Lord above to give me strength. I stopped at the library door trying to think how best to approach Marshall. I'd no idea what to expect from him, let alone how to approach it. I opened the door and walked in.

Marshall sat at his desk with a glass of whiskey in his hand. The decanter sat on top of the desk. His appearance startled me, as he had a black eye and the white of that eye was red.

"Well, well, you've decided to come home, have you?" He sneered at me.

"Marshall, I've been home some weeks now. It's good to see you've returned." He only grunted and took another gulp of his drink. "I have some news I hope will please you." I sat in the chair across from him, and tried to be cheerful.

"How pleased do you think I'll be if the Mansfield school turned you into a slut? That school is a scandal." He stared at me.

"Then why did you arrange for me to go there, if not to be a better wife to you? What did you want me to gain from the training?"

"I heard you sold the wool. Where's the money?" He didn't answer my question.

"I put it in the bank in the city." It bothered me to find it so easy to lie to him.

"You've been to the city?" He laughed.

"No, I made arrangements through an attorney in the village."

"Interesting." He drank from his glass, again. "How many men were you with, Catherine?"

"Marshall, I came back with hope we can make this marriage work." He continued to stare at me. "I hope you'll be willing to work with me."

He stood up and rounded the desk. "Hope? Work? Work with you? You haven't done a day's work in your life." He turned away from me and sat heavily in one of the overstuffed chairs.

I stood up and turned to leave the room. This wasn't the time to discuss anything. He was too drunk.

"What is your extremely pleasing news, Catherine?"

I turned and looked at him. He was half asleep in the chair. "Wool prices are very good. More money for you to drink," I said, under my breath. I don't think he heard me. I left him to his whiskey.

I walked back out to the garden and found Stella trimming back the flower bed. I sat on the rock fence and folded my hands. She looked up at me with a smile. When she saw my face, her smile turned into a frown. "What's happened?" she asked.

"Stella, Marshall's back. He's in his library already drunk. Already drunk? He's always drunk. It's been a long time since he hasn't been drunk."

163

She dropped the shears, took off her gloves and came to sit by my side. She took my hand and asked, "What has happened?"

"He called me a slut. I don't believe he wants to try." I felt tears well in my eyes.

"Did you tell him about the baby?"

"No. If the only reason we stay together is because of the baby, we'll be a very unhappy family." I turned away from her. "If he were to be violent with the baby…I can't let it happen." I looked up at the sky. Storm clouds were rolling in and the breeze picked up. Suddenly, there was a loud crack of thunder, which gave me an ill feeling.

"Stella, I need for you to remember the name Mansfield Hall. Arthur knows where it is. If anything should happen to me, send Arthur to Mansfield. Say it to me."

"Mansfield Hall," she repeated.

"Good. Tell Arthur to speak only to Mr. Mansfield. The gentleman will know what to do."

I ate dinner in the kitchen this evening. Afterward, I came up to my room and locked the door. I have a feeling it's going to be a long night and I'm not going to get much sleep.

Secrets Beyond Dreams

Chapter Seventeen

Whear Hall - July 2, 1920

It's been more than a week since the horrible night at Layne Hall. I haven't been able to sit up long enough to write anything down. The dizzy spells are overwhelming and the doctor I've seen a couple of times, insists I must stay in bed for the baby's sake. Even if I wanted to get up, I don't think I could. The room spins too much. My left arm, left hip and thigh and my face are bruised and very painful. James is here, as is Stella. They've taken good care of me. Some of what I'm about to write is from what they've told me. I don't remember too much.

Early that evening, I told Stella to go to her room and I also retired. I remember locking the door, but it isn't a strong, secure lock. It did make me feel better. The night turned stormy and bright lightning and loud thunder continued on and on. I changed into a nightgown and was writing in my journal when I thought I heard something in the room. I looked around and realized the knob on the door turned and there was a loud bang on the door. Marshall shouted at me through the wood, incomprehensibly. I couldn't understand a word he said and the knob rattled again. He yelled for me to let him in. I backed away and picked up a hairbrush. It was the only thing I could see to defend myself. He started pushing or kicking at the door and it finally gave way, flying in against the wall.

Marshall stood in the doorway and his eyes were both red and bloodshot. "I've been thinking we should put your training to the test. Let's see how much you learned."

As he started into the room, I stopped him by unbuttoning my nightgown. I pulled it off my shoulders, let it fall to the floor and went down to my knees. I set the hairbrush by my leg, and said, "What would you have me do? Is this how you want me, Marshall?"

The sneer on his face turned to anger as I held out my arms. He moved over to me and grabbed my hair. I could smell the alcohol on his breath.

"I didn't ask for them to make you a whore."

He pushed me to the side, saw the hairbrush next to my gown and picked it up. While he looked at it, I got back up to my knees and he swung around, hitting me on the side of the head with the brush.

At this point, all I remember was trying to protect the baby. I curled into a ball on my side. Marshall began to kick me in the back. He stomped down on my hip several times.

I tried to scream, but couldn't find the breath and felt terrible pain in my hip and back. Suddenly, I felt my arm go up and my shoulder snap. Marshall grabbed my wrist and dragged me across the floor. The pain felt so severe. I must have passed out from it and don't remember anything more until a couple of days ago.

What I'm writing now was told to me by Stella and some from James.

Stella and Susan heard the commotion in my bedroom from downstairs. Stella started up the stairs and hurried her pace when she heard my scream. She saw the door broken in and feared the worse. She found Marshall had hold of my wrist and was dragging me toward the bed.

Stella shouted loudly at him. "Mr. Pieper!" Susan followed her and stood in the doorway.

When he saw them, Marshall stopped pulling me and dropped my arm. Stella wasn't certain what he would do next. She feared he might come after them. He stared for moment and then asked what she wanted.

Stella became furious and, these are her words, "shrieked at him to get out of the room." Marshall lost some of his vinegar from the tone of her voice and left the room.

She knelt down to check on me and heard the door to his study slam. Once she determined I was still alive, she covered me with a sheet and told Susan to go find Katie. She also told Susan to bring a pan with warm water and a towel. Susan left the room. Stella then saw the gash in my forehead and the pool of blood on the floor. Pulling a case off of one of the pillows, she put it on my head. Susan returned to the room with Katie, and Stella told the young girl to go to the stable, get Arthur and bring him up to the hallway outside my bedroom door.

Both Katie and Arthur came up to my room and helped Stella and Susan get me onto the bed. When anyone touched near my shoulder, I apparently moaned and Susan said it looked dislocated. They'd have to get the doctor. Stella told Arthur the message I'd given her just that afternoon. She told him to forget about the carriage and go by horse. Ask for Mr. Mansfield only and speak with no one else. Tell him what happened and follow his instructions. Arthur saddled a horse and was on the road within ten minutes. The rain poured down and it took him several hours, but Arthur found his way back to Mansfield Hall. The butler, Thomas, woke up Jacob, who came down and spoke with Arthur. He explained the situation in as much detail as he knew. Jacob sent the boy, Daniel, out with a message. He told the butler to take Arthur to the kitchen to warm him up and get some food. Arthur waited in the kitchen for an hour, when the young boy came running into the kitchen with a very tall, dark-haired man. Jacob joined them and introduced Arthur to James. Arthur recognized him from the day he'd originally brought me to Mansfield. Jacob convinced Arthur it would be all right to divulge the story to this gentleman. Before he could finish the telling, James grabbed Arthur by his jacket and led him out of the kitchen. He turned to Jacob and asked him to get the doctor from town over to Whear Hall. They would be back no later than noon. James' horse was still saddled, and he and Arthur road non-stop through the stormy night here to Layne Hall.

As he got off his horse, James asked Arthur to put his horse on the carriage and have it ready to go. Arthur told him where to go in the house.

James said he took the stairs two at a time and found the room. He opened the door, and saw Stella and Susan putting cold cloths on my forehead and arms. Stella stood up when he entered the room.

James looked at her and said, "You must be Stella."

"You must be James." Stella knew the minute she saw him that he was the one I'd spoken about. "We've sent for a doctor, but that was hours ago."

"It doesn't matter. I'm taking her out of here." He came to my bedside and looked down at me. Stella said he grimaced and sucked in his breath when he saw my face.

"Stella, I would appreciate it if you would accompany us. I'm going to need your help. Your driver is getting the carriage ready. Please, get Catherine ready to travel."

Stella and Susan did their best to get me dressed. It must have been difficult and I didn't help when I continued to fight with them. James pulled the blanket off the bed and threw it over my legs. He started to bend over to pick me up and looked at Stella. "Get your coat, ma'am. We're leaving." He picked me up and headed out of the room.

Marshall heard the ruckus on the stairs and stumbled into the front hallway from his study. He asked James what he thought he was doing. James refused to say anything other than to let us pass.

169

"Sir, that is my wife you are carrying—" Marshall started to say.

James interrupted him. "It may be, but not for long. I don't really care. She needs a doctor and I'm taking her."

"I beg to differ. You'll not leave here…"

James gave Marshall a threatening look, even with me in his arms and said, "If you insist on barring our way, when I put Catherine down, I may have to kill you. If she is injured seriously and does not recover, I will find you and beat you to as bloody a pulp as you have done to her. Am I making myself clear, sir?"

Stella put on her coat and watched all of this exchange with great satisfaction. She felt Marshall needed to be put in his place. He indeed got the message and stepped back to let James pass. They made their way down the rest of the stairs and to the carriage.

Susan stopped Stella and told her as soon as Katie got back from looking for the doctor, and Arthur returned, they would follow. She didn't want to stay in Layne Hall any longer.

On the ride to Whear Hall, Stella mentioned, the only time James said anything was to give directions to Arthur. He wouldn't let me go and she found it endearing in a way.

When we arrived, the doctor from their village waited with Jacob, who was quite upset about the situation.

During the doctor's examination, he found my shoulder was indeed dislocated. Somehow, he managed to get it back where it belonged, but I don't remember. According to Stella and James, I screamed quite a lot. It worried them when I didn't wake up for the next couple of days. Stella said James never left my side and she often found him asleep on the floor by the bed.

Arthur went back to Layne Hall and collected Susan and Katie. Arthur told Stella there wasn't a cook at Whear

Hall and I would need good food to get my strength back.

The little I do remember seemed strange, in a way. At times, I thought I dreamed. I could hear James' voice off at a distance and wanted to tell him I could hear him. My voice was lost. I knew Stella took care of me.

I could feel something in my hand, but when I tried to tighten my grip on whatever it was my hand wouldn't work. I also, heard music, very quiet, somewhere. I wanted to dance to it, but couldn't find where it came from. Nothing seemed real and though I could hear James speak, I knew it wasn't actually him. I knew it impossible.

Then I saw a field with James on the other side of it and I tried to call to him, but still had no voice. In my head, I could feel him hold my hand and kiss my face. I dreamed of James often. At one point, he told me to come back to him and he missed me terribly.

One morning, I opened my eyes and realized I wasn't in my room. I tried to move my head to look around, but it hurt my neck, so I stared at the ceiling. After a few tries, I was able to lift my head off the pillow. Looking down my body, I couldn't see very far with my blurry vision. I saw what looked like a couch, with a very long shape lying back on it. I thought I dreamt again. It wasn't possible James could be stretched out on a couch at the foot of the bed. I remembered hearing Stella berating him a couple of times about needing his own rest, but he refused to leave. I figured I made it up in my mind. He couldn't be here. I hallucinated, but liked it. He looked so good on the couch and I imagined he rested peacefully.

I tried to sit up, but my shoulder and neck screamed in pain which made me moan. This caused James's eyes to pop open and, taking two long steps, he knelt by my side. He helped me sit up and adjusted the pillows gently.

He sat down on the edge of the bed and took my hand in his. He kissed the back of it and said, "Good

171

morning, milady." I could see the concern in his eyes.

"May I have some water, please?" I whispered and stared at him. Was it possible he was here at Layne? I needed a drink of anything, my throat felt so dry.

He put my hand down, got up and went over to a table. Pouring water from a pitcher, he brought the glass to me and held it to my lips.

"Not too much, the doctor said to take it slow." He repeated this a couple of times, then set the cup aside. Taking my hand again, he continued to look down at me.

I reached up with my hand and touched his chest and shoulder. I put my fingers on his face and felt a tear rolling out of my eye. "Are you real?"

"I think so." He smiled and put my hand on his chest over his heart.

I cleared my throat. "I thought I dreamed you were here."

"No, milady, I've been right here by your side."

"James, this isn't my room. Where are we?"

"I brought you to Whear Hall from Layne. You are actually lying in my bed in the master suite."

"I must look wretched," I said, in a raspy voice.

He put his finger to my lips and shushed me. "You are beautiful this morning. I'll hear nothing which will convince me otherwise."

"You are too kind, milord."

"That's better, milady. The doctor has been here a couple of times in the last week—"

I interrupted him. "Week? A week has passed?"

"When he first examined you," James continued, "he discovered your shoulder had been separated from the socket. He found a couple of ribs which might be fractured and isn't sure about your hip. He wanted to have you moved to the city so they could do some x-rays, but then decided the trip would be too long and it would be safer to keep you here."

The memory of Marshall twisting my arm, resurfaced.

"The doctor reset your shoulder, but said it would be painful for a while. He wrapped your chest up like a mummy, which I hate. He also, left some morphine painkiller, but I was reluctant to give it to you. I can have Stella mix it up, if you'd like."

I looked up at him. "No, no. If I stay still I'll be fine. At least it's my left arm. I'll still be able to feed myself. The doctor didn't give me any morphine, did he?" I tried to clear my throat, but started to cough and he gave me another sip of water, which helped.

"No, he didn't think it was a good idea," James said. "Stella went back to Layne Hall and packed up some of your things. She brought your journal, so you'll be able to write in it, too."

"James, was she crazy? What if Marshall had been there?"

James put his hand up and shushed me again. "He wasn't there and she had the assistance of your two cooks and Arthur. I wouldn't want to go up against those three anytime soon. They feel very strongly about protecting you, for some unknown reason. Arthur found Marshall's horse wasn't in the barn, and I'm afraid when he does return, he'll find he has no household staff." James got a mischievous look on his face and sat up straight. "However, it would seem Whear Hall is now amply staffed. I am very short on funds to pay anyone at the moment, but they are so loyal and devoted to you, milady, they have agreed to take a cut for a time—to be renegotiated as things calm down. It would seem I have an instant household. Most importantly, I have a beautiful woman in my bed, who I wish to make passionate love to very much, but I know she is in terrible pain. I will have to be extremely patient." He kissed my hand again.

173

"James, I don't know how I'm ever going to be able to thank you for this."

"I told you before you left Mansfield, I love and adore you. No thanks will ever be necessary. As long as we're together, I will be a satisfied country gentleman with a happy home and family. I'm afraid," he started to whisper. "I've been giving Miss Stella a bit of a headache."

"Oh?"

"The night we brought you here, she let me know about the baby. She wanted me to tell the doctor when he attended to you. She accused me of being too attentive to you and risking my own health, but she just doesn't understand my own devotion, my love. I wasn't about to leave this room..." James stopped mid- sentence. He must have realized I wasn't paying attention.

I looked down at my stomach and released his hand to put it on top of sheet. "James, what did the doctor say about the baby?"

"He assured me the baby is fine. However, to be safe, he wants you stay in bed for another week at least and get plenty of rest. Catherine, what's the matter?"

"James," I whispered. "You're lying to me. I can tell by the look on your face. Is the baby dead?"

He looked down at my hand and then back up at me. "The doctor said he isn't certain if the baby survived. He said it would be many weeks before we'll know anything for certain. If the baby starts moving around and kicking, the doctor said it will be a good sign."

I started to cry and it took a moment before I could answer. "I see, all we can do now is hope and pray he'll be all right." I tried to stop crying. "I was frightened Marshall would hit me so hard, I'd lose the baby. I did everything I could to keep him from hitting my stomach." I continued sobbing and James changed positions on the bed to sit next to me. He put his arm around my shoulders and I buried my face on his chest.

"James, I'm so grateful to the good Lord above for allowing me to survive, but if I lose the baby, it will be too much to bear."

James took his arm from around my shoulder and sat up looking at me, quite serious. "Catherine, we must not lose faith. We have to think positively the baby will be fine. You do realize, no matter what happens with the baby, I'll be more than happy to legally adopt it. Marshall may have a complaint, but after the way he's treated you, he won't have any legal credibility."

It occurred to me what James said and he didn't realize the baby was his. I looked up at him and with my good hand, reached up and touched his lips. "James, you are being silly. This baby isn't Marshall's."

James's brow furrowed. It was apparent he tried to remember and then sucked in his breath and opened his eyes wide. "The child's mine?"

"Of course, milord. The month before I arrived at Mansfield, Marshall had not touched me. I experienced my cycle there during the training. A week or so later, you and I made love in the barn and under a tree. Marshall never touched me when I returned to Layne. There's only one possibility," I whispered.

"Under the tree, along the path." He smiled. "The baby is mine."

"Yes, milord. I hope he's going to be as handsome as you, too."

"He?" James leaned back. "How do you know it's a he?"

"A pox on me if I'm wrong."

"I'm going to be a father."

"Yes."

"I love you. Do you understand that?"

"Yes, I love you, too." With my good hand, I caught

his shirt and pulled him toward me. "James, please kiss me. I know my breath is wretched, but I need a kiss."

He started to lean forward. "I don't want to hurt you."

"You won't." He gently placed his lips on mine and in a split second, my lips parted, and waited for his tongue to enter. It was the kiss I'd been dreaming of and when he pulled away, I sighed. "I think I might live." I smiled up at him.

There was a quiet knock on the door and then it opened. Stella came in wheeling a cart with a large bowl and pitcher on it. James flew off the bed, swept her up in his arms and twirled her in circles. She protested a little, but did get to laughing. When he set her back down, he turned her to me and said, "Look who decided to wake up."

She came to the bed and took my hand. "Oh child, we were that worried about you, weren't we, sir?" she said.

"Catherine." James came up behind Stella and put his hand on her shoulder. "I've already been through this with you. Please, tell Stella it's all right to call me James."

"Stella, you heard him. He hates formality."

Her face began to turn pink. "I'll try, I really will."

James patted her shoulder and said, "I think since Stella is here now, this would be a good time to get cleaned up."

"That's a very good idea, sir." Stella looked at him. James looked back at her a bit surprised. "It has been getting rank in here, James." She smiled.

"Rank?" he asked. He looked at me and winked. "I didn't know I'd gotten that bad. I'll be back shortly." He took another look at me and blew me a kiss.

Stella kept hold of my hand and sat on the edge of the bed. "How are you feeling, my dear?"

I thought for a moment. "Sore, very sore. How very wretched do I look, Stella? Be honest." I looked at her and tried to make my eyes plead.

She put her hand up and moved a stray hair behind my ear. "You've a bit of bruising on your face and a cut on your forehead." I let her hand go and put it up to my head to feel a bandage. "You have some more bruises along your neck, shoulder and chest, but they'll be better soon. The doctor didn't think the cut on your forehead needed stitches and he said the scar will fade with time."

"Is there a mirror in here?" I asked.

"Catherine, you don't want to worry about this now."

"No, I do want to worry about it, Stella. Please, find a mirror."

She stood and looked sad. Walking to the dresser, she opened the top drawer and pulled out my hand mirror from Layne Hall. She held it to her chest as she walked back to the bed.

"Are your sure, Catherine?"

"Yes."

She sat on the bed and put the mirror in my hand. I stared at her. I felt frightened at what I would see. What had Marshall done to me? I lifted the mirror and turned it over. I moved my eyes away from her, looked at my reflection, and didn't recognize myself. Stella had been kind. I felt my bottom lip start to tremble. The right side of my face looked almost black and my eye was swollen and red. I realized my cheek and jaw were also swollen. "Oh, my Lord," I whispered under my breath. A tear rolled down my left cheek.

Stella grabbed the mirror away from me and said, "That's enough for now, Catherine. The doctor is very sure everything will be fine in no time."

"Stella, how could he do this? He's a monster," I said. It occurred to me I couldn't remember what happened. "Tell me, Stella. I can't remember what happened that night.

Tell me."

She put the mirror aside and took my hand, holding it tight. She spent the next half hour telling me a brief version of what happened. How she'd seen Marshall drag me across the bedroom floor. It horrified her and made her feel sick. She told me about the confrontation on the stairs and how she'd realized James was sent by God. Telling me of the ride from Layne Hall and how James refused to leave my side.

"I heard you arguing with him," I said.

"You heard us?"

"I did. I thought I was dreaming. I knew you were taking care of me, but felt it impossible James was here. He can be stubborn sometimes."

"I believe you're very correct with that assessment, my dear." She smiled.

"Stella." I let her hand go and tried to reposition myself. My back felt uncomfortable.

"What can I do, dear?" She helped me roll over on my side a little to get off my hip and back.

"Nothing, I'm fine now. Stella, there is something I need for you to know and understand." I looked back up at her.

"Yes, dear."

"I'm only about six weeks pregnant." I watched her do the figuring in her head.

"You weren't at Layne Hall then, but Marshall was for part of the time."

"Yes," I answered. I prayed she would understand. "Stella, Marshall isn't my baby's father." Stella's mouth opened, but no words came out. "James is the father."

"Ah, I see." She thought about this for a moment. "I think I knew. You told me you had relations with him."

"Yes, I did. I know my relationship with James will be frowned upon. Hopefully, I'm not too wretched-looking and he still wants me…"

"Catherine no, don't say that. If you could have seen him in the last week…I'm sure he loves you very much." She patted my hand.

"Stella, are you very shocked by my behavior?"

"No, child. It makes no difference to me. Mr.—I mean, James—seems a good man, which after that monster Marshall nearly killed you, is such a blessing. He will take good care of you, I'm sure of it."

"There's one other thing I'm going to need you to do, Stella."

She nodded her head and mumbled "anything".

"Is Arthur still here?"

"Yes."

"Good, good," I thought a moment. "Make arrangements with him for tomorrow. Get up early in the morning and have Arthur take you back to Layne Hall. Tell him to be very sure Marshall isn't there. If he is, don't stay, and come back here immediately."

"What is this all about?" she asked.

"If Marshall isn't there or is too drunk to know anything, go into the house, to my room. On the left side of my closet under some boxes, there is a loose floor board. You'll have to move the boxes out and take a nail file with you. The humidity makes the board stick. Open the floor board and you should find another box. It has some things which belonged to my father, but most importantly, it has the money from the wool sale." She let out a breath. "If he's there, don't do it. Come back here and I'll find another way to retrieve the box. Marshall's too dangerous. I don't want him to hurt you or Arthur. Promise me to try, though."

"Yes, but why?" she asked.

"James said he is having some funding problems. The wool money could help him out and I want to help him now more than ever."

"Of course." She thought a moment. "I'll do my best."

"Thank you." I tightened my grip as best I could on her hand. "Be careful."

Stella let me know later in the day, she'd spoken with Arthur and he agreed to have the carriage ready in the morning. She spent the rest of the day helping me. I dozed off and on and Stella told me James came in a couple of times to check on things. When he saw I slept, he went to do some work on his own estate.

Chapter Eighteen

July 4, 1920

Last evening, I could swallow some broth and keep it down. Susan brought some crackers up from the kitchen and I ate a couple of those, too. James came back in as I finished.

"Did I miss supper?" He smiled and leaned over to kiss my forehead. "How are you feeling, my love?"

"The broth helped." I glanced up at him and then away and felt ashamed of the way my face looked. Stella sat in a chair next to the bed, and worked her needlepoint, while I ate.

James touched her on the shoulder and told her to go get her dinner. She left the room and he sat in the chair she vacated. I leaned back and tried to hide my face with my hair.

"It's good to see you sitting up," he said. When he saw what I did with my hair, his smile faded and he looked concerned. "Hey." He got up and moved the plate of crackers to the nightstand. Sitting on the edge of the bed, he tried to move my hair. I looked away from him. "Hey, what are you doing?"

"I don't want you to see this mess," I whispered.

He put his hand on my face and turned my head to face him. "I've seen it, my love."

"It's so horrible." I sobbed.

He smiled at me again. "Catherine, it will go away and you are still the most beautiful thing I've ever seen."

"You're just saying that to make me feel better." I

continued weeping.

"I'm obviously doing a bad job." He turned around on the bed, put his arm over my shoulders, and pulled me to his chest. "There, there, love. It's going to be all right."

He held me for some time and let me finish my tantrum. I could hear his heart beating in his chest and it sounded like music to me.

"James, what am I to do? I can't return to Layne. It's been my home for all of my life and I have memories I'll keep with me forever. The memories of the last three years though, make it a sad place and I don't want to think about it anymore."

"You don't have to think about it anymore. I told you once you could be mistress of Whear Hall if you'd like," he said.

"I can't just move in with you. Think of the gossipmongers."

James stood and struck a serious pose. He put his hand up to his face and paced the room a little. I thought he might not want to involve himself any further in my problems and couldn't blame him. I needed to arrange a divorce and get things settled with Layne Hall. His life would also be turned upside down, with the baby and household staff.

"James, I know this is all overwhelming. I'll understand if you feel you aren't ready for this much commitment."

He stopped pacing and turned to face me. "Catherine," he said, in a very grave tone. "Here are my thoughts on the subject." He walked over to the bed and knelt beside it. He took my hand in his and held it to his face. "If you ever consider leaving me and returning to Layne, my heart will be destroyed. I did consider telling you that I forbid you returning to Layne, but you have to make up your own mind. If you leave, I will have to go to a monastery, confess my many sins and never speak to anyone again. Besides, Whear Hall being empty for eighteen years, it was the home of a bachelor father and his twelve-year-old son and needs a woman's touch now."

I realized at this point, he teased me.

"Catherine, please stay here forever with me. I don't care if you ever get a divorce and the gossipmongers have a field day. I don't care if we live in sin. I love you more than I'll ever be able to show you. Just touching you makes my heart almost explode."

I tried to smile and felt a tear roll down my cheek, again. I touched his face. "You're an old romantic, aren't you?"

"I'll deny it if you tell anyone, milady."

"You may not be aware of this, but I find romantics irresistible and over-powering. I'm certain it's what drew me to you."

He looked at me with those warm, brown eyes. "It wasn't my dashing good looks which attracted you?"

"Would you think me so shallow, milord? You think I would love you purely for your good looks?"

James got up and leaned over me to brush his lips across mine. When he pulled back I asked, "Now what did I do to deserve such a lovely kiss?"

He pulled the chair closer to the bed and sat. "You said you loved me."

"I've said it before."

"Yes, but if I give you treats when you say it you'll continue those wonderful words and I know for a fact, I'll never tire of hearing them."

"I love you, with all my heart, James."

"You keep it up and I may have to kiss you again."

"I do like treats." I moved my battered body to the center of the bed and patted the space I'd left behind. James smiled and pulled his boots off. He sat on the bed, stretched

183

his legs out and put his arm around me again.

"Ah, this is one of my favorite treats. James, when I arrived back at Layne several weeks ago, you know what the hardest thing was?"

"Tell me."

"Not feeling your arms around me in the morning. I dreamed about you one night and as I woke up, I could have sworn I smelled your skin. I think I cried for an hour once I was awake."

"You want to know what the hardest thing for me has been?" he asked and played with my hair.

"Yes."

"Not feeling you in my arms in the morning. I missed washing your hair and putting on your shoes. I remembered every day, the way you played Jacob's piano. We're going to have to invest in a piano. I want to hear you play Daisy Bell, again."

"That would be nice," I think I said, but fell asleep again.

A dream started and I knew it was a dream, but felt frightened. Marshall came through my bedroom door, and called me a slut in a harsh whispered tone. I tried to move away from him, but couldn't get my feet to respond. He brought up his arm and started to swing at my face. I jolted awake and must have shouted. I found James looking at me, concerned. I coughed as I tried to catch my breath. He handed me a glass of water from the nightstand and helped me drink.

"Catherine, what happened? What's the matter?" he asked.

I put my good hand up to my face and shook my head. "A nightmare, it was just a nightmare." I looked up at him.

"Marshall?" he asked.

"Yes."

"He's never going to touch you again, I promise. I'll kill him if he ever comes near you." He sat back beside me and wrapped his arms around me. I put my head on his chest and at some time fell back to sleep. I didn't have any further dreams of Marshall.

Chapter Nineteen

July 7, 1920

James overheard Stella and I discuss draperies this afternoon. After she left the room, he teased me again. "See, we definitely need a woman's touch around the Hall. What do I know about draperies? I know nothing about draperies. I can build bookcases and some odd pieces of furniture, but how to arrange them in a room, I'd be lost."

"James, I only ask one thing. If you ever feel like the women have gotten out of hand with the draperies and such, you'll inform us. I don't wish to over-step my boundaries."

"Catherine, there are no boundaries here. This is your home, now and forever. If you try to assume differently or ever feel any discomfort, I will have to torture you." When he saw me smile, he added, "For hours."

"Thank you, milord. I'll have to keep that in mind."

James can be so very silly at times.

July 8, 1920

I haven't written anything the last couple of days as nothing much has really been going on to describe. I can't get out of bed on my own, and other than sleeping, reading and eating, have done nothing much to write about. Today, I

185

felt well enough to get up and dress.

The day after I woke up, Stella and Arthur went back to Layne Hall. Marshall wasn't there and they had no problem going into the house. She found the loose board in the floor of my closet and the box was still there. She brought it back and it's safe in one of the dresser drawers now. Once my brain is a little clearer, I'll figure out how best to approach James with the wool money. He's such a proud man and I know he's going to be difficult about accepting any money from me. We'll get it worked out.

James helped me put on a lightweight blouse and a skirt. The skirt felt a little tight and I looked rather disheveled by not tucking my blouse in, but knew it didn't really matter. The bruises have faded a little. They are turning other colors besides black. Mostly green, purple and yellow, I still look a mess.

James assisted me in getting downstairs and found a nice wicker chair for me on the patio outside. He put several pillows and cushions on the seat to keep me comfortable. The afternoon was lovely and it felt wonderful to be up and out of bed. My legs are shaky from inactivity, but the sun felt good on my face and hearing the birds sing was very refreshing. I asked him on the way down the stairs, if he would show me around a little, but he refused. He said we could do it at a later time and wanted me to take it easy.

While he potted some geraniums, he kept me company and I watched him work. At one point, I asked if I could help. He told me he would tie me to the chair if I didn't sit still and I knew he only partly teased. As nice as it felt to watch his inspiring body, I knew I'd have to get well soon.

I saw Stella come out to the patio and say something to James. He nodded and wiped his hands off. He came over to my chair and squatted in the front, putting his hands on my thighs. "How are you doing, milady?"

"James, what's going on?" I asked.

"Jacob is here. He's brought a solicitor from the city with him. They're in the living room. Are you up for a visit?"

"Yes, please. We need to get the divorce started as soon as possible." James helped me stand and supported me on the walk through the house.

We entered the living room and I saw Stella had brought a tea service in with some biscuits. Jacob stood by the window with a gentleman I didn't recognize. He turned when he heard us enter and when Jacob saw my face, I could see the shock register in his eyes.

"My God," he said, under his breath. He came over and helped James get me to a seat.

"Hello, Jacob, it's lovely to see you again. How do you like my raccoon look?" I tried to smile and he kept hold of my hand and stared at me. "Jacob, believe me, it was worse last week."

"I'm sorry, my dear. So very sorry," he said.

"Please, Jacob, have a seat." I motioned him to the couch across from me. Stella stood behind my chair and James got a straight back to sit next to me.

Jacob motioned to the solicitor and introduced him. "This is Mr. Snell. Sir, this is Catherine, the woman I've told you about."

Mr. Snell came over and nodded with a slight smile. He and Jacob sat on the couch and he pulled a notebook out of his pocket. He began to take notes, although no one said a thing. Without looking up from his notebook, he said and motioned toward Stella, "Perhaps it would be best if your servant left the room and we had some privacy."

"Sir," I spoke. "This is Stella Taylor and she is not a servant. She is a member of my family and I'll say nothing if she leaves this room."

He made a note on his paper and said, "Very well."

187

Jacob continued looking at me and I could read the shock on his face. His face became a bit pale.

"I want you to know, I hold you at no fault for what has happened, Jacob. The blame is not yours. In fact, I have quite a lot to thank you for." He looked at me with his mouth open. "It wasn't until I came to your Hall, that I discovered the true meaning of a gentle touch as opposed to being hit. Up until recent events, I always hoped to work things out with Marshall, but now I believe I have to agree with your assessment when I first arrived at Mansfield. He is quite mad. Without going to Mansfield, I may not have survived. For this, I will be eternally grateful to you. Always."

"My dear, you let me off the hook too easily. Had I known two months ago what I know now about your husband, I would never have accepted his offer or let you return to Layne Hall. He is a very good actor, Catherine."

"Yes, I, too, am aware of the fact."

Mr. Snell stopped making notes, set the notebook down and cleared his throat. "Mrs. Pieper, perhaps you could go over the events leading up to where we are today."

Something in his demeanor, I found very annoying. "Mr. Snell, before we start, let me correct one thing. You may call me Catherine, you may call me by my maiden name, Layne, but please, I no longer wish to be referred to as Mrs. Pieper. Do I make myself clear, sir?"

Mr. Snell seemed to understand and I began to tell him some of the history of my relationship with Marshall. I spoke uninterrupted for some time. Stella sat down in the chair next to me and kept a handkerchief in her hand.

I felt Mr. Snell, being Jacob's solicitor, must have some inkling of the activities going on at Mansfield. I didn't sugarcoat anything, but I also didn't go into great detail about my involvement in some of those activities. I knew some of the language I used, Stella found shocking, but I would have told her eventually. It would make the whole series of events more clear. She would have to understand.

I explained to Mr. Snell when I left Mansfield Hall, I returned home with the hope Marshall and I could reconcile our differences and work things out. I spoke of the night he returned from the city. How I presented myself to him naked and offered to service him in any way.

"The most surprising thing was Marshall acted appalled at this behavior from his wife. He said he hadn't sent me to Mansfield to become a whore, but in his opinion this it is what I'd become. He hit me and when he saw the brush I'd held for protection, he picked it up and hit me across the face with it. He became furious and continued to hit and kick me." Tears began to roll down my cheeks. "Because I am pregnant, I did all I could to protect my child. I'm hopeful, but I'm still not certain the child is alive. The doctor confessed yesterday, the baby may not have survived. I'm praying he'll be proven wrong.

"Marshall kicked me several times in the back. While on the floor, he grabbed my wrist and tried to drag me to the bed. He wrenched my arm and dislocated my shoulder. The pain was so great I passed out and know nothing more than what Stella and James have told me."

I didn't know what more to say. Mr. Snell scribbled in his notebook again. Jacob stood and went to the window with his hands behind his back. He looked out at the front drive. Stella excused herself crying. James stayed by my side and never let go of my hand.

"I think the tea may have gotten cold. James, could you ask Susan to brew some more?"

Jacob turned from the window and said not to worry myself about the amenities. I looked at James and his face wore pain.

After some time, Mr. Snell looked up. "Catherine, is it possible the day you presented yourself to Mr. Pieper nude, you misinterpreted his intentions?"

Jacob walked to the back of the couch from the window. I could feel James's arm tighten and realized from the look on his face, he didn't like the question. Frankly, I didn't like it either.

"Mr. Snell." I looked at him as serious as I could. "When I first married Marshall, I thought I knew what love was and thought I would have many children and be happy the rest of my life. It comes as quite a surprise, sir, when your husband begins to hit you, drink too much and disappear for days on end. It's also a surprise, when you are informed by your staff, that he is spending his time in the city gambling and whoring. I suppose I should be grateful he took his sexual desires to the city rather than the nearby village. This way, there is some privacy and his name doesn't enter the gossip circles. I suppose I should be grateful he did not scar me too greatly and I still have my teeth. One thing I am not grateful of, sir, is due to Marshall's gambling and whoring, he's ruined my father's estate. If I lose Layne Hall, so be it. Do I have any other regrets? Only one, sir. I wish I'd been smarter when I'd first met him."

After staring at Mr. Snell, I turned my gaze to James. He watched me with a proud look on his face. I squeezed his hand and motioned I wanted to stand. He helped me and then let go of my hand.

I returned my attention to Mr. Snell. I leaned over as far as I could and took hold of my skirt. I lifted the bottom of the hem to my waist and turned so Mr. Snell could see my hip and leg. I watched his eyes take in the black, red, green, yellow and purple bruise.

"All the colors of a rainbow, sir," I said. He looked up at me and I dropped the hem. Turning back to face James, I loosened the buttons on my blouse and slid the shoulders down my back. I heard Mr. Snell take in a breath when he saw the bruising on my back. Maintaining some modesty, although I really didn't care, with my hands holding the blouse around my breasts, I turned back to him and showed him the bruise running up my chest and shoulder to my neck.

"Mr. Snell, I may have misinterpreted Marshall's intentions, but I assure you I didn't intend for him to do this. A part of me, sir, believes I'm lucky to be alive and walking. If not for Stella's quick thinking and sending our stable man for James, I'm fairly certain I would be dead. The fact Marshall sent me to be trained at Jacobs's establishment in the finer points of and different positions of and the openness of fucking, do you still believe, sir, I misinterpreted his desires and intentions? And do you, sir, believe I desired this?"

I turned back to James. He pulled my shirt up to my shoulders and wrapped his arms around me.

"Snell, have you completely lost your mind?" Jacob barked from the back of the couch. The look on his face was ready for battle.

Mr. Snell closed his notebook and put it in his jacket. "Apparently, I have Jacob." He stood and came over to me and James. "Catherine, please, accept my apology for the question and forgive me. I defended a case, several years ago which was similar to yours, but only similar. The wife serviced quite a few men without her husband's knowledge. I compared the cases and should not have. Again, I apologize." I turned back to face him, but he'd nothing more to say. "I'll need to interview Miss Taylor, your cooks and the stable man. I believe their stories will help create no opposition in a court and we can have the divorce wrapped up in six months or less. I'm sure, with no coercion, we could get the woman from the brothel to testify—"

"What's this about?" I interrupted.

Jacob looked at me from the back of the couch. "It's what I meant about knowing then what I know now," Jacob answered. He came back around the couch and stood by my chair. "Please, sit down again, my dear and I'll explain."

James helped me sit back in the chair and sat down himself. Jacob stood by James.

"Marshall's name is not welcome at some of the seedier houses of ill-repute in the city. In fact, he's been barred from several of them. He's beaten a couple of the working women and owes quite a bit. One of the women was taken to the hospital and filed a complaint with the constabulary in the city. He's been having a difficult time getting in any doors down there, which may have made his anger even more volatile." Jacob looked at his hands. "This would be a question a psychiatrist would have to answer. I think it created a type of cascade and, unfortunately, you caught the worst of it. It might interest you to know I've heard in the last week and a half he's been to many of the banks in the city. It's not very clear what he's looking for, but there you have it."

I knew what this was about. He'd tried to find the wool money.

Jacob leaned and put his hand on James's arm. "James will take very good care of you, Catherine. He's a good man. I can tell by the way he looks at you, he loves you more than all else in the world."

"As I said, Jacob, I've been very lucky." I put my hand on top of his. I looked back at Mr. Snell.

"I'd like to speak to your witnesses, Catherine. I won't disturb you any further today. If all goes well, you won't have to appear in court, and we can get the divorce finalized."

James squeezed my hand and stood. "I'll take Mr. Snell to the kitchen. He can interview the others there." He looked down at me. "I'll be right back, my love."

Jacob stayed in the room with me. He sat in the chair James vacated. I took his hand. "Jacob, I can tell by the look on your face, you're still feeling guilt. Please, stop," I said.

"Thank you, my dear, but it's going to take some

time to come to terms with this. I keep thinking, I should have insisted you stay with us at Mansfield. I should have refused to let you return to Layne."

"You simply must stop beating yourself up. There was no way of knowing this would happen and I'm sure you're aware I'm very stubborn. I would have left anyway. Now, I must change the subject and ask your advice. Please, could it stay between you and me, though?"

"Of course, anything."

"You mentioned Marshall was in the city going to the banks?"

"Yes, I've heard that."

"I know what he is searching for in those institutions. A couple of weeks ago, my sheep were sheared and I sold the wool for a pretty penny. When he asked me about the money, I told him I arranged to have it deposited to a bank in the city. However, this I did not do. I still have the money. I know you are aware, James is very proud and will be unwilling to accept any money from me to help with the work needed here at Whear. Have you any thoughts on how I might approach him with the subject?"

Jacob's brow creased and he looked at my hand. "My dear, as you have said, James is proud. He is very strong and proud, indeed. It will be difficult convincing him to accept it. I'm afraid I have no suggestions which will help you. Be honest with him, though. I believe James finds honesty a very important attribute in people. He would be terribly torn apart if you were to keep secrets from him."

"Yes, I agree with you. After all the lies Marshall told, I find James's honesty refreshing."

He smiled at me. "If I think of anything, my dear, I'll let you know immediately."

"Thank you, Jacob. I think I'm going to become very fond of your friendship."

James returned to the living room and Katie

followed him. "Catherine, Katie would like a word with you. Jacob, could I get you a drink in the library?"

"Yes, a drink would be very welcome." He squeezed my hand and smiled.

They left the room. Katie came and stood before me. Her hands were folded in front of her and her head down. She bit her lip and her eyes were flooding. I leaned toward her and reached out my hand.

"Katie, what's the matter?"

She put her hand up to her face and started to cry. "Oh, ma'am, I'm sorry." She took my hand and knelt down at my knees. With tears streaming along her cheeks, she said, "I tried and tried to find Dr. Hansen that terrible night. He wasn't at his house and his manservant only said he'd been called out. I looked all over the village…" She continued sobbing and couldn't speak.

Although I knew it would hurt, I shifted my bad arm and pulled her to me. "Shush, now, my dear. Susan told me you nearly made yourself sick. She said you were soaked clear through to your skin when you came back to Layne."

Katie sat up and tried to control her sobs. "I've been praying for you ma'am, nothing like this should ever happen."

I took her face in my hands. "Calm down. Listen to me. I'm very grateful to you, Susan, Arthur and Stella. If not for you and the others, I wouldn't have survived. You have nothing to be sorry for, my dear." She took a deep breath and I tried to remove some of the tears from her cheeks. "What you did that night, I'm forever grateful for. You and the others are a very important part of my family and I thank God for you every day."

"Yes, ma'am." She nodded.

"Now, I don't want you to fret anymore. Everything is going to be fine."

"Are we going to stay here or go back to Layne,

ma'am?"

I sat back in the chair. "I think we'll be staying here. Is that all right with you and the others?"

"Oh, yes ma'am. I don't want to work for Mr. Pieper no more. He has treated you very ill and Mr. Whear seems a right, kind gentleman."

"Well then, no more tears. We're home." I smiled and she returned it.

"I should get back to work. Susan's likely to skin me and say I'm being lazy. Thank you, ma'am."

"Thank you, Katie." I squeezed her hand and she got up to head for the kitchen.

For a time I sat alone in the library. It felt nice not having Stella or Susan hovering over me. It gave me a little time to think. So many things happened and many changes. I rubbed my stomach, thinking about the baby. Three months ago, this wouldn't have been possible. Saying a prayer, I asked the good Lord to watch over my unborn child and to let him come into the world safe. I thanked Him for bringing me to this place and giving me the strength to have come through all of the good and bad events and I thanked Him for bringing James into my life.

I then looked around the room. I hadn't noticed when I'd first come in, all the windows were bare and nothing hung on any of the walls. I'd forgotten James just reopened Whear Hall, but remembered his comments about draperies. Stella and I only talked about the bedroom windows, but I saw we'd have a lot of work to do.

I heard what sounded like a door close somewhere in the house. I was still unsure of my legs and it frightened me when I thought about getting up to investigate the noise. I then heard a squeak behind me and saw James peek over the chair. At his height, it amazed me how quiet he could be.

"Hi there. Jacob and Mr. Snell have left," he said and sat in the chair still by my side.

"Hello, my love." I found his hand.

He raised his eyebrows. "That was very intense."

"I'm exhausted."

"Would you like to go back upstairs and get some rest?"

"Yes, please."

James stood up and kept hold of my hand. When I got up, my legs began to shake and I held his hand tighter. I began to feel dizzy and he put his hand on my waist. Before I could even think, he leaned over and picked me up. I held on to his neck and tried getting my equilibrium back.

"I think you've had too much excitement today, milady," he said and headed for the stairs.

We met up with Stella in the hallway who was instantly concerned. "What's happened?"

"It's all right. Catherine's just tired," James said and started up the stairs. She followed and I heard him ask her to bring a pitcher of cool water to the room.

James brought me to the bedroom and put me down on the bed. My eyes were closed and I tried very hard not to throw up. I'd began to breathe rapidly.

I felt him put his weight down on the edge of the bed and lean over me. He pushed my hair off my face and said, "Should I send for the doctor, Catherine?"

"No," I replied. "This will pass. I'm just having a bit of anxiety." My breathing became steadier and I began to feel better. "I think my brain had too much to think about and I got overwhelmed."

"We'll have to keep this from happening again for a while. I'll tell the staff to keep it quiet when they're up here doing work."

I brought my hand down and opened my eyes. "James, don't get carried away. It's not anyone's fault, but my own."

He pulled up straight where he sat and frowned.

"Where did that come from?"

I pushed myself up to a sitting position and he arranged the pillows behind my back. There was a knock on the door and Stella came in with a pitcher and a glass. She poured the water and handed the glass to James. He offered it to me, but I only shook my head. I looked up at her. "I'm all right, Stella. Could you give us a moment, please?" She nodded and left the room.

I looked at James who seemed confused. I shouldn't have snapped at him. "I'm sorry for sounding so annoyed. While I sat down in the library alone, I did a little thinking. Jacob feels guilty. Stella and Katie, too. I am assuming, for some reason, you are probably feeling guilty as well." He looked away from me. "You are being too kind and hiding it from me." I put my hand on his chin and turned his face back to me. "James, it's not anyone's fault but my own. It was my own reckless stupidity, which created this situation. I don't know, after three years of Marshall's behavior, what made me think we'd be able to work things out. I fooled only myself."

I could see his eyes welling and put my good arm around his neck. He buried his face in my hair and I heard him sniffle.

"My love, I should have listened to you and Jacob. Can you ever forgive me?"

"Catherine, there's nothing to forgive. You're being too hard on yourself."

I pulled back and ran my fingers through his hair. "Be that as it may, it's still my fault. Now, would you do me a favor?"

"Anything." He coughed and put his head up.

I pointed at the dresser. "Third drawer down in the dresser, is a box. Would you bring it to me?"

He retrieved the box and placed it in my hands. Sitting back down, he put his hand on my thigh. "James, I

197

want there never to be any secrets between us." I stared at him until he agreed. "I did something when I first returned to Layne. I made a decision."

He squinted and tipped his head to the side. I lifted the lid on the box and pulled out the wad of paper money.

James looked at it, shocked. "You decided to rob a bank?"

"No, I had the sheep herd sheared and sold the wool in the village. The foreman of the shearing crew helped me." I tried to hand the money to him.

"Catherine, I can't take this."

"Mr. Whear, I've been in this bed for two weeks doing nothing. When I first woke up, you said it yourself, you now have an instant household staff to feed and house. I'm certain you didn't plan on it. In seven months there will be a baby to clothe and feed, although the first year he'll be on breast milk. James, this money will help the transition go much more smoothly and I'll be able to feel like I'm contributing."

James looked down at the bills and shook his head. "Tell you what. You're going to need to start furnishing a nursery for our little one. Why don't you keep half of the money for the furniture? I'll put the other half in the safe downstairs until we think of a good use for it."

"James, that is a good idea, but you could use it to buy more sheep and expand the herd some."

"That's a thought too, but I'd rather save some of it until you find a use. It is, after all, your dowry."

"Dowry? I knew you were going to be difficult about this."

He took the cash, put it back in the box and set it on the nightstand.

"You just wait until I get back to my full strength." I shook my finger at him.

He put my finger in his mouth and bit down on it.

Grinning, he let it back out. "And just what can I expect you to do to me, my love?" He leaned over me.

"I'm still mad at you, sir. You're not taking me seriously."

"I take you very, very seriously, my love." He kissed my neck.

"Buy sheep, James," I whispered in his ear.

"Yes, dear." He put his lips on mine and kissed me.

I stayed in the bed the rest of the day and took it easy. I don't know if I'd panicked about all the things which occurred and the baby, but thought it best to take it slower over the next few days. I didn't want to throw up anymore. I'm going to have to keep after James about the sheep. He is right about the nursery, we are going to have to prepare for the baby, but we have plenty of time for it.

Chapter Twenty

July 13, 1920

I can get out of bed on my own and the dizziness disappeared. My hip is still sore, but is getting better daily. It still hurts to lift my arm and I can only get it even with my chest. It will take some more work.

Jacob came to visit this afternoon. He and James spent quite a long time closed up in the library. After a time, James brought him up to our room. He found me sitting in a chair and reading a book. I'd finally gotten James to have the couch taken back down stairs and the chair brought up with a lamp. It is much more comfortable than the couch.

Jacob walked into the room and came right to me. He took my hands and kissed my cheek. "Hello, my dear."

"Hello, Jacob. It's lovely to see you."

"How are you feeling?" he asked.

"I'm much better today. Thank you, sir."

James brought the straight back chair over from my vanity and Jacob sat down next to me. James then said he needed to give the workmen some instructions for tomorrow and he'd be back in a few minutes.

Jacob smiled at me and said, "You are looking much better, too. Your eye...what did you call it? Your raccoon eye is looking normal."

"Beautiful shade of yellow, don't you think?" I asked.

"Quite, yes. James tells me all is going well with the estate. Work is getting done at a very good rate."

"Yes, they work hard every day. Jacob, I'm glad we

have this moment alone. I wanted to let you know, I've spoken with James about the money from the wool. He is being quite stubborn about it, but I think if I continue to nag, he may break down just to quiet me." Jacob smiled about this. "Not to change the subject, but I've been wondering if you've heard anything new from the city about Marshall?"

Jacob frowned and looked away from me. "Only the usual stories, my dear."

"Jacob, look at me." He turned his head to face me. "What have you heard?" I pressed him.

"Catherine, I care for you too much to go into the cruel details of your husband's debauchery. I will say, though, Marshall is trying to find you."

I felt my chest tighten. I knew I didn't have to fear, but it didn't keep me from feeling uneasy. Jacob tightened his grip on my hand.

"I've discussed this with James and I believe he is telling the workers now to keep their eyes and ears open. If they hear anything, I'm certain they will tell James immediately. They are very loyal to him."

"Jacob, has Marshall been seen in this area?"

"No, no. He's so far stayed near Layne Hall. He is still searching the banks in the city for the wool money. It concerns me, though. He caused quite a scene at your old church."

"Oh my."

"He shouted with a Father Barnett? I think this was the name. And cursed at him to no end."

"Barrent, it's Father Barrent. Poor man, I hope he didn't have to tolerate Marshall's ill-behavior for long."

"I'm not aware of how long he yelled and only know that he accused the church of meddling in his marriage and other such nonsense."

"I keep thinking I should try to do something, but am at a loss as to what it should be."

"Catherine, listen to me. You've become very important to me and I'm only saying this for your own good. Stay away from him and stop feeling you need to fix him. There's nothing you can do for him now, nothing, my dear."

I felt somewhat surprised by his tone and that he acted so angry. I looked away from him. "Thank you, Jacob. I'll bear it in mind."

"Please do, Catherine." I looked back at him and he smiled, again. "As I said several times already, I care very much for you and James. I don't want Marshall to do you any further harm."

"I second that," James said from the doorway. He walked into the room and placed his hand on Jacob's shoulder. "Is she being stubborn, Jacob?"

"No, not at all." Jacob smiled. "We were just having a very profound discussion."

James squeezed his shoulder and then crossed his arms. "Have you told her?"

"Yes, I have."

"I've spoken with the men. They're going to spread the word around to the others. I feel very sure if Marshall shows his face in our part of the county, we'll know about it before he can cause any trouble."

We discussed this and other subjects for a while longer. Jacob then said his goodbyes and departed.

After James saw him to the door, he came back up to the room and sat in the chair next to me. He looked serious and took my hand between his. "Catherine, I want to tell you some things you can do to protect yourself, just in case Marshall finds his way to Whear Hall."

I folded my hands in my lap and waited for his instructions.

"First, get help. Send Katie or Arthur to find me or one of the workers. We'll be here as quickly as possible. If you're alone in a room with him, scream as loud as you can.

Susan has very good ears and I think she could hear you even if she's in the barn. I wouldn't want to go up against her anytime." He looked at me with his eyebrows up.

"Get help immediately and scream if alone."

"If you should end up in a room with him, keep furniture between you and watch him. If there's something blocking his way, he won't get a hand on you."

"All right, I've got it."

"Talk, ask questions, keep him off balance. The more he has to think about, the more time I'll have to get to you."

"I think I can do that."

"I hope it won't come to this, but I'll do anything to keep you safe, my love."

I looked at him. "James?"

"Yes."

"How do you know all of these maneuvers? Where did you learn them?"

"I learned some of it from the other men who worked at Mansfield, and from estate hands. They're very smart when it comes to defending themselves."

At this very moment, I found James unbearably attractive. "My love, may I sit on your lap?" I continued to be serious.

He smiled. "Of course."

I stood and moved to sit sideways on his legs. I put my good arm around his neck and with my other hand, turned his face up to mine. I kissed him on the lips and then kissed both of his cheeks. "I love you, milord."

He whispered, "I love you, too."

I hugged his neck and he rubbed the side of his face on my chest. Suddenly, he sat up straight with his eyebrows pressed together.

I felt my own brow furrow. "What?"

He brought his hand up to the top button of my

blouse. With one finger he hooked the shirt and pulled it forward and peeked at my chest. "My love, are your breasts growing?"

I grinned and loved how he could be so silly sometimes. "Yes, milord, I'm afraid they have grown a bit. I hope you don't find them too huge and undesirable?"

James eyes snapped up to me. "Impossible, milady. Completely impossible." Outside the blouse, he put his hand over one of my breasts and massaged it. He kissed my neck and whispered, "May I see them, milady?"

"Yes, you may see them, my love," I said and unbuttoned my shirt. James put his hand over mine and started to stand. "Where are you going?"

He led me over to the bed and helped me sit down. Kneeling in front of me, he began working the buttons. "My darling, I want you to understand something I feel is very important." He stood and removed my blouse and helped me lay back. He put a pillow under my head, then shed his own shirt and lay down next to me. He leaned up on his elbow and put his other hand under my expanding breast. "I know when you were with me at Mansfield we practiced several movements with Marco."

I thought I knew what he talked about. "And the men in the barn."

"Yes," he said. "That was a horrible night. I could hear you and knew you were being given much pleasure, but I felt jealous." He looked down at my chest and I felt the palm of his hand cover the nipple. "I hope you won't mind, but I'm never going to share you with another man, ever again. I'm afraid I've become very obsessed with you and if another man ever thinks of touching you, I will have to act."

I smiled and tried hard not to laugh. I knew he wanted to be serious and I loved hearing his thoughts. "My man, that's a lovely thing for you to say. I agree with you and accept your obsession with no reservations."

"Do you feel up to a little coupling, my love?"

Lauren Marie

Chapter Twenty-one

July 16, 1920

Things have settled down some. In the last weeks, my strength has returned and I'm not having anymore dizzy spells. The morning sickness also went away. My breasts are still growing, which makes James happy beyond belief. This makes me happy, too. If I'm still growing, does it mean, perhaps, the baby is all right? I'll have to ask the doctor on his next visit.

It is wonderful waking up with James in the morning. My hip feels better and I'm able to move around now. When we're eating meals, I think he would have me sit on his lap and feed me, if it weren't for Stella. One morning, she asked me if she got in the way. I told her in no way did that happen. James and I will have to behave ourselves better at the dinner table.

I found a pair of James's slacks yesterday and with a belt, I was able to cinch them tight enough to stay on. I went out to the back of the house, looked around the overgrown lawn and tried to find a good area to start a garden. Stella came along to help. We found an area along a stand of trees.

"Do you think James will have a problem if we start a garden?" Stella asked.

"No, I shouldn't think so. We haven't really discussed it. Anytime I bring it up, he changes the subject. I think he worries about my doing too much." I ran my hands over the grass which came up to my thighs.

"Vegetables would be a very good idea, though.

We're a bit late for this year. We could still put in some squash, carrots and potatoes. It would help a little this winter." I looked at her.

"We'd have to pray for a warmer than usual fall," she replied.

"That's true." I looked out at the field and saw James walked in with some of the men. They were coming in for lunch. He saw us and veered in our direction.

"Good day, ladies." He walked up to me and gave me a kiss, then looked down at my legs. "Are those my slacks?"

I held my arms out and spun around. "Yes, they are."

He continued to look at me. "They look good on you."

"Thank you, milord."

Stella rolled her eyes. "I think I'll go see how the girls are coming along in the kitchen." She turned and headed back for the house.

James watched her go and when he couldn't see her any longer, turned back to me. "What, may I ask, are you up to today?" He put his arm around my waist and kissed me, again.

"Well, we were trying to find an area to tear up and start a garden."

"Are you sure you're up to it?"

"James, I'm no longer an invalid. I'm not even having morning sickness anymore. If we get some vegetables put in this month, we'll have enough to can for the winter. It will be a good thing."

"Perhaps we could work something out. I'll ask some of the crew if they'd be willing to help out. Of course, you know, I'd love to help you out."

"Out of my clothes?" I tried not to be too obvious.

He laughed. "Have I told you today I love you?"

208

I thought for a moment. "I think you mentioned something this morning, but I concentrated so hard about a garden, I could have misunderstood."

"Are you paying attention now?" He smiled and started to move me toward the trees.

"If you wish, milord."

He backed me up to one of the trees and put his lips on mine. It was an intense kiss and he took my breath away. He ran his lips along my chin and whispered in my ear. "I love you, milady."

"I love you, too, sir."

After several minutes of this, I asked him if he felt hungry. He got his usual mischievous grin and said he starved and wrapped his arms around me tighter.

"You know what I mean."

"Did you mean food? Of course, yes, I'm quite famished. I did a very hard morning's work today."

We headed arm and arm into the house and got him fed. James went into the town in the afternoon to collect the mail. He handed me a note from Mr. Snell. There was no news yet on the divorce, but all went according to plan and he hoped to have better news soon. The young boy, Daniel, from Mansfield also appeared in the afternoon with an invitation from Jacob to come on Saturday evening for dinner. He included Stella in the invitation, which I found charming. I wondered if there might be an attraction on his part. James sent a message, accepting. Jacob also sent over several books with a note asking to accept these for our library. Jacob is such a dear man.

After dinner, James and I were laying in each other's arms in bed. We were both sweating and breathing hard. He lay on his side with his hand on my stomach, which kept finding its way up to my breasts. I did my best not to deter him.

"You are so amazing to me," I said.

209

"Amazing? How so?" he asked.

"You work tirelessly all day out on the estate and then still have the strength to come in here and satisfy my cravings. How do you do it?" I teased.

"My love, there isn't a part of your body which isn't enticing to me. When I saw you under the trees today, I felt excited. I would have taken you there, but was rather hungry."

"I see, so there are times when food is more important to you than my body?"

He propped himself on his elbow and looked down at me with a grin. "Never. I'd give up nourishment forever if I had to choose between it and your body. Have I mentioned how wonderful your breasts are?" He leaned his head down and kissed my nipple which caused me to catch my breath. He took it between his lips and nibbled. He looked back up at me. "Are you ready to go to sleep, milady?"

"Sleep? Not at this point." I laughed as he tickled my ribs.

We made love again and he certainly does amaze me.

July 17, 1920

James had Arthur bring the carriage out this evening for the ride over to Mansfield Hall for our dinner with Jacob. The evening felt warm and close. I was a little nervous about Stella's impressions. I told her what the Mansfield school taught, but found I'd gotten nervous for no good reason.

When we entered the main hallway, I noticed the paintings I found shocking on my first visit were taken down and replaced with more traditional scenes. During a moment in the evening, when I could ask Jacob about the missing paintings, he said he decided to close the school and have a more respectable home. I was surprised and asked him what his plans were. He said he wanted nothing more than a nice quiet country retirement. He may do some traveling, but has no plans in the immediate future.

Jacob acted attentive to Stella and I believe there is some attraction on her part, too. He asked me if I would grace them with some of my piano talents. I agreed and sat at the piano, playing things which I could remember. For James, I played Daisy Bell. He got a warm look on his face and I think I fell more in love with him. My audience sat around the library and listened. When I finished, Jacob invited me over anytime, but only if I promised to play. I told him James and I discussed briefly getting our own piano, but we have other things which took greater importance at the moment. I told him as soon as we got one, he would be invited to my first recital, but would he find it too boring to come to Whear for dinner sometime if we hadn't gotten the piano just yet? He assured me he would not find our company too boring.

It was a lovely evening and I told James we should plan on having one of our own soon, to repay Jacob for his kindness. James smiled and agreed.

July 21, 1920

The garden is coming along. Some of the men came in early from the fields and helped get the grass cut down. Stella and I marked out the area and we'll go into town tomorrow to see what seeds we can find at the general store.

I've continued to nag at James about the sheep and he assures me every time he is still considering it. Difficult man...

July 22, 1920

Stella and I went into to town today and found some wonderful seeds. We also got some tomato starter plants and beets. I'm hoping it isn't too late in the season for those. This afternoon, we made a lot of headway, and got most of

211

the seeds put in and the tomatoes potted.

We also found some lovely fabric which I think will make wonderful drapes for the living room and library. I believe, after we get the rest of the seeds in the ground, we'll be spending a little more time inside getting the drapes cut and sewn together.

It felt strange in town, particularly in the fabric shop. I kept feeling like I was being watched. At one point, I looked up and noticed two women staring at me. When I stared back, they turned and left the shop. The shopkeeper was very nice, but his wife, I would say, acted downright rude to me and Stella. I suppose some word of my being at Whear Hall has filtered into the town and gossip is in the mill. I can only say let them think what they wish. I'm too happy today to let it bother me.

Today, I feel back to normal. My hip hasn't bothered me at all this week and I can finally get my arm above my head. My shoulder is still a little stiff, but it's better, too.

Secrets Beyond Dreams

Chapter Twenty-two

July 23, 1920

Stella and I spent most of the morning out in the garden. The tomato plants are growing well and we found some squash sprouts today. I think the soil in this area is of good quality and, not this year, but I think with advanced planning in the spring, we'll have a wonderful crop, next year.

I noticed while we worked, Stella kept looking up at the house. When I'd glance up, I couldn't tell what drew her attention.

Toward twelve o'clock, it started getting warm and I decided it would be a good time to go inside and cool off. Stella got agitated and said we should finish the row we'd been working on.

"Stella, the row will still be here tomorrow." I saw her glance go again up to the house and I looked over my shoulder. "What are you looking at?" I asked.

She smiled. "Nothing," she said. "You go on in if you want to."

I felt uncertain about her attitude, but turned and headed back in with Stella behind me.

We walked into the kitchen and I went to the sink to wash my hands. Susan peeled potatoes and without looking up said, "Mr. James is upstairs looking for you, ma'am."

I dried my hands and put the towel on the counter. I knew then he and Stella were up to something or I'd gotten paranoid. James knew I'd be in the garden today. Why would he be looking for me upstairs?

I went down the back hallway to the stairs and started up to the second floor. I found him leaning against the wall outside our bedroom. The door to the room across from ours was open. When he saw me, he grinned and walked toward me. "Hello, my love," he said.

"Mr. Whear. What's going on?"

He took my hand and said, "Close your eyes."

"What?"

"Just close your eyes and behave."

He patted my behind and I did as he said.

"No peeking," he ordered.

He started us forward and after a few steps, turned me to the left and led me forward again. After a few more steps, he stopped and stepped behind me. He put his hands around my waist and said, "Okay, you can open your eyes now."

I opened them and caught my breath. The room had been turned into a nursery. By the windows, there was a bassinette and changing table. Next to the bassinette sat a rocking chair. By the other window was a crib and a dresser and a smaller twin bed, placed next to the inside wall. Sheer drapes were put up under thicker drapes to help keep out drafts in the winter. Next to the dresser and all over the top of the twin bed, were stuffed animals, blocks and other toys.

I put my hands up to my face and searched for words to say. With his hands on my stomach, James asked, "What do you think, my love?"

"James, this is beautiful. How did you do this?" I continued to look and catch each new site with every glance.

"It wasn't easy keeping it a secret from you. I had some co-conspirators in the process." He loosened his hands and turned me around. Standing behind him was the complete house staff, all with broad grins on their faces. "We almost gave it away a couple of times."

I walked over, hugged the ladies and thanked them all. Katie and Susan went back down to the kitchen. Stella stood next to James and both smiled. I turned back into the room and strolled around touching this and that. The bassinette was beautifully made. When I got to the dresser, I pulled the top drawer open and found it full of cloth diapers. I closed it and opened the next one and found tiny garments. I pulled out a T-shirt and turned to them both. "This is incredible. I am so…" I started to cry. Stella came over and wrapped me in a motherly hug. I didn't know what to say.

She kissed my forehead. "I've got some things needing my attention downstairs." She excused herself.

I continued to stand at the dresser and held the little shirt. James came over and stood next to it, putting his elbow on the top.

"When did you have time for this?" I asked and continued to pull out the contents of the drawer.

"Well, as I said, I did have some help. The ladies went a little mad picking out clothes and toys as I'm sure you can see." He attempted to look at me seriously. "I want you to know, I did use some of your money for all of this, though. I hope it meets with your approval?"

"James, of course it meets with my approval. It's beautiful. I wish you'd used it for the herd, though." I put the clothes back in the drawer and closed it. I folded my arms and watched him.

"Well, as a matter of fact, this is something else I need to discuss with you, my love. I did in fact use some of it to purchase about fifty young sheep for the herd."

"That's wonderful," I started to say, but he stopped me.

"Wonderful, yes. We have about thirty ewes, so hopefully in the spring we'll have a good number of lambs drop. I want it to be clear though, I'm considering the money to be a loan. You know I'll make good on paying it back to you. There is still some cash left over, and I think it might be enough to buy a piano. What would you think about that?"

"A piano would be nice, but let's hold off until the spring and see how the herd does. Don't you think it would

216

be good to have something in the till to fall back on?"

"It's your money, my love. Whatever you wish to do, we will do."

I walked up to him and put my arms around his waist. "Besides, I'm going to be far too busy with the baby to have time to play the piano. Now, about this loan business."

"Uh-oh."

"I'm thinking I might be able to come up with a way for you to pay it off." I let one of my hands drop down to his behind and gave it a squeeze.

He opened his mouth with a grin. "Milady, how could you think I'd service you for money? I'm shocked. Just out of curiosity, how long would I be in servitude to you?"

"Let's think, fifty sheep. If the price per sheep was one dollar say."

"Two dollars."

"Ah, two dollars per sheep. If you paid off a dollar a year, times the fifty plus another fifty, I'd say you'd have about one hundred years of service to provide," I said. "Do you find this figure acceptable, milord?"

He glanced up at the ceiling as though doing the figures in his head, and then looked down at me. "Done." He shook my hand. "I think I will still be able to give you an abundance of pleasure in the next one hundred years, milady." He lifted me up and hugged me tight.

"I'm getting excited already," I sang.

He set me down and said, "There is one other thing I'd like to discuss with you."

"That reminds me, I have a topic, too," I replied.

"Milady, come with me and we'll find a comfortable place for a serious discussion."

"Yes, milord."

He led me out of the nursery and we went across the

hall to our bedroom. We stretched out on the bed and he told me to go first.

"I told you once that Stella came to Layne Hall after my mother passed away. She tutored me and produced the great mind you see before you today."

He kissed my head. "I love this mind by the way."

"Thank you. Anyway, I wanted to ask what you would think about asking her to be our child's nanny, at first and then take over tutoring. She's a good teacher and very level-headed as I'm sure you've come to know."

James thought for a moment and said, "You know, that is a very good idea. Do you think she would accept?"

"I haven't said anything to her yet. I wanted to speak with you first. She's good at running the house staff, but she really is a teacher by trade."

"Discuss it with her then. I'm all for it. Stella is a wonderful lady and I think she would care for a child as if it were her own."

"Thank you, my love." I kissed him. "Now, what is your topic to discuss?"

He sat up on the bed, faced me and seemed to be nervous. "It's something I've wanted to discuss with you, but felt I might be too pushy by bringing it up."

I pushed myself up and adjusted the pillows behind my back. I took hold of his hands and tried to reassure him. "James, you can say anything to me. It won't make any difference in how much I love you."

"Thank you, Catherine. I've been thinking about bringing this up for several weeks." He leaned back and put his hand in his trousers pocket. When his hand came out, he held a small black box. "I don't want you to feel I'm rushing you and you don't have to give me an answer right away." He opened the box and let me see what was inside.

A beautiful ring in white gold with a diamond cut into a small oval, sat on black velvet. I stared at the ring. I'd always assumed we would marry, but I never thought he would want to go through the traditional trappings.

"I hope soon after we hear from Mr. Snell the divorce is final, you'll become my wife."

"James, of course." I looked at the ring, again. "There is just one thing I'd like to be clear on. I just want to be sure you understand."

"What is it, my love?"

"I'm only marrying you." James eyebrows folded as he looked at me. "I mean from now through forever, you are the only man I'll ever be with. I don't want anyone but you, my love."

James chuckled. "I understand and agree to your terms."

I looked at him and realized he wasn't being serious. "James, your work at Mansfield…"

"It was a means to an end, Catherine. I never wanted that for life, but it was worth it in the long run. I paid off the debt and got the title back to Whear Hall. I met the woman I'd dreamed of all my life. I couldn't have asked for better." He raised his eyebrows. "However, it won't be a stylish marriage."

I laughed at his reference to the song Daisy Bell. "After paying for the ring, I'm sure you can't afford a carriage."

"I'm still trying to find a bicycle built for two." He smiled, leaned toward me and kissed my lips.

"Good, this was easily taken care of." I sighed.

"Catherine, stay with me and I promise everything will be easy." He smiled and took the ring out of the box. He picked up my left hand and placed it on my finger. It fit a little snug due to my swollen fingers, but he got it on.

I held my hand out and looked at it. My heart raced. "James, this is so beautiful." I hugged his neck, put my hands through his hair and brought his lips up to mine. "I'd never be able to tolerate anyone else's hands on me, my love. How in the world did I get so lucky?"

He rearranged his legs and pulled me down with him. "I think I may be the luckier one here at old Whear Hall." He began to unbutton my blouse.

"Milord, no, we mustn't have a bone of contention to start us out. I believe I've been dealt the luckier hand, though." I pulled the back of his shirt out of his slacks and felt his warm skin.

"Perhaps we could have another serious discussion later about who is the luckier. Right now I have some other business I must attend to. I have to start paying off my debt now," he said and put his lips on my breast.

We made love throughout the afternoon and when we untangled ourselves it was early evening. Neither one of us ate any lunch, which meant we were both starving. We went down to the kitchen and found a few left over items to hold us until dinner. James decided to go out to the fields to see how the work progressed. I tracked down Stella in the living room. She worked on her needlepoint and I sat in the chair next to her.

"I wanted to thank you again for helping James with the nursery. It is so beautiful."

She smiled and put her stitching aside. "It was a pleasure to help, Catherine. That James of yours is a charming man. He kept bringing me lists of things to find. I have to tell you there were times I thought you knew for sure what we were up to."

"I'm afraid with all the work we've been doing in the garden, I've not paid attention to things going on in the house. Stella, I'm also grateful for the order you've been keeping in here."

"It's not too hard to keep things running smoothly. I do have to keep an eye on Katie, but she's doing her share of the work."

"James and I had a discussion this afternoon. We'd like to ask if you would consider being our baby's nanny and as he gets older, be his tutor?" I asked.

"My dear, are you sure? I would think you'd want someone younger to help with the baby?"

"Stella, you are our one and only choice. James agrees with me, too."

"What about the household? Who will care for it?" she asked.

"Let's wait and see what develops. I think with your help, I'll be able to keep an eye on things after the baby comes. You and I were able to keep Layne running and, of course, we didn't have a child in the house then, but I don't think it will hard to keep up. Do you?"

"No, dear. I think we can do a fine job."

"So you'll accept?"

"Yes, I accept. I would love to continue being a part of your family, Catherine. You know that, don't you?"

"I will always want you to be part of my family, always." I looked down at my hand and remembered the ring. Smiling back up at her, I said, "There's something I need to show you." I lifted my hand and showed her the ring.

"Oh, my Lord, he proposed? Finally. He's asked me on several occasions how best to approach you. He acted so worried he'd scare you away." She looked at the ring. "It's lovely, isn't it?"

"Yes it is. He couldn't have chosen anything more beautiful."

"You love him very much, don't you?"

"Yes. He's everything I could have dreamed of."

***

For the rest of July, things at Whear Hall went along quietly. Catherine complained on many occasions about having to let out her skirts and her stomach getting bigger. She worked in the garden as much as she could,

221

but found herself tiring out quicker as the days passed. She mentioned James nagged her to slow down her time outside. Coming to understand Catherine's stubborn side, I'm sure she did as much as she could.

In August, the tomatoes were producing and the squash continued to grow. The carrots came up, but weren't ready to pick and the potatoes didn't develop. She and the ladies in the kitchen did some canning, but the shelves wouldn't be as filled as she would have liked. She mentioned Susan wished they'd had time to bring some of the preserves they canned in May from Layne Hall.

Catherine wrote periodically her wish of hearing something soon from Mr. Snell, but never let what must have frustrated her show in her writing. (note: from Michael Whear - journal editor)

Secrets Beyond Dreams

Lauren Marie

Chapter Twenty-three

August 8, 1920

The most amazing thing happened this afternoon. I've said nothing to anyone about it.

Stella and I were in the living room stitching up some of the seams for the window drapes. I sat in a chair working on a hem, when I felt a tight pinch in my stomach. I realized my baby just demanded my attention for the first time. It was the sign I'd prayed for and waited to happen. He was all right and survived the horrible night from several months ago. I thanked the Lord above and started to say something to Stella, but couldn't. James needed to be the first to be told. I know he's tried to hide his concern.

I wanted to run out of the house and find him, but didn't know what part of the estate he worked today. I'd have to wait for a few hours until he came in for the day. All afternoon, as I stitched, I kept getting little kicks. The baby woke up.

James arrived back at dinner time and so I waited through the meal and listened to him talk about sheep issues. Stella sat across from me and could tell I was agitated.

When James finished his dinner, he pushed his plate away. I stood up, took his hand, and said to Stella, "I'll explain later. James, come with me."

He looked surprised and followed me out of the dining room, up the stairs to our bedroom. He asked on the way, "Catherine, what's the matter?"

I didn't say anything and led him into the room. I

shut the door behind us and locked it. I didn't think we'd be disturbed, but I wasn't taking any chances.

"James, sit down, please."

"Are you feeling a little frisky, my love?" He grinned.

"Please, just sit down." I pointed at the end of the bed.

He began to protest, but I only put up my hand and smiled. He sat on the end of the bed and waited. I unbuttoned my skirt and let it fall to the floor. I knew I must look ridiculous in my blouse and stockings, but I didn't care.

James arched an eyebrow and said, "I guess you are very frisky."

I stood next to him and said, "No." I leaned over and crawled on my knees to the pillows. I turned over and lay on my back.

"No?" he asked and turned to watch me.

"No, not right now, milord." I reached out my hand. "Come here, please."

James took off his jacket and left it on a chair. He slid his boots off and lay down next to me, propping himself up on his arm. "Catherine, what's—?"

"Shush, James." I put my hands up. "Left hand, if you would, please." He brought it up and I wrapped mine around it. With my other hand I lifted my blouse off my stomach. Slowly, I lowered his hand down to my growing bump.

"Now what?" he asked.

"Shush, just wait." It didn't take long. There was a slight lifting under his hand. The look on his face was wonderful and I don't think I'll ever forget it.

"Oh!" He sat up, crossing his legs and leaned over to put both hands on my stomach. Another kick came. He smiled and stared at the bump. "He moved," James whispered to me.

"Yes, he's been kicking and elbowing me off and on all afternoon."

"Why didn't you say something sooner?"

"I wanted you to be the first to know and witness it for yourself. I thought of trying to find you this afternoon, but wasn't sure where you were. I couldn't say anything to Stella until I told you. You needed to be the first to know."

James only half heard me and smiled. "He's alive."

"Yes, I think so, too."

The baby kicked another couple of times, which James could feel. We laughed and cried at the same time.

After a while, James leaned over and kissed me long and tender on the lips. He then stretched out beside me and put his hand back on top of my stomach. "This is a dream come true, my love. I've often wished for a family," he said.

"You did mention to me once about having a herd."

He propped up on his elbow and smiled down at me. "I never thought I would be as blessed as I've been, Catherine. I don't think I could be any happier than I am at this moment." He leaned down and placed his lips on mine, giving me one of the gentlest kisses I think I've ever received.

"You are taking my breath away," I said and kissed him back.

"You take mine, too." He put his head down next to mine, but kept his hand on my stomach.

"We haven't come up with a name yet."

"I've been thinking about it. How would you feel about having a junior running around?"

James frowned a little. "No, I've never really liked the name James."

"You don't like your name? I can't think of any other name I'd love more," I said.

"No. When I was a child, my father insisted on calling me Jimmy. I didn't think Jimmy sounded heroic enough."

"Great God, James, you're six-foot-four and built as tough as a brick wall. You're the only true hero I've ever known." I pinched his ear.

James laughed. "I know, it's silly, but you asked how I felt."

"No James Junior in the house. What if we named him after our fathers?"

"I like the idea. Nicholas Edward or Edward Nicholas? I think I like Nicholas Edward Whear. It sounds good. What do you think?"

"I agree. We could call him Nick when he's being good, Nicholas when he's misbehaving."

"Milady, my son will never misbehave. He will be the best child within millions of miles of these parts. Shouldn't we pick out a girl's name, just in case?"

"No, I'm certain the baby will be a boy. I've also been thinking about something else, James." I sat up and tried to bring my knees up to my chest. When this position didn't work, I bent my knees to the side and put my arm over his waist. Leaning, I looked down at him. "When he's older, what are we going to tell him about how we met? Should we tell him about Mansfield Hall and all that has transpired in the last months?"

"Catherine, I don't think I realized until now how much you worry about future events." He put his hand up to my face.

"James, he'll certainly want to know, don't you think? What will we tell him and any other children we might have?"

"I think if we are as honest as we can be, but not go into details and perhaps keep some of it between you and me alone, it will be enough. If we keep him in the present and well-loved, he may not even think about asking how we met."

"That makes sense," I said.

"Good, now that we have it settled, do we have any other matters of importance to discuss?"

I pursed my lips and looked up at the ceiling. "I have nothing else on my mind at the moment."

"Good, now come down here to my waiting arms. I want to hold you and feel him move some more." James held out his arms.

It is a wonderful relief to feel him moving around in me. I've tried and tried over the last months to not worry about the baby, but there were times when the worries overcame me. Now, all I have to wait for is his birth. In less than five months, he'll arrive, and I can't wait to meet him.

August 16, 1920

James took me with him today to see the new sheep delivered. We rode out to the field on a wagon. It was a bumpy ride, and a cloudy, cool day.

We reached the field where the sheep would be released. There were several men waiting under the trees. One of them had red hair and a beard. I recognized him from the night with the ruffians at Mansfield. I was going to ask James about him, but then decided to leave it. I never told him about the blindfold slipping during that time. James told me they were hard workers and I'll just remember this fact and nothing else.

James helped me down from the wagon and found a nice, shady tree where I could sit and watch the action. He sat with me for a while and confessed he'd brought me along purely to keep an eye on me. He thinks I'm working too hard in the garden.

"James, I'm fine."

"I know you're fine. Please, promise me though, you'll follow the doctor's orders and not push yourself so hard."

"I have to contribute my part. Sitting on my ass all day makes me feel useless. The baby's doing fine, the doctor even said so. You know, I'd do nothing to threaten him."

"Promise me, Catherine."

"I promise." I took his hand and kissed his palm.

"Thank you, my love."

"You're welcome, milord." I heard a dog bark and looked toward the field, not seeing anything. "James, what's that noise?"

He listened and smiled. "I think they're here. You stay here. I'll be back." He stood up and walked down to where the other men were waiting with their sheep dogs.

They heard the noise, too, and looked toward the far hillside. I could hear several dogs barking and the sound of sheep bleating. It was a lovely sound.

Suddenly, the herd appeared heading for the field. There were two drivers whistling and yelling commands to the dogs. The sheep moved forward, some jumping and others trying to evade the dogs. The rovers and dogs were amazing to watch. They drove the sheep down to James and his crew, who kept their dogs down, until the two drivers called the visiting dogs away. Those sheep looked beautiful.

When James and his group took over, he shook hands with the two drivers and then waved them off. The team continued moving the herd onward to an area where they built a pen. I asked James about the pen later in the day and he said they'd stay in there for a week or so to get them used to the field. After time, they'd be released and less likely to roam.

They finished getting the sheep settled and James came back up the hill. He offered me his hand and once up, he stood behind me with his hands around my waist, resting on my growing stomach.

"What do you think, Catherine?" he whispered, in my ear.

"I think those are about the loveliest sheep I've ever laid my eyes on," I replied.

He let go of my stomach and stood beside me with his arm around my shoulder. Looking down at the field, he said, "I think so, too. Strong and healthy, I think we'll have several lambs come the spring time."

I wrapped my arms around his waist. "You astound me, you know?"

He pulled his shoulders back and looked down at me. "Why is that?"

"You handled those sheep dogs like a professional today." His chest fell in and he looked sad. "I'm sorry, but it's not as if you've worked with sheep for the last eighteen years. When did you have time to learn all this?"

He nodded and pursed his lips. "I picked it up from the workmen over the last years. They know what they're doing and I've gotten some pointers from them."

"Ah, milord, I'm a terrible woman forever doubting your excellent mind. I don't know how you tolerate me." I sniffed and looked down.

James arched his eyebrow and said, "Milady has doubted my abilities, once again."

I grinned and recognized a phrase he'd used several months ago. "I'm not worthy of your love, milord."

"I will have to ravage her senseless this evening and put her in her place." He leered at me and seemed to fight off laughter.

"I'm your servant, milord." And we both laughed. We were so loud, the men in the field looked up at us.

When we settled down some, James kissed my hand and asked, "Are you ready to go back?"

"Yes, there's still enough day left, I could do some weeding in the garden."

"Remember your promise, my love."

"I remember."

He helped me back into the wagon and we made our way back to the Hall, to our home.

Secrets Beyond Dreams

Chapter Twenty-four

September 26, 1920

I read in the newspaper today that women were given the right to vote in elections. It was passed by the government last month. I know my old friend, Sylvia, is having a great celebration wherever she is traveling. I'm still not certain what I'll be voting for, but it will be interesting.

When James came in for dinner this evening, I mentioned it to him. He commented it was about time. We discussed long into the evening about the Bill of Right's and he believes it includes women and everyone else across the country. He said he couldn't wait to escort me to the voting station in town during the next elections. I guess I'm going to have to do some studying.

September 29, 1920

I went for a walk through the trees in the back field this afternoon. I knew James would have a fit, I'd gone so far out on my own, but the fall day felt wonderful. Some of the leaves have started turning and in the afternoon light they look like they're on fire. The yellows, oranges and reds are so vibrant, it's awe inspiring.

The main reason for coming out today was that I wanted to find the path which led up the hill toward Mansfield Hall. I hoped I could find the area where James and I picnicked several months ago. I wanted to see if the tall, old oak tree leaves were changing, too.

However, that part of the field and forest hadn't been

cleared since James returned and I found it difficult to tell where any path might be located.

I walked out of the tree line into the field and stood for a moment, feeling the warmth of the sun on my face. I put my arms down by my sides and ran my hands through the tall grass. I didn't have to lean over to touch it.

I walked back to Whear, when I saw James running toward me. For a man so tall, he moved fast. He slowed down when he was about one hundred feet from me and didn't look happy.

"Catherine, what are you doing way out here? What if you'd fallen? It might have taken us hours to find you. I came back in for lunch and no one knew where you were. What are you thinking?"

Ever since Jacob told him about Marshall looking for me, James has become over-protective. It is lovely, his care, but it is getting annoying. I crossed my arms and walked up to him. "Mr. Jailor, it is a beautiful day out here, away from my cell. As you can see, I have not fallen, and all is fine."

James pressed his eyebrows together. "Mr. Jailor?" He looked startled. "Catherine, please don't tell me you feel like this is a prison?"

"James, I love you dearly for all your concern, but you are going to make yourself sick." I continued looking at him. "I went for a walk, that is all."

He crossed his arms, too, and looked down at me. "I love you, too. I don't want you to feel Whear Hall is a prison. I just think it would be wise for you to stay closer to home right now. At least, until we don't have Marshall to worry about any longer."

"My love, I refuse to live any life being continually afraid of some event which may never happen. You've shown me ways to protect myself. I feel I can handle it, but I'm not going to become paranoid and jump at every little noise."

"Oh, my Lord, Catherine…" His face looked amazed. "You do realize we're having our first argument."

"Yes." I started to walk past him. "And you are annoying me, very much."

He clapped his hands together and laughed. I continued to walk away and looked over my shoulder at him.

"You are mad at me," he said, with a grin on his face. I heard him start to follow me.

I turned around with my hands on my hips. He almost ran into me, stopping short. "James, I am not a child. I do not need watching all the time…" He wrapped his arms around my waist and put his lips on mine. Bringing his hand up to my face, he brushed my lips with his thumb and got my attention fully. I opened my eyes and sighed. "I really hate it when you do that."

James grinned. "Milady, I think I may have discovered the way to defuse an argument. If we should have another, I'll know what to do. Just think what a pleasure it will be." He leaned in to kiss me again and I gave no resistance.

After a couple of kisses, we started to walk back to the house, hand in hand.

"Were you looking for something particular out here?" he asked.

"Yes, I was," I answered. He raised an eyebrow with a silent question. I stopped again. "I wanted to find the path which connects Whear with Mansfield."

"Are you planning to visit Jacob?"

"Well, I could, but no." I looked at him. "I wanted to find our tree."

"Our tree?" he asked. "Oh, yes, the tree under which we created our soon to be glorious child."

"Soon to be…in about four months." I turned away from him, again.

James didn't follow this time and I heard him say, "I know where it is."

I turned around and smiled. "My love, why didn't you say so sooner?" I walked back to him and took his hand in mine.

"First, you're mad at me and now I'm your love. What is my child doing to you?"

"I suppose I could be turning into an insane mother type." We started back toward the house.

"Hmmm, will you still be in bed next to me at night?"

"That's part of the madness, you know. Sleep and bed are important." I put my arm around his waist. "And I have to spend a certain amount of time everyday getting angry with you to maintain my balance."

"I see." He looked down at me. "As long as you are in my arms at night, I'll learn to deal with your imbalance."

"And not wandering all over creation?"

"That would be my preference, but I know you're stubborn. I'll just have to keep my eyes on you. Which you know I won't mind at all." He smiled.

"I'll concede and try to behave."

"Thank you."

I shook my head. We walked half way back to the house and James turned me toward the tree line. He showed me where the path was.

"You'd gone out too far," he said.

I looked in the shadows. "It's so dark around those trees. I never would have known it's there." James kept hold of my hand and we started up the hillside. "Have you eaten lunch yet?"

"No and I'm starving."

"Why don't you go back? I can find it now." He looked at me with a raised eye brow and a bit of a leer. "Oh milord, you are evil."

We made it to the top of the hill and followed the path a little ways farther. At one point, I stopped and turned around. I could see Whear down in the valley. It wasn't the view I remembered, but it was close. We continued on, around a corner and came to a clearing where the oak tree stood. We stopped and looked at it. It was turning colors for the fall and looked beautiful. I started to walk toward it, looking up at the limbs so far above my head. I went up to the huge trunk and put my arms around it as far as they would go.

"Thank you so much, James."

He walked up alongside of me and teased. "Am I losing you to a tree?"

I opened my eyes and looked at him without moving my head. "Although this tree is very attractive, there is no comparison. I find your body much more attractive." I tried looking sensual without releasing my grasp from the tree. Being five months pregnant, I wasn't sure I could pull off the sensual look.

James moved behind me and held my bottom in his hands. He whispered in my ear, "I will battle this tree if I have to. I will challenge it to a duel and you will love only me."

"Please, do not destroy this tree. I will love only you. Please, allow it to live. I will show you my love for you grows just as the trees do."

"Then, my woman, hug me as you would this tree," he demanded.

I turned and wrapped my arms around his waist. "Are you happy now?"

James put his face in my hair. "Yes."

"Milord." I looked up at him. "Are you really starving?"

"I could eat something, yes, why?"

I tried to sound disappointed, "No reason, really. I

238

suppose you have to get back to the field. I just hoped to show you how much I love your body."

He kissed me and said, "Might you have some plan?"

"I don't want you to starve." He continued to look at me and I put my hand on his chest and felt his muscles through the fabric of his shirt. I moved my hand down his stomach not taking my eyes off his. Continuing down the front of his leg, I could feel some movement coming from his pelvis. Just as he leaned down to kiss me, I unzipped his trousers and felt inside. His breath caught and he closed his eyes as I put my hand around his penis. I brought it out and moved my hand on it.

James whispered, "Are you wearing under drawers today?"

"No," I whispered back. "Sit down, James." I let go of his member and, while he sat down, I undid my skirt and slipped it off. I then straddled his lap. Feeling his penis slid into me, I let out a sigh and then the baby moved in my stomach. "Oh."

"What is it, Catherine?"

"I think we woke the baby up. He's moving some."

James lifted my blouse, looked at my belly and put his hand to it. "I hope he knows how much I love his mother," he whispered.

It caused me to smile. "I think he knows. He's jumping for joy." I started moving up and down on James lap.

He put his hands on my hips and held me down. Looking up at me, he said, "When was it you first realized you loved me?"

I ran my hands through his hair and held my position. "The morning after the night in the barn with the ruffians, I knew it. It didn't really take hold until the afternoon though when we were here under this tree." I tried to move, but he continued to hold me down.

"Besides being obsessed with my body, why else do you love me?" he whispered.

I had my hands on his shoulders. "I love your eyes."

"They are a part of my body."

"Yes, but it's not what I mean. There are times when you look at me and I can see warmth in them. It's comforting. I can't…I don't have the words to explain it."

He brought his hand up under my blouse to my breast. "What else?'

"I love the way you treat people."

"Tell me." He tightened his grip on my nipple and it made me catch my breath.

"When I see you walking back from the fields with the other men, you treat them with respect. You laugh and listen to their stories. No matter their station you always treat them as equals. I admire you for it."

"What else?"

I tried to move, but he put his hand back to my hip and held me down. His other hand moved and his thumb found my sweet spot. I shuddered a little. "I love the way you tease me. I love your stubbornness even when it makes mad. I love all you've shown me and how you make me feel. You woke up a passion I never knew existed. I'll always be grateful and love you endlessly for it. I love listening to you breathe when you sleep at night. It sounds like music and I noticed it at Mansfield."

He sat up and put his head on my chest. "You listen to me breathe at night?"

"Sometimes. It's soothing." I raised myself up a little and then back down. James let out a small sigh and added pressure to his thumb. "What about me, my love? When did you know you were in love with me?"

Speaking into my chest, he said, "The very first time I saw you in Jacob's office. I admired your courage."

"Courage? I was scared half to death."

"No, I don't think so. There was moment when you looked at Marshall. I knew you were bewildered about what happened, but you looked at him with incredible strength. I silently dared him to speak, but he didn't."

"What else?"

"When you are working in the garden with your shoes off, I hate when I have to interrupt you. You look so content." James let me move, again. "I love the smell of your hair. The way you look up at the sky and the trees…" His breath caught in his throat. He opened his eyes and smiled. "I love to watch you sew. You concentrate very much when you're doing it. I love the way you brush your hair in the morning. Sometimes you look out the window and if the light is shining just right, your hair almost glows. You look like an angle and it's beautiful."

He leaned in and licked my neck. I rocked a little and put my hand on his back, digging my fingernails into his skin through his shirt.

James tensed up and said, "Oh!" His eyes closed, "I really love it when you do that."

We continued whispering for some time and then couldn't restrain ourselves any longer. I told him the oak tree watched over us and gave its blessing.

Sometime later we came out of the path arm in arm into the field, and walked back to Whear.

"Milady, I think this will forever be only our spot. I never want that tree to come down and I never want anyone else owning it. When our child is born we will bring him here only occasionally. It is our place, I want to keep it secret."

"Yes, milord."

"I love you."

"I love you, too."

Lauren Marie

Chapter Twenty-five

November 16, 1920

The most wonderful thing happened today. James and I were eating lunch in the dining room when we heard one of those automobiles come up the drive. It made a terrible roar. We both dropped our forks and headed for the front door. Neither one of us knew who it might be. None of our neighbors owned one of those machines. We went out on the front steps and the driver parked it in front of the house. Looking in the side window, we saw Mr. Snell behind the wheel. He turned off the motor, and stepped out, waved and said good afternoon.

"Mr. Snell, this is a surprise. How are you?" I asked.

He pulled a case out of the back seat, shut the door and headed toward the house. "I'm doing fine, Catherine. Thank you for asking. I have some news and I wanted to tell you personally. I didn't want to trust this to the post."

"Come inside, sir," James said.

The men let me go into the house first and we made our way into the library. On the way in, Mr. Snell said, "I hope I haven't interrupted anything important?"

"We were just finishing lunch, but are free of entanglements this afternoon," James answered.

After we entered, James shut the door. Mr. Snell put his case down on the desk and turned to look at us. I sat down in the straight back chair and waited to hear his news.

Mr. Snell walked toward me, offering his hand. I put mine into his and stared at him. "Catherine." He smiled down at me. "You are a free woman, as of noon yesterday."

My mouth dropped open and I'm sure my eyes almost fell out of my head. James leaned over the chair and wrapped his arms around me from behind. He put his face in my hair and kissed my neck

"Mr. Snell, you said it would take six months or more. I don't understand, how?"

Mr. Snell straightened up and leaned against the desk. "We have the Right Honorable Judge Baker to thank for it. When I realized things were going to drag on longer than they should, I approached him. I told him in sincere confidence about the situation. It seemed to move him and touch his parental sensibilities. He has twelve children of his own, seven of whom are daughters. He got things moving in a better direction and informed me yesterday the decision was finalized." He turned to his case and opened it. Pulling papers from inside, he smiled. "All I need is your signature and it will be finished once and for all."

James still held my shoulders and I put my hands on his. He took one of them and came around to the side of the chair, holding his other hand out to Mr. Snell. "Thank you very much, sir. This is the best news we've had of late. Thank you." They shook hands.

I stood up and moved toward the papers on the desk. "Where do I sign, sir?"

It would be the last time I'd ever sign my name Catherine Pieper and I felt pleased. Mr. Snell handed me a pen and pointed to various lines where I signed my entire name or initialed. I don't think I'd ever used my signature so much. We got to the final page, I put my scribble on it and it was done.

I thanked the Lord above for giving me this lucky break.

Mr. Snell put the papers back in his case and snapped it shut. "I'll file these tomorrow and you'll be clear of this mess."

"Thank you, Mr. Snell," I said. I thought I should say more, but my tongue wouldn't move.

"Now, there is another thing the Honorable Judge Baker did. He wired the traveling judge who comes through this area. This judge would be able to be here in about two weeks time and is willing to perform a wedding ceremony if you should so wish. I have to wire him by the end of the week one way or another. What do you think?"

I turned to James. "Two weeks?" I felt panicky. "I have to tell Stella."

James laughed. "I think that's a yes, Mr. Snell."

"Yes, definitely, sir. Tell the judge yes," I said.

He laughed with James.

"Mr. Snell, have you eaten lunch?" I asked.

"No I have not, Catherine."

"Please join us, we have plenty."

December 3, 1920

The judge, Mr. Mathews, arrived in town on Tuesday and James and I met with him to go over our small civil ceremony on Thursday. He agreed to come out to Whear to perform it. He is a nice gentleman, rather rotund and balding, with a sincere smile. He doesn't seem to have any concerns with my being six and a half months pregnant. He explained all we needed to do and then we bid him good-day.

Yesterday was a whirlwind. It all went by so fast, it's hard to remember. We invited Jacob to come and bring Daniel and Marco with him. Unfortunately, we were informed Jacob sent Marco off to college in the city. It is wonderful Marco will be able to continue his education and move away from his duties at Mansfield. We're very happy for him, but will miss seeing him.

Two weeks ago, when Mr. Snell told us of possibly being married, I didn't think we'd have enough time to prepare. Stella and Susan worked tirelessly. Susan even made a lovely white cake. She is certainly gifted in the kitchen.

I went through my closet, trying to figure which dress would be easiest to alter. I felt beside myself, unable to find anything I'd be happy to wear. Stella understood my unhappiness and a week ago, brought me a box from the dressmaker in town. Inside the box was a gown made of cream-colored linen. It buttoned up the front blouse part and we'll need to let it out around the waist. She even bought some extra fabric if we needed to put in panels. I felt so relieved and cried my eyes out. Stella let me have my tantrum and then we got to work with the dress.

When I put it on yesterday, I almost experienced a heart attack. My stomach apparently grew a little over the last week and the dress was almost too tight. We succeeded, though, and it was a bit tight, but it looked acceptable. She then handed me a beautiful bouquet of roses which came from Jacob's hot house. They were white and yellow and smelled heavenly.

We gathered in the only room in the house I consider completed, the living room, for the ceremony. Susan and Katie decorated the room with ribbons and I felt as if I'd walked into a dream. When I saw James dressed in a black suit, I almost started to cry. He is the most handsome man I've ever seen. He continues to make me breathless in one way or another every day we're together.

Mr. Mathews performed a quiet, simple ceremony and pronounced us husband and wife. I felt a tear roll down my cheek when I turned to James and found his eyes too were welling up. He kissed me, started to pull away, but then grabbed my waist and planted a very non-public kiss on my mouth. Our guests must have gotten an eyeful.

Jacob surprised us with a case of champagne and popped a bottle open. We cut the cake and exchanged pieces.

I sipped on a single glass of champagne all afternoon.

Several times during the day, our little Nicholas made himself known. It's a wonder he hasn't kicked a hole in my stomach and peeked out at us the way he moves around in there.

The afternoon went by without a hitch or problem and was a wedding I won't soon forget.

Last night, after everyone left or went to bed, James and I retired to our room. He started calling me Mrs. Whear, which gave me such a glorious feeling. I asked him, at sometime during our honeymoon, if I was still his milady, though. He said I'd always be his milady and I thanked him.

Lauren Marie

Chapter Twenty-six

December 19, 1920

It's snowing today and the heavy white flakes have carpeted the fields surrounding Whear Hall. I looked out the back windows and gazed at the splendor in the area I could see. It is lovely.

I'm being imprisoned indoors. James doesn't want me to slip and fall in the snow. He's ordered the staff to keep me under close supervision. He can be such a stubborn mule sometimes, but as much as I'd like not to admit it, he is right. I don't want to fall, either.

We've invited Jacob to come for Christmas Eve dinner this weekend. With the snow falling, it occurred to James, we don't have any accommodations for guests to stay over. He's worked all this week to have furniture brought in and set up in time—in case the snows continues and Jacob needs to stay overnight.

James, sadly, brought it to my attention he'd used a little more of the wool money for the furniture. I only smiled and said we'd have to renegotiate the amount of time on his servitude. He patted my behind and whispered, "Perhaps this evening."

December 23, 1920

It turned bitterly cold last night. I don't know what the temperature dropped down to, but it is cold in the house. James brought in several loads of firewood to keep the fireplaces burning continually. We've piled another blanket on the bed and with James's warm body next to mine, I've stayed very comfortable. He did complain about my cold feet. Last night, knowing how he feels about it, I put on a pair of his giant wool socks. He laughed so hard, I thought he would hurt himself. I guess I did look rather silly. I wore a flannel shirt and wool socks with my big belly sticking out.

Tomorrow is Christmas Eve dinner. I'm looking forward to seeing Jacob, and I know Stella is, too. She seems to get an excited light in her eyes whenever I mention his name. I might try to play cupid a little tomorrow evening.

December 26, 1920
The holiday weekend turned out lovely. It's amazing to me how we can go from wonderful happiness to unease and back to feeling easy again so quickly.

Because of the cold weather, the snow which melted during the day, froze solid once the sun went down. The drive out front of the house is treacherous. Around noon time, we heard loud crunching coming from the there. I made my way to the front door and met James in the hallway when he came out of the library.

"What is that noise, James?"

"I have no idea." He opened the front door and we went to the top of the steps to look down the drive.

Coming up was a large wagon, being driven by four horses. There were several men walking alongside of it. They all held onto the load in the wagon to keep their footing on the slick surface. In the front seat, with the driver, was Jacob. He had a huge smile on his face and started saying, "Merry Christmas, neighbors" at the top of his voice.

"What on earth has he done?" I asked and waved back.

The wagon stopped at the bottom of the stairs and the men started to pull coverings off the load. James went down the steps to help Jacob get off of the wagon. They whispered to one another and then James looked up at me and smiled.

"What are you two concocting down there?" I asked him.

"Nothing you need to be concerned with, Mrs. Whear," James replied.

I watched the men pull off the last cover and realized it was the top of a grand piano. I put my hands up to my face. "Jacob?"

He smiled and said, "It's a belated wedding gift, Catherine. I was going to bring it last week, but the weather didn't let up long enough to get it moved."

"Jacob, it's not your piano, is it?"

"Yes, it is. I think it will get better use in a house where someone can at least play. Since I've closed the school, the poor thing only sits and collects dust," he answered. "I realized when I was here for the wedding, there was no music. I did have a splendid time, but if there had been music, you and your husband could have danced your first dance."

I rolled my eyes and thought to myself, I'm surrounded by romantics.

"I also brought the name of the gentleman in town who tunes the thing. I'm sure he will be happy to come out and tune it when you need."

"Thank you so much, Jacob. This is a wonderful gift."

Jacob and James watched as the men unloaded the piano. They were certainly strong and moved it with skill. As they started up the stairs to the front door, James came up ahead of them and opened both the doors to give them enough room. I walked into the hall and found Stella, Susan and Katie, who all looked shocked.

I took Stella's hand and said, "Jacob, it would seem, has brought us a piano."

"Oh, my Lord," Stella said. "Where are they going

to put it?"

"We need to make some space in the living room."

"Not you, my dear." She turned to Susan and Katie. "Ladies, come with me."

"Mrs. Whear, you are glowing today." Jacob came in behind the workers and made his way to me. He gave me a gentle hug and kissed my cheek.

"Thank you for the compliment, sir. You may continue calling me Mrs. Whear as long as you like. I haven't grown tired of hearing it yet." He chuckled, took my arm and we followed the men into the living room.

After the piano was in, one of the men went back out and got the legs. They put them back on and then turned it upright. The ladies moved a table and two overstuffed chairs away from the front window. The men lifted it and moved it to this location. It looks beautiful. The four workmen walked out of the room and shook hands with Jacob on the way out. After a moment, one of them came back in with the bench. He put it down by the keyboard and turned to leave, tipping his hat.

I walked over to it and placed my hands on the wood cover. It felt cold from the ride over from Mansfield. I looked up at James. "Were you aware of this, sir?"

James got a shocked look on his face. "No, ma'am, I'm as surprised by it as you." He came over to me and took my hand. "Although, a couple of weeks ago, Jacob told me of his plan, but I'm still surprised. I didn't realize it would be brought today."

I shook my head. "Jacob, it is an incredible gift. You know, this means I'll expect you here at Whear Hall more than once a month for dinner?"

"I believe I could accept that, my dear. I do love the company of my neighbors," he said, full of charm and grace.

I looked at the room. The furniture arrangement would have to do for this evening. "Let's all have a seat.

James, could you be the bartender this evening?"

He bowed to me. "Yes, my love." He turned and followed Susan and Katie to the kitchen and returned with a bottle of champagne which was left over from the wedding. We sat around the fireplace and chatted for the afternoon.

Jacob asked how I felt and had I gotten excited for the birth of our son? It brought us to a discussion James and I'd been having for a few weeks. There was no better time to broach the subject we'd gone in circles about.

James sat next to me and whispered in my ear. "Are you going to ask them?"

Both Stella and Jacob got curious looks on their faces, exchanged a glance, and looked back at me.

"Perhaps you should do it, milord?"

James stood up, put his hand over his heart and said, "While we are on this subject, Catherine and I have discussed quite seriously about an important topic which relates to our firstborn." He walked to the fireplace, put his foot up on the hearth and looked into the fire. He turned back to them, being dramatic. "Now Stella, I know several weeks ago Catherine asked if you would consider being our child's nanny and tutor. We've given it much consideration and have decided to withdraw this offer." Stella sat up straight and looked surprised. I worried her feelings might be hurt. James continued on. "Jacob and Stella, we love you both very much and we've decided we want you both to be a part of our family." James looked at me and it was my cue to take over the discussion.

"We've discussed it thoroughly and we'd like to ask you both to be Nick's godparents."

I think it took a minute or so for what I'd asked, to register in their brains. Stella put her hands up to her mouth and took in a breath. Jacob sat with surprise and quietly said he'd be honored. They both seemed moved to be asked and are both so dear to us. The mood in the room became rather subdued. Jacob stood and came over to me. Taking my hand, he kissed the back of it.

"This is the greatest gift I've ever received, my dear. Thank you very much," Jacob said and his lips trembled.

"You're very welcome, dear sir. Thank you for the piano." We both laughed.

"Yes, you must play it for us, you must," he said and helped me up from the couch. He escorted me over to it. James and Stella followed and the three of them stood around it while I sat at the bench. I played a quiet piece I'd learned many years ago. I knew it would be short and then I could stop. I wasn't very comfortable playing in front of people.

I ended up playing several other pieces at my audience's request. At one point, Jacob and Stella danced to the slow music. James came and sat by me on the bench and kissed my neck. He put his arm around me and held me tight. I didn't miss a note. I felt very proud of my performance.

During an easy section, I looked at James and whispered, "Would you like for me to play Daisy Bell?"

"You spoil me rotten, my love." He kissed my neck, again. I played the song which had such sentimental meaning for James and me.

When I finished, the three of them clapped and Jacob said, "Bravo, my dear. That was lovely."

Susan came into the room and announced dinner was ready in the dining room. Jacob escorted Stella and seated her. James did the same for me. Jacob said he'd be right back. He left the room for a few minutes and then returned carrying a small white box. He came over to the space between me and James, who sat at the head of the table.

"I became so taken with the music, I forgot another gift I have to give. Catherine, you have honored me very much this afternoon by asking me to be your son's godfather. I thank you very much for trusting me to attend properly to the duty. It was a wonderful surprise. I have a bit of a surprise for you, too."

"Jacob, the piano…"

"No, my dear, the piano was a wedding gift. This surprise is much more heartfelt. I know it is something you wouldn't speak of and am aware it is something you've wanted. After all you've been through and the fact you've forgiven my participation—"

"Jacob, there was nothing to forgive," I interrupted him and looked across the table at Stella.

She smiled at me and said, "Don't look at me like that, Catherine. He's told me what happened. I understand now better than I did before we left Layne."

I sat back in my chair and continued to stare at her. "Jacob, you must never blame yourself."

"That's easier said than done, my dear." He leaned over and handed me the white box. "Open your present."

I looked at James, who said, "I have no idea, milady. He didn't tell me about this one." Jacob patted my shoulder and returned to his seat next to Stella.

They all watched me take the ribbon off and open the box. Inside, I found a set of papers folded into thirds. As I began to open them, James got up and stood behind my chair. I held them up so he could see, too. When I realized what I held, my mouth dropped and I looked across the table at Jacob. I found it difficult to form words.

James gasped, "Jacob! How?"

I held in my hands the title to Layne Hall. With it, were the deeds to all the surrounding property. They were in James's name.

Stella could no longer stand being in the dark. "What is it, dear?"

"It's the title to Layne Hall. Jacob, what have you done?" I asked.

255

He sat back in his chair and appeared pleased with himself. "All of Layne Hall's debt and outstanding promissory notes were paid. You're also free of the tax men coming around for the next year or two. Layne is back in the hands where it really belongs."

"Jacob, this is too much."

"My dear, I'm afraid it's not nearly enough." He looked across the table at me with a serious expression on his face.

I handed the papers to James, who looked at them and sat back at the head of the table. "Jacob, this must have cost you dearly. We'll never be able to repay you."

"You are not going to pay me a cent, do you hear me?" Jacob said. "And you are not coming back to work at Mansfield, young man. You have a family to care for now." I could see Jacob teased James, but he also acted serious.

"When you first came to Mansfield, I knew Marshall Pieper did not think clearly. I remember telling you I believed him to be an ass. The stories I've heard from the city are very disturbing, but what he did to you Catherine...when you showed your injuries. I should never have accepted his contract." He paused and asked for the bottle of champagne from James, pouring himself another glass. He took a sip and cleared his throat. "It seems, too, James and Catherine, since you have settled here at Whear, perhaps you could lease out Layne Hall. The leasing money could help out, I believe." He waved his arm.

I looked at James. He nodded as if he'd read my mind. "Jacob, what have you heard of Marshall from the city?" I asked.

He puffed out his cheeks. "His gambling has overtaken him. He lost the title to Layne in a poker game. It took a little time to track it, but I know the player he lost it to and he was willing to deal with me. The other stories are not fit for discussion at the dinner table." He looked at me and said, "I suppose you could move to Layne and lease out Whear, but I would lose my favorite neighbors and it would be very lonely here without them."

"Moving back to Layne would be impossible, Jacob. Too many bad memories." I tried to smile. "At Whear Hall, we are building new and happier memories. We, too, love our neighbor very much."

Jacob winked at me and took Stella's hand in his. She stayed quiet through dinner and I saw her watching Jacob. I could be wrong, but I think she's fallen under his spell. I hope I'm not wrong.

Lauren Marie

Chapter Twenty-seven

February 3, 1921

I finally delivered my wonderful son, Nicolas, two days ago.

The day started rather strange and no matter how I sat or tried to lie down, I couldn't get comfortable. I'd not been able to work in the garden the past month and, on that day, I just didn't feel like myself.

In the afternoon, I felt something like heartburn coming on. As I walked down the hallway to the kitchen, I felt a terrible pain stab me down in my pelvis. I leaned up against the wall, panted for a few minutes and then felt water run down my legs. I knew then I was in labor.

At that time, I heard footsteps behind me. Katie changed the sheets upstairs and brought the old ones down for washing. She walked up to me smiling. "Afternoon, Missus." She saw the look on my face and stopped smiling. "Missus, what's wrong?" she asked.

"Katie, get Stella. Tell her my water broke."

She dropped the sheets and ran to the kitchen. Within a few seconds, Stella and Susan had their arms around me and helped me up the stairs to the bedroom. Stella said she'd sent Katie after James and Arthur, and she'd sent someone to town to get the midwife.

They got me lying on my side in the bed and Stella kept an eye on the second hand of her watch, timing the contractions. Every five to ten minutes, the pains would start up. Susan brought some pitchers of water and clean sheets up to the room. She also got the blankets from the nursery.

259

When the baby got to kicking, the pain felt so severe. I tried to curl into a ball, but my stomach was too big and I could only get so far. Stella sat on the edge of the bed rubbing my back. She talked to me through the whole thing.

The door flew open and James stumbled into the bedroom. He knelt beside the bed and took my hand. His face looked red and he breathed hard. "Catherine, tell me, is it time?" he asked, between puffs of air.

"Yes," was all I got out before I started panting, again.

"Stella, what can I do?"

"Just hold her hand, James. There's a pan there with some cool water and a cloth. Put it across her forehead, it will help." She seemed calm, which I took as a comfort.

Every time a contraction kicked in, James got a terrible look on his face and started babbling, which wasn't all that comforting. This went on for some time and I finally told James to hush. He'd begun to drive me crazy. I grabbed his hand with both of mine and squeezed as tight as I could through the pain.

Finally, the midwife arrived. She made James leave the room and then spoke to Stella, who said my contractions were less than two minutes apart. The woman smiled at me and said she'd arrived just in time. She did an examination and said she could see the baby's head. Rearranging my legs, she asked Stella to sit behind me. She put the clean sheets to the side of me and told me to start pushing.

After pushing for a time, I felt the baby slide out of me into the midwife's waiting hands. Of course, I began to cry, and tried to sit up to see him. I didn't have any strength left and needed to be patient. She cut the cord and held him upside down. Before she swatted the baby's bottom, my little son let out a yell all on his own. It made me cry harder and I held out my arms. The woman did a few more things and then wrapped him in a blanket. Looking back over my knees, she said, "May I present your son, Mrs. Whear?" and handed me the bundle. I looked down at his sweet face and kissed his forehead. Stella, sitting behind me, cried, too, and kept saying, "He's beautiful, just beautiful."

I understand from Susan, James was beside himself in the hallway. Although he only waited about forty-five minutes, he nearly lost his mind with worry. She said he wore out the runner rug pacing up and down the hall. When they heard the baby cry, he froze and stared at the door. He refused to move.

When the door opened, James pushed his way past the midwife and came in. I sat up and held my hand out to him. Stella got out of the way just in time, and James sat on the edge of the bed, gazing at his son.

"May I introduce your son? This is Nicholas Edward Whear, milord." James looked at me as though I spoke a foreign language. I saw tears running down his cheeks and smiled. "Father, say hello to your son."

James looked down at Nick and I don't think he realized the waterfall his eyes produced. "Hello there son, aren't you something?"

I sat a little straighter and put the bundle into James arms. He held Nick without too much force. I put my arm around his shoulders and leaned my head on his arm. "Isn't he beautiful?"

"He is indeed." James looked back at me. "Good job, Mother."

"Thank you."

After some time, the midwife felt things were stable enough to leave. She told Stella she'd check back in the morning, but if anything should come up during the night, to just send for her.

James watched while I breast fed Nick for the first time. He jokingly said, "The doctor told me we wouldn't be able to have relations for several weeks, but my son gets to enjoy my wife's breast on a regular basis. A man could get very jealous of this behavior, you know?"

I laughed and knew he teased, but thought there could be a serious note in his voice. "I'm sure he'll share eventually, my love." I kissed James on the cheek.

"Now don't start, milady. Don't get me all excited."

"Milord, I have only one word for you, 'hands.'"

James smiled, and looked almost embarrassed. "Milady is evil." He got a more serious look on his face. "Speaking of evil, why did you tell me to hush? And why did you almost break my hand? I was doing a very good job."

"You did a wonderful job, James. The midwife said Nick is twenty-three inches long, which is above average for a first child. Now imagine twenty-three inches trying to get out of your pelvis in a hurry. I'm afraid I got cranky, but it was the circumstances. Please forgive me."

"I forgive you. My hand will heal in time." He tried to sound pathetic, but only came up with laughter.

February 22, 1921

Another one of those strange days yesterday. I only hope one of these days, Marshall will realize he's no longer wanted anywhere in my life.

I spent the afternoon in the nursery and finished feeding and rocking Nick. He fell asleep and as much as I didn't want him out of my arms, I thought it would be a good time for me to get a nap. The last two weeks have been exhausting.

Starting to move toward the small bed which we'd put into the nursery for just such a reason, I caught sight of myself in a mirror hanging on the wall. I've gained some weight while carrying the baby and it sits mainly in my breasts and waist, but I noticed my cheeks and neck looked thicker, too. I lost a few pounds with Nick's birth, but I still have a way to go. My breasts are huge and, as I looked at the mirror, I almost thought it would be too bad to lose them. James seemed to like them very much.

As I looked in the mirror, I heard the door open. Stella's head poked around it. When she saw me, she entered the nursery and I could tell something terrible happened. The first thing I thought was that James might be hurt.

"Stella, what is wrong?"

"Catherine, please forgive me. I didn't mean to let him in," she whispered and looked at the bassinette.

"Let who in?" I took her hand.

"Marshall Pieper. I heard a knock and opened the door before I realized it was him. When I tried to close the door, he pushed his way in."

I walked over to my son and looked down at him. He slept soundly and looked so peaceful. I thought for a moment, and then turned back to Stella. "Where is he now?"

"In the living room. I told him I wasn't sure where you were," she answered.

"Stella, go down the back stairwell to the kitchen and tell Katie to get Arthur and send him into the house. Then she should find James. Tell her to have Arthur say he's unaware where I am. Then come back here."

She nodded and left the room. I turned back to Nick and tucked the blanket tighter around him. "Oh, to be so peaceful."

I walked over to the window and looked out. Within a few minutes, I saw Katie fly across the patio and head toward the back fields. She is a good runner, and it made me feel better to have Arthur in the house.

The door opened again and Stella came back in. "I saw Katie run out. Does she know where to find James?"

"Arthur was pretty sure he knew where they were working today. He gave her directions." Stella came up beside me and took my arm.

I pulled the house keys out of my pocket and handed them to her. "When I leave, lock the door behind me. Open it only when James or I come back up. Do you hear me?"

"Catherine, please, don't go down there. Not after the last time. He doesn't look well."

"James told me things I could do to protect myself. He said to not sit down and, if possible, keep a piece of furniture between us. I think I can stall him." I started toward the door.

"Be careful. He really doesn't look well."

"I think I'll be all right." I opened the door and turned back to her. "Watch after Nick, Stella. Keep him safe."

"I will."

I walked into the hallway and waited until I heard the lock click. Then I turned, making my way down to the kitchen. When I walked in, Susan stood at a chopping block, cutting up potatoes. She looked up and nodded with a serious look on her face. Arthur leaned in the doorway with his arms crossed. I began to step toward the door which would take me to the living room and stopped, turning back to our cook. "Susan, if you and Arthur would do me a favor, please?"

"Yes, ma'am." She put her cutting knife down.

"Come with me and bring your rolling pin."

"Yes, ma'am." She opened a drawer and took out her large wooden rolling pin.

Susan and Arthur followed me to the back entrance to the living room. We stopped outside and I motioned for them to wait.

I took a deep breath and opened the door. Walking into the room, I realized the sun shone on the other side of the house. The living room looked dim. I stopped just inside the door and waited for my eyes to adjust. Leaving the door ajar so Susan and Arthur could hear, I looked around the room and felt safe if Marshall became violent.

"Hello, slut," I heard his voice.

"Marshall, if all you're going to do is call me names, I may as well leave."

He stood up from one of the high back chairs in the middle of the room. "Hello, Catherine. Ready to come home?"

I stood my ground and made no reply. I knew he no longer lived at Layne Hall, the title being in the safe in James's library. Stella was correct when she said he didn't look well. He'd lost some weight and his hair was long. He hadn't shaved in some time. The suit he wore looked worn.

"Oh wait, you're living here with the staff from Layne Hall and sleeping with the master. Is he fucking you? Are you sucking his cock?" He moved around the chair and stood in the middle of the room.

"What do you want, Marshall?"

"You're my wife, I want you."

"We've been divorced since November. I'm no longer your wife."

His voice rose. "Remember the vows, slut, 'til death do us part?"

I just watched him with no reply. There were a set of chairs between us and I reminded myself to keep them there. I felt safe for the moment, but I watched Marshall and knew he could move quickly.

"You nearly killed me, Marshall," I said.

"Yes, well, you were acting like a whore, now weren't you?"

"I thought it's what you wanted."

"I have plenty of whores in the city, why would I want one for a wife?" He moved forward a couple of steps.

"Why did you send me to Mansfield then? Did you think they would train me to set a better dinner table?"

"You give up too easily, Catherine. Why did you walk out on me?"

"Marshall, if you will remember, I came back to Layne. I waited almost a month before you decided to come home. You took your anger out on me and beat me. How is that giving up?"

He smiled, but looked aggravated at the same time. "I understand you've had a child. Is it mine?"

"No."

"See, you have become a slut. You let some strange man plant his seed in you."

"I begged him to cum in me, Marshall."

He looked at me with his eyebrows creasing between his eyes and I realized I hit a nerve. His hands were clenching into fists by his sides. "You begged?" He arched an eyebrow. "You're sure the baby's not mine?"

"I'm sure."

"You should know, I've lost Layne Hall. I sold it to pay off some debts. Where is the money?" He watched me and I think he waited for some reaction. I didn't give him the satisfaction, knowing he lied.

"What money?"

"From the sheep's wool. I understand you got a pretty good price for the wool in the village."

"I told you I put it in a bank in the city."

"It belongs to Layne Hall."

"Marshall, you said you lost Layne Hall, what do you want?"

"I told you. I want you." He grinned and his voice rose. "I want to fuck you and hear you scream again." He moved forward.

"This is my home now and you are not welcome. Please leave, Marshall."

"Where is the child? Is it in the house?" He looked up at the ceiling.

I turned to leave the room, but he moved and blocked the door. I backed around the chair and put it between us.

"Do you want to beat me again, Marshall?" I stepped away from the chair, toward the middle of the room and held out my arms. "Here I am. You want to hold my nose and make me suck your cock, again? Here I am." I saw a shadow cross his face. "Drop your trousers, sir. Let's do it, but I should warn you. My husband, the master of this hall, will kill you without a thought and I will spit on your grave." I glared as hard as I could at him. "So, you can fuck me, but then you'll leave and never return, because you'll be dead."

"You see, you have become a whore. Such language, Catherine," he said, with anger.

"I was trained properly, Marshall. Mansfield is a very good school. They teach it all. Do you want sodomy, again? I've experienced many men in my ass, yours will be nothing."

I think my last statement surprised him. He started to reply, but stopped. I could see the wheels turn in his head and he got a very excited sneer on his face. Starting toward me, he stopped again when he heard the floor creak behind him. He turned and found Susan who held her wooden rolling pin in the doorway. Arthur stood next to her.

"Mrs. Whear has asked you to leave, sir," she said.

Marshall looked back at me. "Mrs. Whear? You bitch," he hissed.

I heard the back door of the house slam open and several heavy feet stomped toward the living room. I stepped back toward the piano.

James pushed past Susan into the room. He looked at me with a question on his face and I nodded I was fine. Three of the field hands entered the room behind James and moved toward me. Two of the men carried shotguns. The third man with red hair and beard was the man I'd seen when the blindfold came down in the barn at Mansfield. His name was Heck. He stood in front of me and faced Marshall.

James turned to Marshall and said, "Sir, you are not welcome in my home. You'll be escorted to the gates and I ask you to leave peacefully."

"Your home? You are the master of this dismal place?" Marshall pointed his finger at me. "You married this whore?" he shouted.

I'd never seen James angry before and hope I never witness it again. He grabbed Marshall's jacket with both hands and held him close. "Sir, I believe you owe my wife an apology."

Marshall struggled, but couldn't remove himself from James grip. "I owe her nothing. She's a whore. She offered to suck my cock."

James looked over Marshall's shoulder at me and raised an eyebrow. I merely shrugged my shoulders.

James turned to the other men and said, "Gentlemen, show Mr. Pieper to the gates." He looked back at Marshall. "Please, point him in the correct direction to get back to town. Mr. Pieper, if you ever step on my land again, you will regret it the rest of your short, pathetic life." James released Marshall's jacket and pushed him away. He moved around Heck, toward me and took my hand.

Marshall gazed around the room with a crazed look on his face. He pointed at James. "You sir, are the one who will have regrets. You've married a slut. She offered to let me sodomize her in this very room."

Heck moved toward Marshall, brought his fist up and punched Marshall in the stomach who doubled over, losing his breath. I didn't like the violence, but for a moment thought it nice Marshall knew now what it felt like to lose his breath.

Heck bent over at the waist trying to go eye to eye with him and said, "'Twasn't a very gentlemanly thing to say, sir." I recognized his voice. He'd moved me to the hay and told me not to remove the blindfold. He grabbed a handful of the back of Marshall's jacket and pushed him toward the front door. He and the other two men saw my ex-husband out to the drive.

James and I followed to the front door and watched as they led Marshall down the steps. James kissed my hand and said, "Did you really offer to suck his cock?"

I looked down at his hand in mine. "Well, yes, I did say that, but was…What's the phrase you used? Yes, I was buying time. I stalled him," I answered.

James laughed a little and put his arms around me. "You are such a good student." He looked down at me and raised his eyebrow. "We'll have to try it sometime."

"Yes, I think we should."

He kissed my lips and said, "I'll be right back." He patted my rear and turned toward the library.

I continued watching the men from the front door. The air felt chilly and I began to feel cold. I heard the library door close and James came back out, carrying a small bag. He passed me and went down the steps calling out to Heck. The red-headed man turned around and walked back toward James. They spoke for a few minutes, then James handed him the bag. I recognized it from James's desk and new it contained a good number of coins. Heck opened it, looked inside and then nodded. They shook hands and Heck pocketed the bag and tipped his hat to me. He turned and moved to catch up with the other men.

James watched them go. I turned back into the living room and went to stand by the fire. I found Susan still by the door with her rolling pin.

"Ah, Susan. I can't thank you enough for backing me. It gave me a very safe feeling."

James came up behind me. "I have to thank you, too, for your courage, Susan," he said.

"Glad to be of service, ma'am, sir." She nodded.

"Susan, I also want to apologize that you had to

Lauren Marie

overhear such language. Please, do forgive me."

Susan thought a moment and smiled. "I've heard those kinds of words before, ma'am. I've heard worse from the men out in the field." She laughed and turned back to the kitchen.

After she'd left, I turned and grabbed James around the neck. I put my lips on his and gave him the most passionate kiss I could muster. He wrapped his arms around my waist and lifted me up. He walked us toward the couch and sat me down. He squatted down in front of me and looked into my eyes. "You're shaking."

"Marshall has gone mad, James. If he continues with such behavior, I'll never feel safe here or anywhere. What are we to do?"

"You've nothing to worry about, my love. I don't think Marshall will trouble us again."

I looked at James and knew I didn't need to be frightened, but there was something else. "James…"

"I'm riding into the village tomorrow and filing a formal complaint with the constable. I think if he gives Marshall a warning, he'll leave us alone."

"James." I pulled him up to the couch next to me. "The man you were speaking to outside, the one with red hair, you gave him the bag of coins. I recognize him."

"You do?"

"I saw him the night in the barn. You told me to be sure the blindfold stayed in place, but when they moved me to a bench, it slipped up and I could see him. I managed to get the blindfold back down with my arm. I also recognized his voice. What did you pay him for?"

"It was for the work they'd done this week. Since we came in from the field early and they won't be back tomorrow, I thought it was the best time to pay them." He looked away from me. "After all that happened this afternoon, I gave them some extra for their help."

270

I don't know why, but I knew James lied to me. I couldn't say what the lie was, but something told me he didn't tell me everything. It was only a feeling from the way he wouldn't look at me and he only did it to protect me. Sometime in the future, I'd ask him about it, but for now it was over.

I remembered Stella waited upstairs with Nick. I got up from the couch and looked back at James. "I have to let Stella know everything is over. She's protecting Nick." James took hold of my hand and wouldn't let it go. I turned back to him. "James?"

"I love you, Catherine." He looked up at me.

"I love you, too." I leaned over and kissed him.

He continued looking up at me and then let my hand go and stood next to me. "I think I'll come with you. I haven't seen much of Nick today."

Lauren Marie

Chapter Twenty-eight

March 29, 1921

Stella and I walked into town today. I needed to find some fabric to make Nick some more clothes. For only two months old, he is growing.

When we arrived back at Whear Hall, we entered the main hall and Susan came out from the kitchen, wiping her hands with a towel.

"Ma'am, Constable Hunter is here from town. He's in the library. He's been waiting for a bit. I asked Arthur to go out to the field to get Mr. Whear."

"Thank you, Susan," I said and took off my coat.

"What do you suppose he wants?" Stella asked.

I handed her my bag and coat, and turned to the library. "I have no idea."

I found the constable looking at the few books on the shelves. When he heard me enter, he turned and smiled.

"Mrs. Whear, I'm Constable Hunter. How very nice to meet you, ma'am." He came forward and bowed an old-fashioned bow.

I asked him to have a seat and offered to bring some refreshment. He agreed a cup of tea would be lovely.

I went back out into the hallway, where Stella and Susan stood and asked Susan to brew up some tea and bring it in.

When I went back and sat, Constable Hunter said, "It's very nice to have Whear Hall opened again. For a time, there, I thought it would be taken over by the grass and vines. It's looking quite beautiful now."

"Thank you, sir. My husband has worked hard and it is coming around."

"Have you been in the area long, Mrs. Whear?"

"No. I'm not from here. I was born and raised at Layne Hall about three hours away."

"Ah, I see." He looked back at the bookcase.

"Mr. Hunter, may I ask what brings you here today?"

Before he could answer, Susan came in the door carrying a tray with cups and a pot of tea. I stood and went over to pour. I asked if he took cream or sugar, but he said no. I poured the tea and took him the cup. As I picked up my own cup, the door opened once more and James came in. He'd washed himself off and still dried his hands. Mr. Hunter stood to greet him.

"Sir." James tucked the towel into a pocket in his trousers and put his hand out to shake. "I'm sorry, I was delayed. I hope you haven't waited too long?"

"Long enough to meet your wife, sir." He sat back down and took a sip of his tea.

I asked James if he would like a cup, but he said no. Bringing the cup with me, I sat in the chair across from the constable. James leaned against the desk and crossed his arms.

"Mr. Hunter, is there something we can help you with?" James asked.

His eyes looked back at us both and his brow creased between his eyes as he glanced down at his tea. "Well, sir, I'm afraid I'm here today with what might be some bad news."

James nodded and we waited.

"A body washed up to the shore of the Tulle River last week. It was a man. Now, some folks in the town are saying it could be your ex-husband, Mrs. Whear. There has been a rumor he created a disturbance here at Whear some

274

weeks ago."

"Yes, he did. It was a month ago, at least." I looked up at James.

"I see, ma'am. Well, since there is no family for Mr. Pieper in this area, we would like it if you'd come into town tomorrow and see if you could identify him."

"Mr. Hunter, I wish I'd known, I was just in town this afternoon," I said.

"Sir, instead of upsetting my wife with this, since I have met Mr. Pieper, would it be possible for me to see if I could identify him?"

"Mr. Whear," the constable replied. "This would be very good of you, but I'm afraid we need someone who is...or was, a relation. Since Mrs. Whear is as close a relation as we can find, I'm afraid it will have to be her."

"Marshall did have a sister up north. I never had the opportunity to meet her. Her name is Claire Pieper."

"That's very good. After you tell us if you recognize him, we can try to contact her, if you have her address, ma'am."

"Of course."

"Constable Hunter, may I accompany my wife tomorrow?"

"Of course, sir."

"Is there any idea of what may have happened to him?" I asked.

"He did come to his end in a most foul way, ma'am. Since his wallet was empty, we do think it may be a robbery. Perhaps he put up a fight, there are some nasty bruises on his middle section." He went silent for moment. "Mr. Whear, I understand you've got a group of traveling workmen living on your property?"

"Yes, they helped us out in the fall to clear the fields," James replied.

"You paid them a wage?"

"Yes, sir. I'm afraid they've left for the season, though. They may return during summer, but it's hard to say."

"Yes, I see. Mr. Whear, you are aware those types of people are known to be thieves and ne'er-do-wells?"

"Mr. Hunter, the men who have worked here at Whear were recommended by Mr. Jacob Mansfield. They worked for him for many years and he trusts them completely. If Mr. Mansfield trusts them, so do I."

"Of course, sir, of course." Mr. Hunter stood. "Well, this should do it for now. What time might I expect you tomorrow?"

James looked down at me. "Ten o'clock?" he asked. I nodded.

"Fine, I look forward to seeing you in the morning, then."

James showed the constable to the door and then came back to the library. I got up to pour myself another cup of tea and sat back on the chair. I could see he was thinking about all this.

He finally looked at me and smiled. "Good man, Mr. Hunter."

"Yes, he is. James." I set my cup down, stood and clasped my hand in front of me. "I have only one question to ask you."

He put his hand up. "Catherine, my love, no questions, not yet. I think its best you don't ask me anything. After tomorrow, we can have a discussion. Just know, I love you more than anything and I'd never jeopardize that."

"I know, James." I continued to look at him, let out my breath and walked to him. I wrapped my arms around his waist. "I love you, too."

March 31, 1921
Yesterday, James and I took the carriage into town

to meet with Constable Hunter. His office is in a low, one story brick building on the main road. We entered through the front door. Mr. Hunter's office sits at the front of the building. We asked for him and after a time he came out to meet us.

Mr. Hunter offered us a seat in the waiting area and said it would only take the staff a moment to prepare the remains to be seen.

After a time, he returned and walked us to the back of the building where there was a make shift morgue. On a table in the middle of the room, lay a body covered by a sheet. The smell was appalling. James put his arm around my waist and I grabbed onto his hand. I'd seen my father's body after his death, but he'd been laid in a casket in his Sunday suit and it happened briefly before burial. This all seemed very surreal to me.

Mr. Hunter walked to the table and pulled the sheet back from the head. It took me a moment to realize what I saw. After a month or more in the river, the skin was pale and looked as if it were chewed on by fish. I stared at it, but could suddenly take it no more and turned my face into James's chest.

He put his hand on the back of my neck. "Catherine, are you all right?" he asked.

I opened my eyes and said, "Yes, I'm fine." I looked at Mr. Hunter. "Sir, I'm afraid I can't say if this is Marshall or not."

The constable nodded and put the sheet back over the head. "Mrs. Whear, I'm just wondering. Did Mr. Pieper ever wear any jewelry?"

"Yes, he did. He had a ring he wore most of the time. It was gold with a Masonic sign on top. There was also a diamond in it. I'd forgotten about it." I pulled my head away from James's chest and waited.

Mr. Hunter moved down the table and pulled the

277

hand out from under the sheet. The ring gleamed on the third finger. It was Marshall. I thought I should be having some sort of reaction, but felt nothing.

We walked out of the morgue, back to Mr. Hunter's office. I sat down in a chair. James sat next to me and held my hand. One of Mr. Hunter's assistants brought me a glass of water.

"Mrs. Whear, as far as you know, did anyone hold ill will against your ex-husband?"

"The gentleman who drives our carriage, Arthur, has worked for my family for many years. He mentioned early last year he'd been taking Marshall into the city to gambling halls and brothels. I'm not aware of what transpired. Mr. Mansfield brought it to our attention that Marshall lost Layne Hall gambling. I'm sure he owed a lot of money. It's likely he owed the gambling establishments. It's been over a month since I last saw him and I could tell he'd been drinking. Mr. Hunter, is it possible this was an accident?"

"Mrs. Whear, anything is possible. However, I don't believe this could have been an accident. The cut across his neck is too clean. There are also too many bruises to consider."

"I see," I replied.

The ride back to Whear seemed very long. Although James kept his arm around me, we didn't speak much. I started to ask questions, but never got the words out. When we arrived back, he went out to the fields and I went inside to check on Nick.

Secrets Beyond Dreams

Chapter Twenty-nine

April 1, 1921

Things were quiet around Whear Hall today. Stella and I spoke a little about the plans for the garden. We'd like to get some things put in next week. I'm glad we got the bulbs put in when we did.

James got up and left the house early this morning. He never came back in for lunch. Something must have come up with the sheep or grass cutting. I'll look forward to seeing him this evening.

April 3, 1921

I couldn't bring myself to write anything yesterday. I'm at a loss and not sure what happened.

I fell asleep before James came back in the night before last. Sometime during the night, I woke and found him lying next to me. Rolling over, I put my arm across his chest. He sighed and then he moved my arm and turned away from me. I looked at his back.

James never did this before and it unsettled me as I lay awake the rest of the night wondering what I'd done. He got up early again and left the room.

I didn't get up for a long time, but then needed to go to feed Nick. I did all my motherly duties in shock. I spent the day in the nursery with Nick. I couldn't speak to Stella. She knew by the look on my face something was wrong, but didn't ask.

Nick took in his nourishment and looked so peaceful. My heart felt cut in half and I couldn't stop crying.

I slept in the nursery last night and was thrown when James didn't come in to see the baby in the morning.

Today I'm so afraid. What if James has finally gotten tired of me because of my messy first marriage and what he's been through? Have I not been grateful enough? The questions keep running through my mind. I'm so lost, but I have to be able to care for Nick.

April 5, 1921

I didn't see James at all yesterday. I stayed in the nursery, again. Stella came in midday with concern on her face.

"Catherine, is Nick all right?" she asked.

"He's fine," I replied from the rocker.

"Is there anything you need? Why have you been staying up here?"

"There's nothing I need."

Stella adjusted the blanket over Nick and looked back at me. "Did you and James have an argument?"

"No." I felt the tears coming again and pulled my knees up to my chin. "I can't...discuss this right now, Stella. Please..." I couldn't be so rude as to ask her to leave. I couldn't talk.

"I'll bring you some tea in a little while," she said, and left the room. I heard her footsteps going down the hall to the stairs.

I can't lose James.

Chapter Thirty

April 6, 1921

These last few days have unsettled me to no end and James is working hard getting things ready for the shearing in another couple of weeks. I know he's tired and coming in late. He's barely said anything to me and he hasn't seen or played with Nick at all. I haven't eaten much. If I try, my stomach just burns and I have felt very nauseated. I'm beginning to wonder if I might be pregnant again. It's possible.

On top of this, Nick started coughing this morning. I'm praying he only has a cold and nothing more serious. I fed him this evening and he fell asleep quickly.

James came in from the fields earlier today. I caught him looking at me over the dinner table, but we conversed very little. After we had finished, he went into the library and closed the door.

I put Nick down at seven o'clock. I couldn't stand it anymore, I needed to talk with James and get the air cleared. I wanted to understand what I'd done to cause him to turn away from me and Nick. I dreamt this morning that James turned into Marshall and I jolted awake. I can't stand another day without hearing his voice.

I left the nursery and went down the back stairs to the kitchen. The ladies sat around the table and talked. I looked at them and felt jealous of their conversation.

I tried to smile. "I'm sorry to interrupt. Stella, could I speak to you a moment?"

"Of course." She got up from the table and we

walked into the hall.

"Stella, I'm going to be in the library for a while with James. At least, I hope it will be for a while. We're not to be disturbed unless it's an outbreak of war. I fed Nick and put him down. Could you check on him in a little bit?"

"Yes, of course. Catherine, is everything all right?"

"I just need to discuss some things with James."

I turned away from her and walked down the hall to the library. I opened the door and entered.

James sat at his desk, looking through some papers. He glanced up when I closed the door and smiled when I locked it.

"Hello." I walked up to the desk and didn't move my eyes from his. His smile faded when he really looked at my face.

I sat in the chair across from him and realized James would think I wanted to discuss what happened to Marshall. I didn't want to talk about that subject. We stared at each other for a moment.

"James." I broke the silence. "I'm sorry." I started to feel my throat tighten. I'd promised myself I wasn't going to cry. I thought I'd used up all my tears over the last few days.

James stood up and came around the front of the desk. He leaned on it and crossed his arms. "Sorry for what?"

I took in a breath. "I know it must be rather tiresome, to be so concerned about me. I just want to apologize to you, I know you never would have planned…I mean, I know you love me, but I can understand it must have annoyed you. It has put you in a terrible position and…I hope you don't regret marrying so soon…I just want to apologize…" A tear slid down my cheek and I realized I wasn't making any sense.

James brow furrowed and he brought his hand up to his mouth. "I asked Heck to find a way to keep Marshall from troubling us again."

I shook my head and interrupted him. "No, I don't care what happened. Marshall was cruel and quite mad. I won't ever care what happened on that day. I'm grateful he's no longer alive to torment us."

He continued to stare at me. "I was afraid you were angry with me. When you weren't in the bedroom the last several nights, I felt sure you might be having your own reservations. I was afraid to say anything about it, certain you'd find me disgusting."

I frowned. "How could you ever think I would be angry with you? I know you only did it to protect your family. James, I could never find you disgusting. I just don't want you to tire of me. Marshall's gone now. There isn't anything else which will be a problem from my past, I'm sure. Please, give me another chance and don't give up on us."

James looked startled by my last sentence. He said, "Oh my Lord!"and threw up his hands.

I remained silent and waited.

"We've got to be the two dumbest people in the county, my love. I've spent the last few days worrying you would find what I asked of Heck disgusting and perhaps rethink your coming here, our marriage, everything. And"—he squatted down in front of my knees—"correct me if I'm wrong, you've been worrying I'd grown weary of you because of it?" He pulled me up and put his arms around me holding tight. "We should have spoken last week. Here we are two intelligent people. You'd think we'd know better." He pulled me back and looked in my eyes. "My love, I will never tire of you or have any regrets. I love you more than anything I ever thought possible. We should never, ever lose faith in each other and never stop talking."

I pulled myself back to his chest and the tears came again. "Nothing, and I mean nothing, frightens me more than even the smallest thought of losing you. I couldn't live if that happened."

"I must assure you, too, Catherine, there is nothing about you which will ever make me weary. You have, in fact, quite the opposite effect on me." He tightened his grip on me. "Hey, you're shaking."

I couldn't stand it any longer and started to weep uncontrollably. Once I could speak, I said, "I'm afraid I let my mind get carried away this week. I couldn't figure out why we weren't speaking and I hated it." He wiped one of the tears away and kissed my cheek. I moved my hands up his shoulders to his neck. "I also don't want to become spoiled. I know you have work to do, but when we're in bed at night, please never turn away from me. It almost made me insane with fright."

"Catherine, please, forgive me. I wasn't aware I'd done that. I must have been asleep, but I'll never do it again, I swear."

"Thank you." I put my forehead on his chest and just closed my eyes. Taking a handkerchief out of my pocket, I dried my eyes and blew my nose turning away from him. I put the hankie back and turned around to him, again.

"James, there is another thing we need to discuss."

He nodded and said, "A whole week without discussion, I imagine you've saved up."

I put my hand on my hip. "Are you saying I talk too much?"

"No, no, no. I know you tend to think a lot." He must have noticed the frown on my face. "Oh dear, I'm digging a deeper hole, aren't I?"

"Yes, I'd say so." I tilted my head and raised my eyebrows. He visibly relaxed and smiled. "I'm not certain how aware of this you are, but in my other life"—I put my hands together—"I had a very difficult time conceiving a child. I always assumed it was my fault, however, now, I

285

think there may be a reason to doubt that assumption."

James stood and looked at me curiously. "Milady, what are you saying? Are you pregnant again?"

"I am saying it might be so, milord. I've been nauseated the last week and I'm late. If I am, I'm not very far along. We did break the doctor's rules earlier than he recommended."

Before I could say another word, James put his arm around me and spun. When he slowed down, he kissed my lips, then put me gently back to the floor.

"Catherine, did I ever mention to you since I was an only child, I'd always dreamed of having many children of my own?"

"I think you may have said something about having a herd and such."

He looked down at my stomach. "You don't look very big."

"I may only be a month or so. James, I may not even be pregnant."

He put his hand on my stomach and his other around my shoulders. "Have you told anyone else?"

"No." I frowned up at him. He leaned in and kissed me. I smiled.

"That's better. I hate it when you frown. I promise, no more tears, my love. If I realize we're acting like children, we'll sit down and get things sorted out."

"This week turned out awful." I pulled back and took his hand. "Your son misses you, too. Can you spare a moment this evening to spend some time with him?"

"That is a wonderful idea."

We left the library and went up to the nursery to look in on Nick. He slept. His cough cleared up and I felt thankful. James sat in the rocker holding the little bundle in his arms. He rocked his son for some time. It was a joy and relief to watch.

Secrets Beyond Dreams

Chapter Thirty-one

May 1, 1921

I walked out of the back of the house this morning, heading for the garden. When I looked toward the barn, I saw James speaking with Constable Hunter and stopped in my tracks. What did he want? I felt my stomach start to churn.

Deciding there wasn't anything I could do at the moment, I continued toward the garden. I spent some time getting the plants watered and pulled some weeds.

My mind turned over all the possible reasons Constable Hunter was here. I couldn't come up with any good explanation and kept seeing a terrible vision of James being arrested. The tomato plants took my attention for the moment and I needed to think about the garden.

"Damn," I said, aloud. I'd pushed aside some of the leaves and discovered cut worms. They were big, fat and enjoying the leaves.

"Catherine, I hear you. Is there a problem?" I turned and James stood at the end of the row.

"Cut worms. I'm going to have to mix up some bran and molasses. We didn't have any last year, why on earth are they here this time?"

"I suppose they could have come in on the sprouts." He walked over, bent at the waist and lifted the leaves. "Looks like they're getting a good meal." He let the leaves down. "I'll have one of the men help you." He straightened and came toward me. "I saw you come out of the house."

I brushed off my hands. "What did Constable Hunter

want?"

"He had a few more questions."

"This is the second time he's been here with a few more questions. I wish he'd let go of it." I looked at James.

"I think Hunter is something of an old dog with a bone. He keeps chewing on it. There's nothing to worry about. The ruffians are gone and there's no proof of anything." He looked down at my stomach and put his hand on it. "How's Nick's brother doing today?"

"Fine. It's interesting he doesn't kick around the way Nick did, but he still lets me know when I'm doing something I shouldn't."

"Such as?" James arched his eye brow.

"You've changed the subject on me again. How do we get Hunter to stop looking into this business?"

"By not worrying about it. He'll get over it when he finds nothing." He kissed my forehead. "He did say he wanted to speak to you again. He was going to do it today, but I'm afraid I lied to him and said I didn't know where you were."

"Did he say what he wants to ask? I just want it to be over and never think about it again."

"Catherine, be honest with him. There's no reason to be concerned." I pulled away from James and started walking toward the house. "Where are you going, my love?"

"I have to go mix bran and molasses. We can't have worms eating our tomatoes." I stopped and turned around. "When am I supposed to answer his questions?"

"He said he'd come back around tomorrow. Hey." He walked toward me. "Are you mad at me?"

"No, I'm…no. I just want him to leave us alone and…" I looked at him. Walking to him, I put my hands around his waist. "I'm not mad at you, my love. The situation and"—I pointed at the plants—"those stupid worms, I'm finding very frustrating today."

"Okay, what can I do to help eliminate your frustration?"

"Let me think. I know, swim with me at the lake tonight."

"I'll be there." He smiled and kissed me.

"Good." I started back to the house. "Susan's going to love the mess I'm going to make in her kitchen. It's probably a good idea to be out of the house tonight. See you later." I waved at him.

The thought of meeting with Constable Hunter tomorrow plagued me the rest of the day. I knew if I wanted any sleep tonight a good swim with our usual activities would wear me out.

May 2, 1921

This morning turned out better than I had ever hoped.

Constable Hunter arrived promptly at ten o'clock. He spoke with Susan, Stella and Arthur briefly, asking them a few questions.

James and I waited for him in the library. James paced the room, while I sat and watched him going back and forth.

Finally, the door opened and Stella showed the constable into the room. He and James shook hands and he greeted me cordially. Stella left the library and James leaned against the desk.

Constable Hunter grasped his hands in front of himself. "Mr. Whear, I wonder, would you mind if I spoke with your wife privately?"

"Is it necessary?" James asked.

"Yes, sir. I just need to confirm a couple of things." Mr. Hunter sat in the chair next to me.

I looked up at James and could tell he didn't like this. I put my hand on his arm. His gaze turned to me and he furrowed his brows and then smoothed them out. He nodded and left. I knew he'd be out in the hall pacing.

I felt an odd calm come over me. After all the emotional upheaval over the last year, I felt I could get through this. I folded my hands in my lap and waited for Mr. Hunter to start his questions.

"Thank you for agreeing to speak with me, Mrs. Whear. This won't take very long," he said and pulled a note pad out of his pocket. He looked at the paper. "Now, your cook Susan said the day Mr. Pieper was here at Whear Hall he acted abusive to you. She also thought he'd been drinking. Do you have any idea what was angering him?"

"Mr. Hunter, I think you need to be aware of a few things. My ex-husband was always verbally and physically abusive to me. He drank too much on a regular basis. His behavior that day was just more of what I'd already experienced many times. I asked him several times what he wanted, but he never made it clear what was his reason for coming."

"I understand. Did you feel threatened by him at anytime?"

"He always threatened me, sir."

"I understand your husband and Mr. Pieper exchanged some words?"

"James asked Marshall to leave peacefully and not return. When Marshall began to call me profane names, my husband took exception of this behavior. He did grab Marshall by the jacket, asked him to apologize and told him if he ever returned he would beat him. That was all."

"After Mr. Pieper left, where did Mr. Whear go?"

"We spent the rest of the afternoon in the nursery with our son." I looked straight at him. "Mr. Hunter, I would like to be very candid with you, but I want your assurance what I'm going to say to you goes no further than this room."

291

"Of course, Mrs. Whear."

"I'm counting on your discretion, sir."

He nodded.

"Mr. Hunter, as I'm sure the gossipmongers in town have let you know, I came here under terrible circumstances. I'd returned to Layne Hall after being away for a time. Marshall had not been there and let some of the estate's daily and weekly duties fall by the wayside. In particular, the flock of sheep. I made arrangements with a crew in the village near Layne to come out to shear the sheep. They kindly assisted me with the sale of the wool. Prices were very good and the money I received would have supported Layne for at least the next two years." I shifted in my seat and held my hands together. "When Marshall returned and discovered what I'd done he became angry and he became considerably more furious and violent when I would not tell him where I put the proceeds from the sale of the wool. If it had not been for the quick thinking of Layne Halls staff, I might very well be dead. I'm fortunate to be acquainted with Mr. Mansfield, who introduced me to my husband, James. He made the arrangements for a doctor to come and care for me after I'd been beaten by Marshall."

"Ah yes, Mr. Mansfield," Mr. Hunter started to say.

I continued to stare at him. "Sir, Mr. Mansfield is quite the world traveler and is aware of the kind of character Marshall presented. Jacob said Marshall caused terrible trouble in the city, but, because he is a gentleman, felt it not decent enough to be repeated in my presence."

"Mrs. Whear, I'm sure you are aware of the rumors about the goings-on at Mansfield?"

"I haven't the time to listen to gossips. What has that to do with the death of Marshall?"

"Quite correct, Mrs. Whear. I apologize. When Mr. Pieper came here, did he ever mention the money?"

"Not that I remember."

"He didn't say at all what he wanted?"

"As I said, he did not. No."

"Did you know of anyone who might have been angry with Mr. Pieper?"

"No, I do not. Mr. Mansfield may be the one to speak to about that. He's more aware of Marshall's behavior when away from Layne Hall than I, sir."

"I've spoken to Mr. Mansfield a little. He is reluctant to give many details."

I knew Jacob didn't give details to protect me. "Mr. Hunter, Marshall was cruel to me. I hope you will understand what I'm about to say. Whoever killed him has my admiration and I hope they are happy wherever they are." He looked at me a bit aghast. "Really, sir, I could care less if you ever find out who did it. I hope this doesn't shock you, but Marshall ill-treated me and got what he deserved. I know I sound crass in my own right, but his behavior... I'm sorry, sir. I don't mean to carry on."

Mr. Hunter let out his breath and closed his notebook. "Mrs. Whear, I only have one more question to ask and I wish to apologize ahead of time for it. I don't mean to cause you any worry."

I continued to watch him, but said nothing.

"Have you any reason to think Mr. Whear, or the traveling workmen he hired, may have had anything to do with Mr. Pieper's death?"

"I know of no such thing, sir. As I've already told you, my husband was with me and our child the rest of the afternoon on that day. Our son had a cough at the time and we were quite concerned for him."

Mr. Hunter thought for a moment and then stood. "Thank you very much for your time, Mrs. Whear. I'll see about speaking again with Mr. Mansfield. As far as I can tell, Mr. Pieper was a gambler who got himself tangled up with the wrong people. I hope all this hasn't been too much of an upset for you."

"No, Mr. Hunter, thank you for your concern." I stood and we walked into the hall. I showed him to the front door. Both James and Stella were in the living room and came to the doorway.

The constable stopped and smiled at them. "Mr. Whear, Miss Taylor, thank you for your time." He turned back to me. "Mrs. Whear, I appreciate your candor and guarantee my discretion." He nodded and went to the front door.

After the door closed, I turned to James and Stella. "He's going to ask Jacob some more questions."

"What did you tell him, Catherine?" Stella asked, as we walked back to the living room.

I sat on the couch next to James, who held my hand. "I was honest with him and told about what occurred last spring. I told him about Marshall's drinking and gambling. I may have withheld some of the details, but there are things I'm not about to share with the constable."

Stella smiled and said she wanted to let Susan and Katie know. They'd been anxious for some word. She excused herself and left the room.

I leaned toward James. "You're very quiet, my love."

"I'm sorry." He put his arm over my shoulder. "It's just….you are continually surprising me."

"How so?"

"Remember when I told you, I first fell in love with your courage?" I nodded. "Today was another example of it. I knew by the look on your face everything would be fine."

"I was rather crass, though."

James creased his brow. "Crass? I don't believe it for a second."

"I told Mr. Hunter, Marshall got what he deserved and I didn't care."

"I don't see that as being anything but honest," James replied.

"I also said I admired whoever did it and hoped they were having a happy life."

James laughed. "I don't believe it qualifies, either."

"I guess I don't have it in me to be crass, then. I'm relieved in a way. I don't like not caring much."

James kissed my hand, leaned toward me and looked mischievous. "You know, milady, if you'd like to practice some crassness with me, I'd be more than willing to help you with technique." He started to kiss my neck.

"We should work on it now, milord. In another month or so, I'll be having problems moving around," I said and patted my stomach.

May 15, 1921

I was sitting in the nursery this afternoon feeding Nick. We rocked and I hummed a song to him, when I heard the door creak open. Looking up, I saw James put his head around the door and smile. He came in the room and squatted down next to us, touching his son's head lightly.

"Lucky boy." James smiled up at me.

Nick gurgled and let go of my breast, turning to look toward his father. James put a blanket on the floor and took Nick out of my arms. I closed my blouse and watched them play. James got the baby laughing before long and, at one point, Nick grabbed James's hair in his little hand.

"Ouch, hey, you got me," James said.

Nick squealed with delight, kicked his feet and then put his hand on James's nose.

James entertained Nick for a bit and I watched them. After a while, James gave Nick the pacifier and put him in the bassinette. The baby cried a little, but soon drifted off. We watched him sleep and James put his arm around my waist.

"Milord, what made you come in so early this afternoon?" I asked, taking his hand and lacing my fingers through his.

He turned toward the door and led me out of the nursery, across the hall to our room. "I was having so much fun with Nick, I almost forgot." He sat me down on the bed, took off his boots and slid back onto the pillows holding his arms out. I felt a little suspicious, but crawled up to him and put my arm over his stomach. "I thought you'd want to know Constable Hunter was back earlier."

"Oh dear, what few questions did he have?" I felt on edge and sat up.

James sat up too and leaned against the headboard. "No questions really. He spoke with Jacob who gave the good constable all of the lurid details of Marshall's city escapades. He wanted to let us know the case has been closed, unsolved yes, but closed for good."

I smiled. "What a relief."

"Are you pleased, my love?"

"Very pleased indeed. In fact, I never want to think of it again. I say a pox on anyone who mentions the name to me ever."

James looked up at me. "Do you not want to know the details?"

I crawled onto his lap and straddled his legs. I grabbed the upper part of his shirt, pulling him to me and said, quietly, "I would prefer to not see you afflicted with a pox, milord."

He sat up and put his arms around me. "I understand, milady."

"Good." I touched his lips with my thumb. "Answer me this, are you going back out to work this afternoon?"

James glanced at the window. "I see there is still daylight. I suppose I could, but I sense there might be something else you would like for me to do."

I felt his hand on my breast. "It's funny you say that. I do believe there is a project I could use your assistance with."

He started kissing my neck. "What might it be?"

"I'm feeling desperately in need of a bath and my hair could be washed. It's been a time since you've done it."

"You know, it would give me nothing but pleasure to wash your hair. I am your servant, as you are aware."

I moved off of his lap and stood. I held out my hand. "Come with me. I want you now."

Lauren Marie

Chapter Thirty-two

1976

Nick turned onto the highway that went out to Layne Hall. He'd set up a meeting with his brother, Michael, to answer a question that came up during the readings.

He and his siblings spent the summer and fall reading their mother's journals. The post office got many letters from them and long-distance charges on their phones were up. They all read through the pages and gained a better understanding of their parents' past. Many subjects their mother and father refused to discuss, became clearer. The most important part of their story was how much they loved each other.

On the drive, Nick thought about all the memories his mother wrote about. Some, he remembered, and others not so much. The things that brought a smile to his face were of his parents and the children sitting around the fire in the evening talking about their day at school or playing out in the fields. His parents paid close attention to every word and thing their children said and did. Father would have his arm around Mother, or they'd hold hands. When they'd walk out onto the patio, they were never far apart. All of the children remembered almost caught moments. He never told his siblings about the time he caught his mother and father in the barn. He was sixteen years old and he'd been shocked to find out his parents still had sex. Nick was in the middle of young man hormones and catching them made his curiosity worse than ever.

There were so many things he laughed and got choked up about. He'd forgotten when his brother, Michael, got hit in the nose once and it gave him a black eye. They'd been playing Musketeer's with their brother, Jason, when things got a bit out of hand. Their father made them swords in the wood shop and dubbed them all knights of the Whear realm. His brother Jason said he was being bossy and an argument began.

Nick was helping his younger brother Michael through the door. Michael's nose was bleeding and he could see the start of a black eye. He almost had a heart attack.

He remembered leading Michael to a chair by the table and sat him down. Mother raced to him and Susan handed her a towel she put under his nose.

"Tilt your head back, sweetheart." Susan got another cloth wet and put it behind his neck. "What happened here?" Mother asked.

Nick looked at Jason who stood behind their mother. He wore a scowl on his face.

"One of you say something, please," Mother demanded.

"Nick was being bossy and I told him to stop it, he wasn't the leader," Jason started, but Nick, feeling he needed to defend himself spoke at the same time.

"Wait a minute, one at a time. Jason, you first."

"Nick said I was a no good traitor for not taking his orders and he was going to ask Lord James to demote me from Musketeer to a common guard. I was going to hit Nick, but he ducked and I hit Michael. It was an accident."

"You hit your brother with your sword?" Mother looked stunned.

"No, with my fist," Jason answered back.

She stood and stared at him. "You raised your hand against your brother?"

Jason started to say something, but when he saw her face, must've thought better of it and stayed silent.

"Mother, it was an accident," Nick remembered

saying.

She looked at him and said, "It wouldn't have been an accident if he'd hit you, Nick." She squatted back beside Michael. "You two, I want you to sit at the dining room table and work on your studies."

The three boys protested it was Friday night and they could do their work over the weekend. She gave them a glance which hushed the complaint.

When their father came in from the fields, they'd gotten a good talking to about fighting. It made sense that they needed to defend each other and not be jealous. On top of that, they'd been grounded from playing Musketeer's and their swords were put away. They sat at the table every day when they came home from school and did their homework and spent the weekends working in the fields with their father. Although their father thought it was punishment, they all liked working with him.

Finding out how much their mother worried about her oldest boys during the war years, came as a surprise. She'd been a strong woman and he never knew about all the things she'd been anxious about. He'd loved his parents and missed them more than anything.

Nick drove up the long drive to Layne Hall and saw his brothers, Michael and Jay, waiting by the front doors. After parking his car, he got out and joined them.

Layne Hall had sat empty for many years. Nick remembered his parents talking about leasing it out to a family which he thought they'd done. Now, it looked worn and tired. Vines covered the windows and the grass had grown waist high.

They spent some time going from room to room on the second floor. They wanted to find the loose floorboard in their mother's old closet. They weren't certain which room their mother grew up in and in the second to the last, Jay opened the door and squatted down. He pulled a Swiss knife out of his pocket, pried one of the boards, and it came away easily. Underneath the floor, they found a box. Jay brought it out of the closet and held it for Nick to open.

Inside they found their Grandfather Layne's pocket watch, some pictures and a stack of money. The bills were very old and faded. They were in an envelope with their father's handwriting on the outside. It said Catherine's Dowry.

Nick looked at it for a long time and thought his father put all the sheep money back inside. Michael opened the pocket watch and found it still worked. Their mother traveled back to Layne on several occasions in the later years, but never mentioned putting this box back into the floor in any of her journals. They never could understand why she did it.

They drove back to Whear and started to prepare a pot of coffee, but decided they all needed something stronger. They went out to the patio in back and sat with a bottle of whiskey, silently sipping.

Michael explained he'd spent some time trying to track down the tribe of ruffians who lived on the property for a time. Given the circumstances, it was impossible to find any records of them and he gave up. He did some more searching, but wouldn't divulge what he'd found.

"Where's Karen?" Nick asked, about Michael's girlfriend.

Michael smiled as he poured them more drinks. "She went into the city to get some better linens for the beds and bathrooms. The ones here are pretty worn." He looked at his brothers. "We've made a decision."

Nick accepted the drink and took the bait. "Are you two staying together permanently?"

Michael sat down and continued smiling. "Yes, we're together permanently, brother. In fact, she got me to propose last night. And I have a proposal for you guys and the rest of the clan. We've talked about it and would like to move in here to Whear for good."

"Can you afford the taxes?" Jay sipped his drink and then set the glass on the table between them.

"Not really, but part of the proposal would be to sell off some of the land surrounding Whear. Since we don't have sheep anymore, it seems like someone could put that acreage to good use. The money from the sale would be set aside in a trust and should take care of taxes for a long time to come."

They clicked the glasses together and Nick congratulated him. If Karen could get him to settle down, Nick would be the first one amazed.

"What are you laughing about?" Michael asked.

"I'm sorry, I just can't believe what I'm hearing. You have mellowed, Michael. I never thought I'd see the day you'd settle down. I'm very proud of you."

"Shut up. She has me wrapped around her little finger. She's never met our parents, but loves them both dearly from reading the journals. She is a wonderful woman."

"Are you going to move into the master suite, upstairs?" Nick always stayed in his old room when he visited.

Michael said, "After all I've read about our parents' activities in the suite, I don't think I'd get a decent night's sleep. We bought a new bed and have moved into the room next door."

They talked a little longer about the date for the upcoming wedding and then Michael turned serious.

Michael looked at them and told him another idea. "Since I'm a writer I've been tossing around the thought if maybe publishing mother's journals might be interesting. I'm not sure anyone would believe they were real and would think I'd made up the whole thing." He sat back in his chair and shook his head. "It's only an idea."

"They were respected in this area. I'm not sure how the folks around here would feel about knowing about Mother and Father's bedroom adventures," Nick said.

"I thought that, too. I'd have to do a ton of editing." Michael looked at the back property. "It would have Mother's voice say something about what happened with the family after the days of trouble. To just cut it off in 1921 wouldn't give the readers an ending. They need to know about our parents love and how it survived long after. Apparently, trying to find a definitive ending date would be hard. You guys have read the journals. Mother noted down everything. First steps, first words, first teeth, plus all the pages about the gardens, and the sheep. I think maybe it would be more fascinating to focus on when Father brought home the first truck. Since motor vehicles weren't seen much during their early days, readers would find it enjoyable."

"Yes, but would you edit out the parts at the lake, in the woods and barn? Don't you feel people would want to know our parents' love endured well over fifty years?" Nick asked.

"I think from what people read in the earlier entries, they would know. If they read about Mother's first ride in a car, they would understand it without having to be told. Besides, at some point, I'd have to give Mother her privacy back. I know it's strange, but there are times when I'm not sure we knew them well at all."

"I think you'd have to put in some of the tricks Mother played on us. I would have been only seven or eight, but I remember the pine cone hitting me in the butt. Who knew Mother had such a good arm?" Jay said.

"I think I gained more respect for our Mother when she did it." Michael laughed.

"I don't know if it's a good idea. We'll have to let

the others know and see what they think. They may not like opening that can of worms." Nick looked at his brothers. "We're you at all disappointed with them? Finding out about Marshall Pieper and his death?"

"No. His death means nothing." Michael stood and started to pace. "I think our parents had some advantages with the training from Mansfield. They knew how to enjoy one another. I don't think any of us suffered at all because of it. We knew they loved us, there was never a time I doubted it." He stopped and looked at them. "Did I mention I finally found some information about Pieper's death?"

"No, do tell." Nick felt excited.

"As you know, I've been doing some research. I was able to contact Constable Hunter's granddaughter. Her father, the constable's son, moved up to the north. She got him to contact me and I discovered the son had all of his father's old records boxed up and collecting dust in his attic. He agreed to let me go up and see what I could find."

"You never said a word about this, Michael."

"If I mentioned it and then found nothing, I think everyone, particularly Stella, would have been upset. Ever since she went back and graduated from law school she's been insufferable. I think John even gets upset with her sometimes." Michael walked to the rock wall and leaned against it. "Anyway, I drove up north and spent several lovely, dusty days in the gentleman's attic going through pages and pages of notes." He put his hand in his jacket pocket and pulled out some papers folded into thirds. "I did find some interesting things. For some reason, Constable Hunter held onto several hundred death certificates. The son said they were mostly unsolved cases. I'm not certain I'll ever understand the reason for this, but yes, I did find Pieper's certificate. You'll never guess what it said as the cause of death?"

"Murder most heinous?" Jay guessed.

"No." He grinned. "It said only one word. 'Mischief.'"

"You're joking?"

"No, really." He opened the papers and pulled one out, handing it to Nick, who looked at it and then, passed it to Jay. Sure enough, on the line for cause of death it said mischief.

"Also, in the boxes were some of Hunter's handwritten notes and yes, I found notes with Mother and Father's names."

"No!"

Michael handed over the rest of the papers. "Yes, I got copies of everything I could get my hands on."

Nick read through the papers. What it basically said was Constable Hunter didn't think their mother and father had anything to do with Marshall Pieper's death. The law found several gambling establishments and whore houses in the city which said nothing good about the character of the man. Pieper also owed large amounts of money.

Nick nodded his head and looked at Michael. "I would love to see Jeff Snell's notes. I'd love to see his notes on Mother's bruises."

"Lord only knows where those notes are. I couldn't find anything. Snell left the city for destinations unknown. The law firm he worked for doesn't exist any longer. One other thing I did find was quite surreal. When I saw it, I could almost hear the ruffian's voices."

"You went to Uncle Jacob's barn?"

"Yes, it's still standing. The new owners were curious why I'd want to look at it, but they let me. The post is still there. The benches were pulled up at some point, but that post...it was weird." Michael poured himself another drink and offered one to Nick, which he accepted. "I was also able to locate Daniel Goodhue. He's in his seventies and has retired up north."

"Remind me, who is Daniel Goodhue?"

"He was the young boy who took Mother's message to Aunt Stella when she first went to Mansfield. He also is the one Uncle Jacob originally left Mansfield to in his will."

"Oh yes. What did he have to say?"

"He said good things about all involved. Did you know Uncle Jacob sent him to college? He only saw Pieper briefly the first day Mother arrived at Mansfield. He said he remembered thinking Pieper looked like a dandy, but had no other impressions. He remembered Mother and Father. He said Mother always treated him kindly when he'd do work here at Whear. He spoke some about Heck, mostly because the ruffians scared him. His parents passed away when he was ten or eleven and he considered Uncle Jacob a decent guardian. Daniel wanted to participate in the school, but Jacob refused. He was very good in mathematics and after graduating from college, like you, brother Nick, was a teacher. He very seldom returned to Mansfield after he'd graduated, but came back for Uncle Jacob's funeral in 1933."

They spoke for another couple of hours about the things discovered about their parents. Michael didn't think the others would have a problem with not selling Whear Hall, but felt unsure on how he would approach them. It was hard to tell how their siblings would feel about it.

They agreed that James and Catherine never tried to steer the children toward anything particular. They let them choose what they wished and only supported them on their endeavors. Nick thought his mother would have been proud of them all.

As it started to get late in the day, Nick wanted to head back to the city to take his family out to dinner. Michael walked him and Jay out to the drive and asked, "You guys don't have any problem with Karen and me living here? Yay or nay?"

Jay shook his head. "You'll probably need to update the plumbing. I have a vague memory of Mother saying there was a leak somewhere in the upstairs bathroom. She said it never did get put in right."

"You and Karen have my blessing. I'm sort of relieved that family will still be living here and I can come back to visit. It's home, always will be." Nick thought about each one of his brothers and his sister. He thought of their families and how publishing this story might affect them.

He looked back up at Michael. "Let's talk some more about how to go about editing the journals. I'm sure Stella will have a fit, but this might be a good time to let the world know what went on back in those days. How a load of secrets could be hidden so well, but dreams came true."

"Thanks, brother. Are you becoming an old romantic? Remember I write horror stories." Michael put his hand out and Nick shook it.

"I think if you do it, you'll put it together properly. Just don't include ghosts." He smiled and got into his car.

Driving away from Whear Hall gave Nick some satisfaction. He knew he'd be back, but for now, he felt he understood it better.

ABOUT THE AUTHOR LAUREN MARIE

Lauren Marie lives in Western Washington State with four cats, Agamemnon, Jericho, Jasper and Shiva. She started writing Secrets Beyond Dreams eleven years ago and finally finished it this year.

OTHER BOOKS BY LAUREN MARIE

Going to Another Place - revised edition released 2018
One Touch at Cobb's Bar and Grill - Montana Ranch series, short story

Lauren Marie

Loves Touch - Then and Now
Love's Embers - Canon City series book 1
Love on Ice - Canon City series book 2
I'm Not What You Think - short story
Golden Ribbons - The Miss Demeanor Detective Agency
series - short story
Big Mike, Little Mike - short story
The Haller Lake series - A Demon Scheme
The Haller Lake series 2 - Magick's Pathway
The Haller Lake series 3 - Portal Hop

YOU CAN FIND LAUREN MARIE HERE:

twitter- Lauren Marie @HallerLake11
https://www.facebook.com/lauren.marie.963
https://www.facebook.com/lauren.marie.books
laurenmariebooks.com

Books to Go Now

You can find more stories such as this at
www.bookstogonow.com

If you enjoyed this Books to Go Now story, please leave a review for the author on a review site where you purchased the eBook. Thanks!

We pride ourselves with representing great stories at low prices. We want to take you into the digital age offering a market that will allow you to grow along with us in our journey through the new frontier of digital publishing.
Some of our favorite award-winning authors have now joined us. We welcome readers and writers into our community.

We want to make sure that as a reader you are supplied with never-ending great stories. As a company, Books to Go Now, wants its readers and writers supplied with positive experience and encouragement so they will return again and again.

We want to hear from you. Our readers and writers are the cornerstone of our company. If there is something you would like to say or a genre that you would like to see, please email us at inquiry@bookstogonow.com

73673363R00188

Made in the USA
Columbia, SC
05 September 2019